THE ACCIDENTAL ELOPEMENT

BEVERLEY OAKLEY

THE ACCIDENTAL ELOPEMENT

CHAPTER 1

Katherine wasn't usually frightened of the dark.

And certainly not when she could still hear the strains of the lively polka she was supposed to be dancing with George.

However, as she felt her way along the dark corridor behind the ballroom of Lady Braxton's London townhouse and the sounds of the orchestra grew fainter, some of the courage for which Katherine was renowned drained away.

For a moment she contemplated turning back.

However, returning to the dancing meant she'd have no choice but to partner her dreadful cousin and Katherine would rather frighten herself half to death in a deserted corridor than do that.

Except, she soon found to her dismay, that it wasn't deserted.

And when she stumbled over a large, unidentified object and landed with a painful jarring of her wrists upon the cold, hard flagstones, she was sure she was about to be kidnapped by pirates and never see any of her loved ones, ever again.

Until she remembered that she was a young lady about to make her debut, and not a child any longer.

"Good Lord!" came a disembodied young male voice in the dark before a groping hand located a piece of Katherine—a carefully arranged ringlet of hair—which caused her to shriek even louder when it was quite unnecessarily tugged. Whether this was to establish who or what she was, she had no idea, and perhaps neither did the tugger, for immediately a profound apology was issued before the groping hand was operating with complete abandon in the dark.

It found Katherine's breast just as the voice said in tones of utter mortification, "Forgive me! Are you hurt? Take my hand. Really, I can't apologise enough."

Katherine had made one unsuccessful attempt to stand, but it was a struggle in her flounced skirts and multiple petticoats. She swatted away the supposedly helping hand and hissed something unintelligible—since unladylike language seemed less of an offence when she couldn't see to whom she was speaking.

But when the disembodied groping hand entered her orbit once more, in fact brushing the bare flesh above her garter and getting in a good squeeze of her thigh flesh, her temper, which had never been one of her strong points, snapped, and she lashed out with a sharp slice through the inky air.

A loud yelp made her realise she'd perhaps been a little peremptory and certainly too violent in this unladylike action, and even though she felt disinclined to apologise, she did say, ungraciously, "I'm sorry I hit you, but a lady can only take so much of all this groping in the dark. I mean...what were you *doing*?"

"I could ask you the same thing," came the response, now at ear level. In fact, she could feel the soft whisper of breath against her cheek, which made her step back, saying, "I asked first."

"I was chasing a cat. Bending down, in fact. And then suddenly something crashed into me. Or on top of me."

"That was me."

"Of course it was you. There's no one else here, is there?"

Katherine bridled at his tone. She was unused to being found at fault. "Then how thoughtless it was of you to crouch down where anybody could simply crash into you."

The response was whip-fast and enragingly superior. "Anybody—or rather, anybody *else*—would be carrying a candle. I think I have every reason to be deeply suspicious of the motives of anyone who is not."

"Well, *you* don't have a candle. And I would suspect the truth of anyone hiding away in the dark, claiming they were crouching over an imaginary cat," huffed Katherine, smoothing her skirts. "In fact, I'd wager there was no cat here at all. No, you were sneaking away from something, weren't you?"

"And if I was, what business is it of yours? Whoever you are."

Katherine could not imagine the audacity. "I could ask the same question. You certainly are no gentleman to speak to a lady in that fashion."

"Since that lady hasn't bothered to declare herself, I think I could be forgiven."

"A gentleman would have declared himself first," Katherine said hotly. "What were you sidling away from? There's a noisy ball going on in the next room. If you were a gentleman, wouldn't you be gallantly asking the ladies to dance instead of hiding in the dark? Perhaps there's someone you're afraid of seeing? A lady who has expectations of you behaving towards her as a *gentleman* would." Katherine said this triumphantly before elaborating on her theme. "My guess is that you've given some poor young lady the idea that you'll dance with her all night, and now you've changed your mind and are sneaking away."

"And I'd suggest you're trying to sneak away from a gentleman to whom you've already promised two dances. Meanwhile he, poor fellow, is searching for you vainly in the ballroom while you're here making a mockery of him."

"He can do that all by himself," Katherine sniffed. "But I never promised him anything, and I never will."

"Ha! I was right." The anonymous young gentleman sounded very pleased with himself. "Well, I feel sorry for this chap without even seeing what *you* look like, miss. Poor fellow!"

"Poor fellow, indeed. George can pine til the cows come home. I'd even suffer talking to you than have to spend another five minutes with his sweating hands squeezing mine and his cow eyes boring into me...and his horrible, putrid breath choking me and his—"

"Poor George! I was just starting to feel sorry for him until you described the exact George I, too, am so at pains to avoid tonight." The voice became more confidential, and the mood relaxed.

"Well, you have described my cousin to a very fine point." Katherine laughed. "And if you are as well acquainted with him as you seem to be, then you obviously know exactly why I am here in the dark."

There was a small silence. And then, "Your *cousin?*"

"Yes, my Cousin George."

"George...who?"

"Lord Quamby's son. Lord Quamby is married to my Aunt Antoinette who's the sister of my mother who—"

"I know exactly who you're talking about. And we're talking about the *same* George!" The voice sounded stunned.

A quick gasp from both of them was followed up by a delighted cry in unison.

"Jack!"

"Katherine!"

Katherine laughed at the ludicrousness of it. "I can't believe it's really you, Jack!" When the seeking hand came in contact with her cheek, Katherine gripped his wrist to hold it in place as she raised her hand to feel for his face.

Of course, it was terribly unladylike behaviour, and had there not been the mantle of darkness lending their reunion such an air of unreality, she'd not have been nearly so forward. But, with their hands on respective cheeks and around waists, such a greeting seemed quite natural.

"I can't believe it's you, Jack. I haven't seen you for five years, and I certainly didn't expect to see you tonight."

"That's because my mother is visiting Quamby House, but as we arrived late, she decided to remain at home while I said I needed activity after the long drive."

"Mama said nothing about *you* coming. I knew she was expecting visitors and I do remember her mentioning your parents, but then she said you'd not be accompanying them so I lost interest, and in fact didn't even consider the visit might be this weekend."

"You lost interest? Do you mean you were interested before?"

"Of course!" Katherine laughed. "I wanted to see if I could still make you do whatever I told you to, now that you were grown."

He laughed too. Katherine had been notorious for sending Jack on all sorts of errands when he was just the foundling child visiting Quamby House before he was adopted by the well-to-do Eliza and Rufus Patmore. She and Jack had spent a great deal of time together as children before Jack had left the district with his parents. Katherine's last visit to Patmore Farm had been when she was twelve.

"Is that what you thought, eh?"

"I could always make you do what I wanted you to, Jack." She heard the edge of wickedness to her tone and tensed in expectation of having her hair pulled. There'd been a lot of chasing and tumbling on the ground when Katherine had been seven and Jack eight. Even during that last visit, when she'd been on the cusp of adolescence, seeing Jack again was like having a lamp turned on, warming the little heart that was in danger of becoming too caught up with adult cares.

"You'll never know, will you?"

"Are you daring me?"

"Of course."

Katherine thought. She ran her hand over his cheek, the pads of her fingers keenly attuned to the light dusting of stubble. Then she slowly contoured his jawline. She felt him shudder slightly though he didn't move. With a flat hand, she gently contoured his shoulder line. It was a broader shoulder than she remembered. The cloth of his well-cut coat was smooth and rough at the same time, and she felt the sharp line of his collar.

He seemed to hold himself rigid. Rapt. She was sure a small sigh of disappointment escaped him when she removed her hands.

"All right, but you must *promise* you will do as I say before I tell you what you must do."

"Hmm." She felt his breath in the cold air between them, and her mouth stretched into a smile of anticipation as she waited for him to reply. Jack had been her willing slave, fulfilling her every demand with the utmost good humour until he'd reach a point where he'd declare his chivalry was at an end and she could ask until the cows came home, but he'd not pick another apple or climb to the highest branch of the fir tree at the bottom of the garden of Quamby House before his next visit from the foundling home.

"I'm afraid I'm old enough and wise enough to no longer agree to carry out promises that are not reasonable ones. You taught me a lot, Katherine, including that I must be wary of what I promise. Otherwise, I could end up plunging my hand into a basket of spiders or a hornet's nest."

"I never made you thrust your hands into a hornet's nest!" Katherine was indignant.

"But you did have me thrust my hands into a basket full of spiders. I do remember that."

Katherine remembered it well. It had been at the pinnacle of her power when she was eight and Jack was going through a stage of wanting to prove how brave and strong he was. This was just after the Patmores had adopted him. "All right. What if *I* promised that my request would be something I knew would be good for you. What if I said that, like you, I'm no longer a foolish child but an adult of good sense who would only order you to do something that I knew you would not regret, or cause you harm."

"Hmmm." The considering tone came again. "Yet you want me to first of all promise you that I will do the thing you request of me."

"Yes. I've never done you harm. So it's not an unreasonable request, is it?"

"Knowing you as I do, it's not unreasonable at all. And taking very large risks is something I pledged I'd always be prepared to do for you, right from when I was a boy. You know I've always been your slave, fair Katherine, so yes, I will promise to carry out this request, or at least attempt to. And now I wait in anticipation to hear what it is. Even if it means going back into the ballroom and being chums again with Young George, which I know I should be. He's not a bad fellow, but tonight I think he's out of his depth. He doesn't know how to behave when he's all at sea and then he becomes quite ridiculous."

"I won't send you back to George." Katherine smiled into the dark, her heart starting to hammer as she considered the very big request she was about to make of him. It hadn't occurred to her until just this moment, but the intimacy between them, based as it was on a lifelong friendship, didn't make it seem outrageous in the slightest. "I want you to kiss me."

"Kiss you?" He laughed. "That's very brazen. Can I first ask you why? You haven't seen me for five years. I might have ghastly spots all over my face, and lost my front teeth and likely cause shivers of revulsion to run down your spine if you were observing me in the lamplight right now. Why, I might even be more unprepossessing than Young George."

"I don't think that's possible. But, have you?"

"What?"

"Got spots all over your face."

"I'm not going to tell you. That'll mean you're the one taking all the risks. I've just warned you of the potential dangers, and now you have to think the worst while I kiss you so that you can hold firm to your dignity and control your horror when we both get into the light again."

Before Katherine had a chance to reconsider, she felt the tips of his fingers lightly brush her cheeks before he cupped her face. Her breath caught in her throat while the blood rushed to her head causing pins and needles along the way. Too intrigued by her body's alien responses, she wasn't going to back out now.

After a second's agonising anticipation, his lips gently touched hers.

It was as if a thousand butterflies had been unleashed in the dark. Katherine was enthralled. This was much nicer than she'd expected. Jack's strong young body felt like a rock of sanctuary in the darkness when she'd felt as out of her depth in the ballroom as Jack had just suggested George felt. She twined her arms behind Jack's neck, eager to deepen the kiss as his tongue gently breached the seam of her lips. He smelt nice: of pepper and sandalwood soap overlaid by the familiar smell that was just him. Katherine shivered, opening her mouth wider as the sensory delight grew more intense.

Too soon, he stopped and, with a sigh, Katherine sagged slightly as he drew back, his hands clasping hers and squeezing them in the dark.

"You did that so well," she told him approvingly. "Have you done it much before?"

"A few times." He paused. "But I never enjoyed it as much as this time."

"Is it very different kissing different people?"

"You've never kissed anyone, I take it?"

"No. That's why I asked you to do it. So I'd know what to expect. I'm going to London in a month to be presented, and Mama and Aunt Antoinette have been drilling me like sergeant majors on how to make the most of myself in order to make the best match I can."

"You always were ambitious, my dear Katherine."

There was something about the way he used the familiar term that made her feel quivery all the way down to her feet.

"I just know what I'm worth." She said it in a proud, haughty tone, but she was smiling. "That's what Antoinette says I must think every time I weigh up an offer." She giggled. "You'd remember my aunt, of course!"

"Lord, how could I forget the redoubtable, scandalous Lady Quamby. Your mother and her sister were the ton's reigning beauties."

"And don't you dare suggest in front of them that they're anything less, today," Katherine teased.

"As a gentleman, I am well versed in tact."

"You always were. And now I really should return else Mama will tear strips off me. I've been gone far too long as it is." She put her hand on the cold plastered wall and half turned. "Are you coming?"

"I think I'll make my departure now and find a hackney to take me to Quamby House. I expect I'll find Mama will still be up playing cards with the earl. He was very delighted to see her again, and not the slightest bit disappointed that Uncle Rufus couldn't accompany her. Lots of stories to share." He paused. "Unless you'd like me to return to the ballroom with you."

Katherine considered then shook her head, even though she knew he couldn't see her. "No, I'll go alone. You can be my special secret. I'd rather no one knew we'd stumbled upon each other here in the dark when we meet back at Quamby House tonight."

His soft chuckle followed her as she groped her way back to the bright lights of the ballroom. And it sustained her with a happy internal glow as Young George's face lit up when he encountered her at the supper table.

"You look very pleased with yourself, Katherine," he remarked, touching her elbow. "Anticipating the final dance of the evening with me?"

Katherine sighed but kept her smile in place. "All right, George. If that'll please you."

Her lips were still thrumming with pleasurable delight at the memory of Jack's kiss, but now the idea of being in George's cloying waltz hold would remind her of how important it was to find herself a husband who made her feel the excitement and pleasure Jack's touch inspired, rather than the weary resignation she felt being with George.

CHAPTER 2

Katherine wasn't sorry when it was time to leave the ball. But it was only a country affair, she supposed. London would be so much more exciting.

"Darling, you weren't very kind to Cousin George when you haven't seen him in such a long time," Katherine's mother said under her breath as she followed her daughter and sister into the carriage, tucking aside her blue silk skirts as the door was closed. The gentlemen, who had stayed on to finish their game of cards, would be coming later in the barouche.

"It takes more than plain speaking for George to get the message," Aunt Antoinette said breezily as she arranged her voluptuous, shapely frame against the far side of the carriage. She smiled as she toyed with the feathers of her headdress. "My poor son can be rather a buffoon when he's had a couple too many as he clearly has had tonight."

Katherine shot a glance at her aunt to see if she were funning or perhaps taking offence on George's account. This was her first visit in a year to Bath to stay with her aunt and Lord Quamby, but her last was memorable for making her debut at the Assembly Rooms. There, a gentleman had asked Aunt Antoinette if she were Katherine's sister, declaring her 'a golden-haired' manifestation of Katherine. The remark had delighted Aunt Antoinette, shocked Katherine, and prompted her mother to use it as an example of why her daughter should not be trusting of gentlemen who were only after 'one thing'. This cryptic phrase, with no elaboration, had been confusing, but the incident had made Katherine more observant of her aunt who seemed to lead her life as if it were one great big adventure with nothing more important than drinking champagne and being feted by gentlemen.

"Antoinette, you mustn't speak about the boy like that in front of Katherine," her mother now said before asking briskly, "And did you see any handsome gentleman whose acquaintance you'd like to further, Katherine?"

"Bearing in mind they must also have a nicely plump pocketbook. Such a sighting would save your parents the cost of your London season," her aunt responded with a laugh. "You'd be very welcome to remain here and further any acquaintance you desire as long as they are quite of the Upper Five Hundred. Or, since your mama declares she wants you to follow your heart, the Upper One Thousand."

Lady Fenton ignored her sister, her gaze still focused on Katherine. "Darling, I'm being serious. *Did* you meet anyone? And don't listen to your aunt. You know your father and I want you to wed only when your heart is properly engaged."

Katherine played with her reticule while she formed a careful answer for her mind was filled with thoughts of Jack. "No, Mama, I didn't see anyone."

"So, it's off to London in a week then!" declared Aunt Antoinette gaily. "I'm so glad. I'd have hated to be deprived of my fun in the metropolis."

Katherine let her mother and aunt converse on either side of her while she continued to dream of the young man she'd not seen but with whom she'd shared such an exciting kiss in the dark. It had been as pleasurable and as exciting as she'd imagined it would be, though she was aware the sensations might have been heightened by its illicit edge.

When the carriage drew to a halt in front of the portico of Quamby House where she and her parents would stay until they travelled to London, her heart suddenly began skittering around her chest cavity. It was silly, she berated herself, because she'd known Jack for years. Admittedly, when she'd last seen him they'd initially been wary of each other until one of the earl's dogs had gone missing. During the subsequent search, however, they'd reestablished the old rapport, daring each other to more outrageous exploits, balancing on overturned tree trunks to cross streams and climbing overhanging tree branches. They'd been filthy when they'd returned but very happy, the bonds of old friendship fully restored.

"Come along, Katherine. Don't keep everyone waiting!" Her mother was waiting for her by the carriage while Aunt Antoinette was already being admitted through the double doors. "The Patmores are here already. Please be kind to Jack. You treated him so abominably as a child as I recall, but do remember he's officially adopted. He's not the foundling boy you had at your beck and call when you were younger."

That was what her mother thought, Katherine mused as she followed her mother. Jack would always be at her beck and call. Why else would she like him so much?

Annoyed to find her heart positively racing by the time she neared the drawing room door, she wondered why since she was neither embarrassed nor feeling ashamed of her behaviour with Jack. She supposed it was because Jack had entered into the experiment with his usual good humour. And that's what it had been: an experiment, not a romantic adventure.

"Katherine, you've turned into quite the beauty!" declared Eliza Patmore as Katherine curtsied demurely in front of her and her husband. Although Katherine had been aware of the young man beside them who had risen at her entrance, she hadn't yet ventured a look in his direction.

"Thank you, Mrs Patmore," she murmured, before turning slightly and inclining her head. "And you must be Jack." Suddenly, her heart was in her mouth and hammering like a tin drum though she kept her voice level and cool. "So nice to see you again."

He was nothing like the thirteen-year-old she remembered. The feel of his jawline and the touch of his lips in the dark had provided no inkling of what he'd look like when under scrutiny. His hair was the light, curling brown she remembered, but his lips were a more interesting shape. They were curved into a smile, now, his sparkling eyes boring into hers as if he were sharing a private joke with her, except that she wasn't ready to enter into the fun. In fact, she wasn't sure what to think for she'd always had the upper hand, and yet now, Jack Patmore was no longer the poor boy with no family; he was a young, handsome man of good standing.

"Did you not recognise me?" he asked.

Yes, she recognised him, but there was a jaunty confidence that was nothing like she'd expected. Of course, he'd always been easy-natured. Katherine had had a hard time whipping up his anger when she'd played a childish prank on him. For the most part though, she'd co-opted him into high jinks that had Cook running after them waving her wooden spoon, or Nanny shrieking with terror at a mouse the children had dropped into her work basket. So, while Katherine had never seen Jack lose his temper, she'd not expected he'd be so at ease in these surroundings. Yes, that's what it was. He was the fortunate boy who'd been allowed a taste of the good life at Quamby House. He was supposed to be grateful and subservient, but now he was smiling and acting as if he were Katherine's equal. It irritated her. Yes, that was the feeling that was niggling at her, she decided. Irritation. "Barely, for it's been a long time since I saw you…"

"Yes…a very long time." He frowned. "When *did* I last see you?"

"Five years ago," she said quickly.

"Five years ago. That's a very long time. Surely we've… bumped into one another since then?"

She felt the warmth in her cheeks. She, who never blushed. "Yes, five years ago I saw you. When I was twelve," she said airily. It was ridiculous, but she suddenly couldn't think of anything the least bit clever or lively to say.

The look he sent her was wicked but Katherine was not going to pretend to share the humour. Of course, she shouldn't have kissed him in the dark. She'd thought herself terribly clever, but now she felt she'd played into his hands.

"We're unleashing Katherine on local society so she doesn't embarrass her poor parents when she goes to London, isn't that right, Fanny?" Aunt Antoinette appealed to her sister, waving at the servant to pour the claret.

"When have I ever embarrassed them before?" Katherine retorted, gaining courage and taking a glass of claret before her father plucked it from her hands. Nevertheless, this is what he did, saying, "You may have attended your first ball but this is for grown-ups, my dear."

"Papa! I might be married in a month!"

"That would be working fast, my dear," said Aunt Antoinette. "Even faster than your mother when she was unleashed on London society all those years ago. Not that she was distinguished by her speed. More, her tenacity and daring. It took her a full two seasons to snare handsome Fenton." She flashed a smile at her brother-in-law before greeting her son who'd just walked into the room. "George, you've returned at last! Say hello to Jack. It's been a long time since you've seen him."

"You were at the ball." George pointed an accusing finger at Jack as he ran a chunky, ring-adorned hand through his fashionably curled hair. "As soon as you saw me, you disappeared. It *was* you, wasn't it?"

Jack looked innocent. "Lord, how rude of me. Was that *you* coming towards me? Truth is, I lost my nerve when I found myself surrounded by strangers." He sent the other youth a disarming smile. "Every young lady in that room seemed to look down her nose at me, so I decided to beat a hasty retreat. If I'd known it was you, George, I'd have asked you to introduce me to some people. Maybe someone whom I could have asked to dance."

George pursed his lips and swivelled his eyes between Jack's earnest face and his mother's smiling approval. Won over by the fact that Jack appeared to look up to him, he said reassuringly, "Course I would have, Jack. I always stuck up for you when we were children. Don't know what you'd have done without me looking out for you if the truth be told."

"I don't know, either," Jack agreed.

George stuffed his thumbs into his waistband. "Cousin Katherine was forever planning something devious to shame you, Jack, just because you were an orphan." He jutted out his jaw and looked collaboratively at Jack before frowning at Katherine and saying upon a sigh, "The number of times I stopped her from tormenting you when you had no one"

"Yes, yes, George, I'm sure we all remember those days," his mother interrupted, raising her eyes to the ceiling and fanning herself. "But let's turn the topic to the plans for fun and excitement we've devised for our guests here the next few days. I expect you to be on your best behaviour and to be the perfect host. We don't want poor Katherine rushing off to London thinking she couldn't have escaped fast enough."

Aunt Antoinette smiled at Jack. "And your presence will be much appreciated, Jack, because we've hired a dancing master for Katherine only George says he won't dance. So, I hope you don't mind"

"I *will* dance," George objected.

"You said you'd refuse, darling, because you had more important things in town and you'd be leaving tomorrow."

George rolled his shoulders. "Well, I've changed my mind," he muttered. "That was before I met Katherine again after so long and...and realised how grateful she'd be to have a dancing partner. I'm not about to shirk my duties as host while Katherine and Jack are here. Not when it could be just like the wonderful old days."

And as Katherine glanced between George and Jack, she felt she really was returning to those wonderful old days where Jack was her friend and ally and teasing George promised to be so much fun.

CHAPTER 3

The wonderful old days had been anything but wonderful as far as Jack was concerned. Life at the foundling home was spartan, and survival depended on charming the wardens and being a step ahead of the children who would snitch or steal for an extra spoonful of gruel.

The only wonderful highlights of Jack's years from infancy to when he was eight years old were his thrice-weekly visits to Quamby House. The supervisor at the foundling home had told Jack a permanent position as a bootboy might be in the offing. However, the earl and his countess, who seemed to him like genial royalty, insisted instead that Jack must 'play'. Jack soon learned that the words work and play were interchangeable. Jack's job was to 'play' with the earl's son, George, a large, lumpish, spoiled, and self-absorbed boy, who was an only child and needed a playmate. Apparently, in the eyes of Lord and Lady Quamby, this constituted work as their son was, they told him, 'not an easy boy'.

George had been resistant at first, and had Jack feeling disinclined to court the society of a child who was so unappreciative of his good fortune, but Jack soon learned that trailing the bigger boy was an assured way of getting lots of good food. Unaccountably, the cook formed a fondness for him, and never did he return to the foundling home without a covered basket full of treats he would share with the other children, thus shoring up his power and popularity there.

Not that Jack had sought power for any other reason than to get enough to eat, but now that he was eighteen and would soon be proving himself in the West Indies, he realised his early days had provided useful training in understanding how children and adults manipulated one another for different objectives.

George was clearly keen to impress Katherine and prove his dominance over Jack—just like the old days—so it was easy to slip back into the old patterns that had worked in the past.

Maturity, of course, altered matters a little. Katherine was conscious of her blossoming beauty, he could see, while George remained as unaware of external forces as he had ever been.

Chief among these pleasures was eating, though it appeared he'd suddenly discovered a passion for dancing, and squiring Katherine in a polka or waltz was, he declared, an important cousinly duty.

"She's quite green, so she'll need a bit of dash if she's to carry it off on the dance floor," he told Jack the morning after Jack's arrival at Quamby House.

"And you're just the man to ensure she shows herself to advantage," Jack responded as they tucked into the peach tart Cook had made. He found it touching that the old dear had remembered it used to be Jack's favourite. "You're the counterpoint to her grace, charm, and elegance."

"The counterpoint, yes," George repeated, leaning back in

his chair in the conservatory, though he sounded a little uncertain as to what Jack actually meant.

"She appears so vibrant when she's next to you," Jack explained. "You're bringing out her best."

George seemed to like this before asking if Jack would like to observe from the sidelines how he executed his clever moves on the dance floor with Katherine. With a smug grin, he added that he wasn't one to keep his tricks to himself and, in view of their long friendship, he'd be pleased to teach Jack everything he knew.

So, now Jack was reclining on a red-velvet-upholstered sofa he'd dragged into the vast, empty ballroom, and was nodding approval as George swung Katherine round and round the room to a less than perfect piano accompaniment.

Almost perfect, in Jack's eyes, however, was Katherine whose transformation from a spirited twelve-year-old to a beautiful and self-assured young woman was almost complete. He didn't think she could be any lovelier, and he still couldn't get over that he'd shared his first proper kiss with her the night before in the dark. He'd kissed girls before, though he decided these didn't count since none of the consequent effects had been remotely like the incendiary response he'd experienced with Katherine.

Not that Katherine appeared to consider it an earth-shattering experience. In fact, she'd been making it quite clear all day that their sensuous encounter in the dark had been nothing more than a piece of fun for her. At breakfast, she'd tossed her elaborately plaited and braided hair and raised her nose to the ceiling when Jack had said good morning, murmuring that she hadn't been up long enough to tell. Jack wondered if the fact she wasn't able to look him in the eye was because she was embarrassed, or if she really did think herself his superior.

Her attitude amused him, which was why he'd dragged the old red velvet sofa into the ballroom. Watching so slavishly from the sidelines would surely annoy her.

And, clearly, it did.

After the third time that Jack complimented George on his technique and criticised Katherine on hers, she snapped.

"Maybe you should try for yourself, Jack, instead of offering everyone else good advice."

"I was just offering *you* good advice," said Jack innocently. "Not *everyone*."

"So, George doesn't need improvement but I, who am to be launched in less than five days, have a long way to go? That's what you inferred, Jack, and don't you deny it. Are you so perfect that you've never stepped on anyone's toes?"

"I wouldn't dare try what George is doing," Jack said hastily. "The man's a cream puff in trousers, and I'm nowhere near the expert he is. I'd only show what a clumsy oaf I am by comparison."

"Go on, try then," George dared him, dropping his hands from about Katherine's waist and shoulders and signalling for Jack to take his place. "Though what you say is true. Many a young lady, and not so young, has complimented me on how well I take the lead while ensuring she has such a pleasurable experience along the way." He glanced at Katherine as if to gauge the effectiveness of his words, and Jack caught Katherine's secret eye roll as she tilted her face to glance at her new partner. A moment of shared hilarity reverberated through them as Jack rose and took George's place, truncated with great effect by Jack's loud objection that Katherine had started before the proper beat.

"Do you really have two left feet, Jack?" Katherine said crossly as he pulled her closer to him, pretending to try and keep his balance.

Together they lurched about the dance floor until the music finished after which Katherine threw up her hands and declared, "You'd have to be the worst dancer I've ever had the misfortune to partner."

"Jack! Jack, old chap, do watch more closely," George admonished as he returned to squiring Katherine about.

"But just for this one last dance," warned Katherine. "My feet are bruised all over from Jack stepping on my toes, but George is such an athlete it quite takes my breath away. Really, George, with the pace you set, I truly can only manage one more dance."

Outside, alone together as George had reluctantly answered a summons from his uncle, Jack and Katherine had to hurry behind the broad trunk of an old oak tree before they collapsed into laughter.

"Goodness, did you see how smug George looked when I called him an athlete!" Katherine giggled.

"And how he loved to put me in my place," Jack replied.

"George is so easy to manage if he thinks he has the upper hand." Katherine wiped the tears of laughter away from her face with the back of her hand and, still breathing rapidly, said, "Do say you'll come to London with us. George is coming, and I don't think I can bear even a week staying at Uncle Quamby's townhouse if it's just George and me. Didn't your mama say it was a possibility?"

"A possibility, but one already discounted," Jack said feeling disappointed. "I board my ship for the West Indies in ten days, and I'd decided to forgo London and return home to pack."

"Then change your plans."

The way Katherine looked so imploringly up at him decided Jack in an instant. He shrugged. "All right, I will. Mama and Uncle will be in London in any case, though I can only stay a couple of days before the house is overrun with the Hampshire cousins.”

“Then you can stay at Uncle Quamby’s townhouse, I’m sure.”

Jack saw that her suggestion was genuine. “In that case, we’ll all go to London. It’ll be grand!”

CHAPTER 4

"So I have day dresses, two spencers, two walking dresses, three shawls, one opera cloak, four pairs of dancing slippers, one pair of walking boots, three bonnets—" Katherine broke off her inventory to greet her aunt while her maid laid out each item of her lavish wardrobe on the bed before folding it to put away in the wardrobe. "Aren't I going to be the best-dressed debutante in all of London, Aunt Antoinette?"

Katherine was feeling remarkably chipper this morning despite the hour at which she'd returned from her very first London ball. After their day of travelling between Bath and London, they'd only reached Mayfair at four o'clock the previous afternoon, and Mama had said that of course it was too late to look in at Lady Eddison's Assembly Ball. However, Katherine had had her way, partly because the Patmores had already arrived and Jack had turned up on their doorstep with all the encouragement needed. Which wasn't much. For Mama was tired and Jack was persuasive, saying his own mama hoped very much for Katherine's company, which was all it took to make a compelling case.

It had been entirely worth everything. Aunt Antoinette had accompanied her to last night's ball, naturally, though Katherine suspected her aunt had her own scheme for the evening already laid out if the warmth of Aunt Antoinette's familiar greeting of a young man considerably younger than herself, who had then paid her a great deal of attention all evening, was anything to go by.

Katherine had only been to London once, and she'd been too young to dance though she'd attended a few quiet house parties.

This was different, though. She was officially *out*. A debutante. And it only took last night to realise she was a popular one.

This, it transpired, was the reason for her aunt's visit to her bedchamber now.

Aunt Antoinette draped herself across a chair she pulled at right angles to the bed, looked at the selection of clothes and accessories, and said, "I think my favourite is the crimson silk."

"Though I shall wear the pale blue, naturally, since Mama will be accompanying me."

Her aunt nodded approvingly. "Of course. Your mama was such a wicked girl in her day but, of course, now that she has her own daughter, she is as overprotective as a mother hen."

Katherine rubbed the side of her nose, not quite thinking this an appropriate analogy, though it was true that her mama had shown herself surprisingly cautious and occasionally critical about the way Katherine's conducted herself in public.

She sat down at her dressing table and picked up a rabbit's-foot brush. "I can't believe the things you say about my mama, sometimes. About her being wild. She seems so... proper." Katherine was fishing for more tidbits, it was true, but true also was the fact she found it hard to reconcile her mama—devoted wife and mother who had eyes only for

Katherine's papa—with the bold and beautiful debutante she'd learned had scandalised society with her antics.

"Marriage has made her proper."

"Marriage didn't make you proper," Katherine dared, with a smile. She'd always been aware that Aunt Antoinette was 'different' and that her marriage to the Earl of Quamby was 'different' yet she still didn't quite understand it.

"Oh, being proper is only for people who have to be," Aunt Antoinette said airily. "The ugly girls, the wallflowers— they can't get away with anything. Last night made it clear you'll never fall into that category, my dear, which is why I've come to talk to you."

Katherine straightened. "Goodness, that's very...direct, Aunt."

"Well, there's no point in fostering your ignorance and then regretting I'd not spoken to you earlier when it's already too late."

"What's too late?" Katherine bent forward in alarm.

"Nothing's too late. Not now. But that's only because I'm speaking to you of matters your mama wouldn't dream of bringing up with you—even though it's what nearly caused her own downfall. And mine." Aunt Antoinette raised an eyebrow. "Well, aren't you going to quiz me?"

Katherine blinked. "Wouldn't that be impolite? I was going to wait for you to tell me."

"Oh, but you *are* a well-brought-up little miss. The trouble is, Katherine, one day you'll get caught by surprise with those...feelings there..." she said directing a searching look at Katherine's bosom, "and there..." She dropped her eyes lower. "You probably won't think to behave in any manner other than what your heart and body and those feelings direct you to. At least, you won't if you're anything like your mother and myself. Which means, Katherine dearest, that it is my duty to explain to you the dangers of being under the control of love, passion, and desire. It's quite likely you'll entirely lose your head and throw caution to the wind, and then where would we all be if I hadn't warned you?"

Katherine stared at her, puzzled. "Warned me? But you just did. About these feelings you say I'll feel when I fall in love. I've felt some of them already but they didn't make me lose my head. I certainly shan't make foolish decisions when it comes to choosing a husband. It's my most important consideration now that I'm in London."

As Miss Fenton, Katherine had a world of limitations placed upon her, but she'd seen how entirely different it was for the young matrons of her acquaintance to order their households and servants, and that's exactly what she couldn't wait to do.

Aunt Antoinette let out a tinkling laugh. "Oh, my dear girl. If only it were that easy! Do you really think you'll just fall in love with the right gentleman and get married?"

"Georgiana Rice did. And so did Miss Marcia Heaslip. And Miss Juliana Macefield and"

"Well, those are the girls you know who did what was expected of them and good for them that it all went so swimmingly—if it did." Aunt Antoinette shrugged. "But what if you fall in love with someone entirely disreputable?"

"Like Cousin George?"

Antoinette snorted as Katherine clapped her hand to her mouth. "Forgive me, Aunt. It was very rude to speak like that about your son." When she saw that she'd caused Aunt Antoinette no offence and, in fact, that her aunt appeared to endorse her feelings, she went on hesitantly. "I meant Cousin George cultivates an air about him that is disreputable, but he's the last man I'd fall in love with." She thought a moment. "I suppose you might mean someone like Mr Marwick who danced with me twice last night."

"Exactly!" Aunt Antoinette gave a decisive nod, as if she'd

been waiting for Katherine to mention his name. "He is *exactly* the kind of gentleman I'm here to warn you about, and if you can't heed anyone's warnings—because let me assure you, your mama will be on the warpath since Mr Marwick is the nephew of a fellow she was secretly betrothed to—I shall have to advise you how to manage matters so you don't land up in the kind of trouble I did."

Katherine glanced at the door and prayed her mother wouldn't choose this moment to enter. She knew Aunt Antoinette was the wilder of the two sisters, but her mother — clearly reformed if her aunt had been truthful about the early days—seemed determined that her sister not spend too much time alone with her niece.

"What kind of trouble, Aunt?" she whispered. She knew it was death to a young lady's reputation to be unchaperoned when alone with a young man, though she'd never been entirely sure why if kissing was the worst that could happen. If Aunt Antoinette could elaborate, it would be hugely helpful.

"The kind of trouble I worry about you getting into with a rake like Mr Marwick."

"But I only danced with him twice, Aunt."

"And I saw the way his eyes followed you around the room for the entire evening. Believe me, Katherine, he wants to do more than just dance with you."

Katherine shivered with pleasure. She glanced at the red silk. Perhaps she would wear it, after all. Mr Marwick looked the kind of gentleman who'd appreciate a bolder entrance than she'd make in the more demure pale blue. "You think he might want to marry me?" She was surprised when Aunt Antoinette made a derisive snorting noise that did nothing to detract from her shining beauty and aplomb. There really was something of the ripe peach about her. Katherine had over-heard those words used more than one gentleman. And it was true that Aunt Antoinette looked rather exotic with her golden ringlets escaping from the fashionable and elaborate style now in fashion. So, still thinking of this expression, she asked, "Do you mean he regards me like a peach, ready for the plucking?"

"Good Lord, where did you hear that term?" her aunt cried, looking both shocked and delighted. "You overheard Lord Brentwood say that about me, didn't you?Such a nice gentleman." " She sighed fondly before adding briskly, "No, your beauty is different and, as you're an unknown quantity, you are a source of great fascination to a man like Freddy Marwick as well as to his friend and rival, Lord Derry. So, beware, Katherine. Mr Marwick is the kind who'll take any opportunity to whisk you into a dark corner, or away from the hubbub, and you might think it a thrilling idea at the time." Her aunt frowned heavily. "But do not go anywhere alone with Mr Marwick for he is not a reputable gentleman. I've made enquiries, and for fear of making you do exactly the opposite of what I tell you, I must warn you about him."

Katherine opened her mouth to protest that she had no intention of going into any dark corners with any gentleman, though she liked Mr Marwick who was charming and attentive and, indeed, rather intriguing in a dangerous kind of way, but her aunt cut her off. "But, if you do, and if matters proceed in a manner that is...unwise...then know you can always come to me for help."

Katherine was about to ask her to clarify what she could possibly mean but her aunt rose and said, decisively, "And that is all I have to say on the subject for fear of your mama boxing my ears for putting ideas into that pretty little head of yours."

"And was that all you came to tell me?"

"Absolutely. You need to beware of Mr Marwick, but if you do something you regret, come to me, rather than your mama." She put her hand on the doorknob and was about to leave the room when Katherine's mama swept in, a lovely smile making her even more of a beauty than her sister, Katherine thought in that moment. But then, while she was enormously fond of her aunt, she was devoted to her mother, despite their occasional differences of opinion. And as her mother seemed so very pleased with Katherine's choice of attire when she asked what Katherine wanted to wear to Lady Maxwell's that night, and so satisfied with the reports of her daughter's general conduct the previous evening, Katherine decided that her trip to London was going to be the most marvellous success. She'd make both her parents proud, and be, herself, the happiest bride sometime during the next few months, she supposed. For there really was a vast array of choice, with seemingly every eligible gentleman in the land here in London for her to choose from.

Mr Marwick was dangerous and exciting and clearly mad for her; Lord Derry was courteous and intense and also clearly mad for her. Already she had two potential suitors.

And that was only after her very first ball.

CHAPTER 5

Katherine only realised what a sedate affair the previous evening had been when she and her parents were announced by Lord and Lady Maxwell's butler, in stentorian tones, to a vast assembly of guests.

"You look very beautiful, my darling." Her father leaned over to whisper in her ear. "Now, smile. It's not often I don't see that wicked glint in your eye, but I assure you, nobody's going to bite you."

This made Katherine relax and, with a laugh, the very first person she was presented to was, to her surprise, Mr Marwick.

"Miss Fenton. I am enchanted," he murmured, kissing the back of her hand. And indeed he really looked to be. His dark eyes sparkled, and his glossy moustache tickled in the most interesting way as it touched her flesh, sparking the sudden idea that it would be interesting to know what it felt like caressing her lips.

Almost immediately she saw Jack, who was of course the only man she *had* kissed, and since Jack's presence had the effect of making her feel comfortable and at ease in this alien company, she didn't object when her mama truncated Katherine's conversation with Mr Marwick and steered her in the direction of her old friend, saying, "Jack, you look very dashing this evening. Won't you lead Katherine into the next dance? This is all very new to her, and with you, I know she'll be in safe hands."

Katherine couldn't resist a quick glance over her shoulder at Mr Marwick before she surrendered herself to Jack. When she saw that the tall, slender gentleman with such dangerously alluring saturnine looks was staring intently at her, heat burned her cheeks and her heart rate accelerated wildly. As their glances interlocked, he kissed the tips of his fingers and offered her a very elaborate bow.

"I see you have a new admirer," Jack remarked as she turned back to him. His eyes were warm. "Not that I'm surprised. You're far and away the most beautiful girl in the room."

Delight fizzed through Katherine but before she could reply, Jack seized her hand and pulled her away.

"Heavens, Jack, that's no way to manhandle a lady!" she said crossly.

"Sorry! Your Cousin George was making a beeline for you, and I thought you'd feel safer on the dance floor with me and out of his orbit."

"Well, if it's a choice of having you step all over my toes or to have to suffer George's arms around me, I don't know what I'd choose," Katherine grumbled. But it wasn't long before she was tipping up her face to say admiringly, "You're actually quite a marvellous dancer, Jack. You haven't stepped on my toes, once."

"Oh, that was all an act for George. Surely you knew that?"

"But you were so convincing."

"Of course. A foundling home lad only survives through pretending to be whatever is required at the time." His grip tightened about her waist, and he drew her closer as they negotiated a manoeuvre between a couple who'd left them little space. Katherine reflected that while it was wonderful to be admired by Mr Marwick, everything about the London social whirl was still rather daunting, and having Jack close was more of a comfort than she would have believed.

"And what is required of you tonight that you must pretend?" she asked playfully.

He appeared to consider this. "I must be a fine upstanding gentleman, older than my years if I'm to compete with all the other rich, titled, and experienced fellows currently admiring you throughout the room. And I must definitely not step on your toes in order to maintain your current high opinion of me which I know will be in shreds the moment I say something to make you cross. I might look at my ease but inside I'm quaking, walking on eggshells."

"Goodness, was I such an imperious child?" She laughed as she was assailed by fond memories of those distant days. "Yet I don't recall that you were ever angry with me."

"Again, that's due to the skill required of a foundling home child. I learned how to manage you, Katherine. And really, I quite enjoyed doing your fetching and carrying which, might I add, I only did because I wanted to."

"Wouldn't you do whatever I asked...even if you didn't want to?" she asked slyly. "You only do things that you want to do? Is this your way of telling me you're a man of unyielding principle?"

"I like to think so though perhaps it's not yet been put to the test." He grew serious. "It's one of the things I intend to work on when I'm away. I don't want to be known as the foundling lad who was only able to make his mark through the support of his generous adoptive parents. I want to come home having made my fortune through my own efforts, and known as a man of honour and principle."

"Fine words, indeed, but I can't bear the thought you're leaving in only five days. I *will* miss you, Jack."

"Will you, really?"

Katherine glanced up, surprised at his tone and the intensity of her own feelings. She swallowed down the lump in her throat. "It was lovely having you there at Quamby House, and it would be so nice to have you here throughout the season as...well...a comforting presence as I"

"Navigate the multitude of gallant offers from so many gallant men," Jack supplied for her. "No, thank you. I don't think I could bear the jealousy. But, here is the first of those gallant admirers ready to seize his moment now that our waltz is over."

He dropped his hands from Katherine's waist. "Good evening, George. What a relief it will be for Katherine to swap her dance partner for one who really can dance."

Katherine flashed a colluding smile at Jack. "Really, I don't know how I'll be able to walk tomorrow after what you've done to my feet, Jack!"

George nodded. "We can't all be good at everything." He gripped Katherine's hand and pulled her into the centre of the dance floor. "Let's show Jack how it's done, eh?"

Jack shook his head. "I'll just bow out gracefully and see what other enticements are on offer. As it happens, I've spied a very pretty girl by the supper table who looks like she needs some company."

Katherine followed Jack with her gaze from over George's shoulder as he waltzed her about the room. She was surprised by the chagrin that welled up inside her as she saw the responsive smile the aforementioned very pretty young lady directed at Jack. Mr Marwick, who was waltzing with a plain ginger haired girl passed, by. His glittering black eyes bored into hers and his moustache twitched as he whispered, "Promise you'll reserve the next dance for me, Miss Fenton."

The thrill of being singled out by such a dashing gentleman, both rich and in line for a title, restored her spirits. Tonight, she decided, she would make advances in properly assessing whom she'd consider a suitor. Aunt Antoinette's words had bolstered her confidence. She'd said Katherine could have her pick of the gentlemen, but Katherine needed to assess who was worthy. It was important to discover what it felt like to kiss a gentleman with a moustache before she furthered that acquaintance. What did it matter that she'd only met Mr Marwick last night? After all, she had only a few weeks in London to make the most important decision of her life.

She had to start somewhere.

SURPRISINGLY, HER OPPORTUNITY CAME EARLIER THAN expected, and immediately following her dance with Mr Marwick who'd held her thrillingly close. The unexpectedly soft brush of that magnificent moustache of his upon her jawline as he'd turned his head to point out something to her had caused her to jerk up her chin. His assessing gaze and the quirk of his lips told her he'd done it on purpose.

She couldn't help herself, but her mouth turned up in secret acknowledgement and her heart seemed to leap about as he increased the pressure of his hand around her waist.

"Your mama is nowhere to be seen, and I can't possibly leave you here alone," he remarked, glancing at the supper table on the other side of the room, then leading her in that direction but hesitating as they approached. He scanned the room quickly, then said under his voice, "If you glide through that knot of people, there's a door into the passageway beneath the Holbein and you won't be noticed though it's a public door, leading to the ladies sewing room."

Katherine glanced down at her gown and he laughed. "Nothing torn. Everything in perfect order, in fact. But if slip into the passage, I'll join you there in the shadows so we might…discuss our evening. We'll only be gone thirty seconds, and your mama won't even notice."

Katherine wasn't going to let this opportunity pass her by. She agreed with a quick nod, and within less than a minute, she was in the dark passage and in Mr Marwick's arms, the pair of them tucked behind an imposing coat of armour, while Mr Marwick kissed her with haste and enthusiasm.

Katherine sighed with pleasure. She'd enjoyed kissing Jack, and this experience was an interesting contrast. Her body was doing all the same things: her heartbeat was growing more rapid, her skin felt heated, and there was an urgency all about her. But the moment he withdrew to take a breath, she wasn't visited by the urge to throw her arms about his neck once more and drag his mouth back to hers. He was a very adept kisser, and the experience was definitely worthwhile, but she certainly had some more research to do before she decided on her future husband.

It was he who hurried her back into the throng once more, saying words that suggested he was as concerned for his own reputation as for hers.

But before he had the opportunity to remark upon their quick kissing tryst—which he was clearly about to do for his eyes kindled as he lowered his head to hers—Katherine was nearly startled out of her wits by a familiar hand upon her upper arm followed by a slight tug. Raising an indignant chin, she found Jack nodding at Mr Marwick and thanking him for his attendance to Katherine on the dance floor. His manner indicated clear dismissal.

Not that the older man was going to be fobbed off by

such a greenhorn—at least, that's the impression Katherine gained as the two regarded each other.

"And who might you be?" Mr Marwick asked, quite rudely, Katherine thought, wondering how Jack would describe himself.

"Mr Jack Patmore, Miss Fenton's proxy cousin. My family accompanied hers to London and assigned me the duty of ensuring she was properly attended."

Katherine liked that assessment. Yes, Jack was like a proxy cousin: stalwart and dependable and there to see to her interests. She wasn't at all disappointed when Mr Marwick bowed in dismissal and left, she discovered.

"What have you been up to, Miss Fenton?" Jack asked with mock severity. "Tell me, or I shall have to report to your mama that you've lost one of the pearl earrings she lent you for this evening."

Katherine put her hand to her earlobe with a gasp and grabbed Jack's hand. "It's in the passage just beyond. I have to fetch it. Come with me, Jack. Hurry!"

She was panting with terror when she reached the door beyond. Jack stopped in the passageway when she dashed behind the coat of arms.

"*What* were you doing with Mr Marwick all the way up here, alone?"

Katherine stepped back into view and met his censure with defiance, though the truth was she felt a little embarrassed having to admit the truth. "Really, Jack, it doesn't concern you, but since I've nothing to be ashamed of, I kissed him. Or rather, he kissed me. Just like you did."

She glanced nervously up the passage to where the door was quite likely to admit any visitor heading to the mending room.

He gave her a considering look. "And?"

"And what?" Katherine fanned herself, returning to his

side for the earring was not where she'd hoped to find it. "It was very nice, actually. I liked the feel of his moustache. If he's going to be my husband, I'll want to know that I like it."

Jack looked startled. "But you only just met him."

"Clearly the reason he's in London is the same reason I am." She pushed back her shoulders. "I've decided I need to kiss every man I think might be my husband. Naturally, I have to compare."

Jack nodded, stroking his chin. Then he stared at the floor and took a few steps away.

"What are you doing?"

"Looking for your earring, of course."

"Aren't you going to ask if I liked kissing Mr Marwick as much as I liked kissing you?"

"I'm not sure I want to."

"I liked kissing you very much."

He straightened, his bright smile suddenly taking on a decisively sly cast. "Do you not think that in order to make a truly considered assessment you ought to kiss me one more time?"

Katherine met his look and shivered in anticipation. With Mr Marwick's kiss fresh in her memory, Jack's suggestion sounded perfectly reasonable. Her gaze travelled the length of his long, lean legs and lingered on his mouth and without saying a word, she stepped into his embrace, closing her eyes as a sweet, pleasurable sensation poured through her at the touch of his lips.

His arms tightened about her, and she felt as if she were melting into him. He was more slender than Mr Marwick but of course at least six years younger, so that was hardly surprising. But she liked the strength of him, the width of his shoulders, and again she was flooded with happiness at memories of their long-ago shared companionship.

Until her body started to behave in a very strange manner,

and suddenly the kiss seemed to only touch the surface of what she needed right now. Tiny prickles of sensation speared her all over, and there was the strangest roiling in her lower belly. As she deepened the kiss and ran her hands over his coat and down his back, she was delighted to hear his own breathing grow more laboured. Her breasts grew tingly, and she wished he would put his hands there but he was ever the gentleman.

Katherine desire for exploration soon had her running her fingers through Jack's hair, contouring his waist, skimming his hips, but when her hand inadvertently came in contact with an unexpected swelling at the front of his trousers, she opened her eyes in surprise.

He broke the kiss, stepping away quickly. "Heavens, Katherine, you can't do that to a fellow," he protested, blushing furiously.

"Do what? What was I doing? And what *was* that?" Katherine was confused but before she could say any more he gripped her wrist and pulled her after him, back towards the ballroom which was just as thronged with people as before, and no one seemed to pay them any heed as they slipped past a group of gentlemen loudly talking politics.

"There's your mama. I'll leave you in her capable hands while I go back and look for your earring—properly, this time," said Jack, and was gone before she could stop him.

CHAPTER 6

"I don't know where you find the energy to stay up so late every night and still want to go riding in the afternoon, Katherine?" her mother remarked as she and Aunt Antoinette idly went over Katherine's various items of clothing to see what needed mending or cleaning. The late morning sun cast fingers of light across the counterpane which Katherine mused were rather like fingers of happiness. It was what she was feeling as she sat on the edge of the bed enjoying a discussion on the previous evening's entertainment.

"I'm more interested in who Katherine has set her sights on," murmured Aunt Antoinette, fiddling with the pearl earring on the dressing table which Katherine was praying she'd not pick up and then wonder aloud where the second one was. Jack had failed to locate it, and Katherine knew it would only be a matter of time before her mama asked for it back.

"Is Mr Marwick still a contender? He's been very attentive the past two nights," said her mama. "I know I took against him on account of his connection to his uncle, Lord

Slyther, whom I was *not* very fond of, but Mr Marwick does seem rather a different kind of fellow."

"He's very charming," Katherine agreed, sorting through her jewellery box for a chain to wear about her neck.

"Well, I'd say that doesn't augur well for him at all given that degree of indifference." Aunt Antoinette stood up to help Katherine with the clasp of the chain she'd chosen. "What about Lord Derry? He's not as rich, but although he is very intense, he has displayed a nice sense of humour on occasion, and that's most important for a gentleman. Remember, you'll be spending a very long time keeping each other company."

Frustrated, Katherine sat back down and sent them both a plaintive look. "Exactly! And that's what's so troubling. I expected it would be easy to find a husband, but it's not at all. There are many, many charming gentlemen, but none of them makes me want to spend the rest of my life with them. How did you know, Mama? And you, Aunt Antoinette?"

Her mother smiled. "You've been in London barely three days."

"Well, I've never found anyone I wanted to spend the rest of my life with," said her aunt. "But that hasn't stopped me having the most enormous fun!"

Katherine still couldn't fathom why her Uncle Quamby was so tolerant of his wife's many gentlemen callers.

"Enough said about that!" her mama said with a smile. "As for me knowing that your papa was the right one. Well, I knew it instantly!" She tempered her pleasurable recollection with a frown. "I was very reckless though, and I don't recommend doing half what I did, though I shouldn't even say it. I was just lucky my high-spirited antics didn't get me into terrible trouble and ruin my reputation. A young lady only has one of those, and I certainly hope you're behaving yourself, Katherine."

"Oh, I've made sure Katherine knows to be careful," said her aunt. "No disappearing into darkened chambers alone. Isn't that right, Katherine?"

Katherine smiled weakly and stood up again. She felt suddenly stifled in her small bedchamber and was afraid she'd feel similarly stifled in tonight's ballroom, which surprised her, because before she came to London, she thought she'd never get enough of dancing and ballrooms.

Her request for someone to accompany her for a walk in Hyde Park was met with lukewarm interest from her mother but her perceptive aunt stood up, saying, "Just a short one for I daresay a little fresh air would be good for your complexion —though not mine at my age. I daresay you're hoping you'll see Lord Derry"

"I like Lord Derry, but I hardly imagine I'll know if I want to marry him before the end of two weeks," Katherine grumbled, later, as they promenaded along the neatly brushed gravel paths beneath the oaks, garnering a good deal of attention. "These things take more time than two weeks, surely?"

Her aunt gave her arm a comforting squeeze and sighed. "My poor Katherine. I can see that in your case you'll need to be struck by lightning if you're to be satisfied you've chosen the right man. Clearly, you are more like your mama than you are me, and a good thing that your mama was so fortunate and did find her match." She touched her niece's cheek as they continued to stroll. "And you don't have to make any decisions this season."

"If I like the way a gentleman makes me feel when he kisses me will that tell me if I'm making the right choice?" Katherine sent Aunt Antoinette an anxious look. "That's how you said I should test if he's the right husband. Because obviously there'll be a lot of kissing if we're going to be married for the rest of our lives. And as long as he kisses nicely then I can feel confident in my choice. Am I right?"

Aunt Antoinette slanted her a troubled look and Katherine pounced. "I knew there was something you weren't telling me. Mama said she'd sit me down for a long talk on marriage responsibilities after I got an offer because different husbands needed managing in different ways."

"She's right about that." Aunt Antoinette looked up at the sky as if she was going to leave it at that but Katherine persisted. "There's more than just kissing though, isn't there? When I was kissing Jack, I felt"

"You kissed Jack!? Good lord, Katherine, you're not falling in love with Jack, are you?"

"Of course not," Katherine protested. "I just asked him to kiss me so I had something to compare it with when the man who asks me to be his wife kisses me."

Aunt Antoinette looked dubious then said almost crossly, "Fanny asked me specifically not to talk details to you about everything—or anything—involved in marriage as she believes that, given your nature, you'll behave just as recklessly as she did."

Katherine widened her eyes. "Isn't it better to know what to beware of? I mean" She stopped to reassure herself they were far from being overheard but, as it was not yet the fashionable hour of the day for promenading and the avenue was empty but for them, went on in a rush, "When I was kissing Jack I noticed that I felt like it was not enough. That there was something more. And Jack was definitely affected...in unexpected ways." She blushed hotly. "I may be an innocent, Aunt, and I know Mama and Papa have taken every care to ensure I'm sheltered, but I'm not stupid. What about the farmyard animals? Of course, I know what stallions do to mares to produce a foal. Only, when I mentioned it to one of my governesses, she said animals and human beings are entirely different."

"So they are." Antoinette smiled. She paused to take her

niece's hand and gave it a quick squeeze. "And now I'm going to tell you everything your mother is so terrified of you knowing because, right now, I believe your understandable curiosity is more important than her unfounded—in my opinion—fears."

Relieved, Katherine looked enquiringly up at her aunt as she halted in the middle of the gravel walkway. "So, my future husband *will* want to do more than just kiss me?"

"If you choose the right husband, you'll want to do those things, too."

Katherine thought of the way her heart had skittered all about her chest when Jack had kissed her. She'd wanted him to touch her all over. Even the thought of their brief tryst in the passage made her breathless.

Her aunt sent her a knowing smile. "I won't go into details —for the sake of my promise to my sister—but suffice to say that it's only when a certain...nakedness...is achieved, that the marriage act is consummated. Very coy, I know, but I trust you'll use your imagination."

Katherine looked about to make sure that not another living person was in sight before she asked, "What does consummation involve?" She tried to recall her history lessons in the school room. "I've heard it used in a way where I thought it was a legal term and nothing about being in love."

Her aunt laughed. "You might say that the physical act where the husband lies on top of his wife, just as the stallion does the mare, *is* the legal side of consummation, whereas any love and pleasure that goes with it is just good fortune. You, my dear, are in the very happy position of having a substantial dowry, which means you can choose a suitably connected husband who makes your heart do all the right things. In other words, you can marry for love."

Katherine nodded and pressed her lips together, glad she was talking about this to her aunt and not her mama. "I think I understand. I remember learning about King Henry VIII who tried to have his marriage to Katherine of Aragon annulled so he was free to marry Anne Boleyn in order to have a son. Miss Matterson wasn't very good at answering my questions because of course I knew King Henry and Katherine of Aragon already had a daughter. But you've explained it much better. So, I understand that a marriage needs to be consummated in order to have a child." She bit her lip as she reasoned it out, adding, "Which, of course, means *you've* consummated the marriage act twice, and so has Mama because both of you have two children each."

"Stop! No, there's something missing." Aunt Antoinette, looking flustered, put her hand to her bonnet as a gust of wind threatened to blow it away. "Goodness, Katherine, I've never considered myself the slightest bit prudish, but we live in less...liberal times, now, perhaps. And it certainly is no easy task talking about this to an innocent, particularly when that innocent is the gently reared child of my sister, who is adamant your delicate ears aren't sullied by my crude talk." She drew in a deep breath, then said, "There is enormous pleasure in the marriage act though, ideally, a child only results when it is desired. Otherwise, my nursery would be overflowing," she added with a smile. "So, suffice to say that you must choose a husband who makes your little heart want to shoot to the stars—and if you want to minimise your nursery, you can talk to me about that later."

She said this under her breath but Katherine, thoroughly excited by her candour, tugged at the lace of her aunt's modish mauve silk gown and asked, "Please tell me now. I... I'm not sure I want to start my nursery the day I marry. Truly, I had great reason to consider this when I stayed at my friend, Miss Larson, at the vicarage in Tunley. Her mother had nine children, and when I heard her bemoan the fact she was soon to have a tenth, I wondered why she didn't do anything about it."

"Poor woman. Such ignorance! But as few prospective brides are given the slightest bit of useful information before marriage, it's hardly surprising. Well, Katherine, suffice to say there *are* ways to minimise the number of children brought into the world, but we'll talk about that when you're about to walk down the aisle. Now, if my eyes aren't deceiving me, I do believe I see young Jack up ahead. I know he was in Oxford Street outfitting himself for his departure to the West Indies next Monday."

CHAPTER 7

Jack was surprised he hadn't noticed Katherine before her aunt hailed him. He was usually extremely conscious of Katherine if she was anywhere in the vicinity.

At the very moment his attention had been caught by Lady Quamby's elegant wave, he'd been walking quite quickly through Hyde Park, deep in thought. How many trunks should he transport and what, exactly, should he put in them? Disconcertingly, he was experiencing a sudden and unexpected lack of faith in his ability to fulfill the ambitions of his mother and uncle, and everyone else who believed that he could be an effective overseer for such a large enterprise as the tea plantation to which he was destined.

"You look like the birds of paradise I'm told I'll see during my travels," he told them, doffing his hat upon a gallant bow. "And let me say how much I admire your bonnet, Katherine. If I'd come much closer without knowing it was you, I'd have imagined myself walking towards a rose bush."

He liked the coquettish way Katherine patted the profusion of blooms nestled beneath the brim of her elaborately trimmed straw hat and said, as he offered her his arm, "Allow me to escort you to the gates before I return to the duties that lie heavily upon my shoulders."

Katherine rested her hand lightly upon his forearm. "I trust you're coming to the ball tonight because I told George he couldn't escort me as I'd already promised you."

Jack felt a ridiculous jolt of pleasure. "I wasn't intending to go with so much still to organise, but as I'd hate to see you complicit in unladylike lies, then I'll look in, if only for an hour or so."

"If only all gentlemen were so gallant," sighed Lady Quamby, turning as an acquaintance hailed her. And as this particular acquaintance was in possession of a pair of fine muscular shoulders padding out his superfine coat, and intense dark eyes above a wolfish smile, Jack was not surprised when she made her excuses, telling him that he'd now have to see Katherine home as she "hadn't seen Mr Montgomery in a full two months", inferring there was a great deal for them to catch up on.

"My aunt is very popular with the gentlemen," Katherine remarked, as she and Jack strolled beneath the trees.

"And you appear to be so, too, if the three evenings I've observed you holding court like a butterfly queen is anything to go by."

"Oh, Jack, that was remarkably poetic. I do like it when you say things like that to me!" She squeezed his arm then sighed, so of course Jack needed to find out what was troubling her.

"But you're enjoying yourself? You seem to be."

She gave him a wicked smile which he returned, because of course she was silently alluding to their kiss which, if truth be told, he couldn't stop thinking about, which was most inconvenient when there were so many more important matters he ought to be attending to.

"Yes, but the choices, Jack! There are so many men who have just the right address, whom I know I could marry, and who've shown a decided interest in my company and"

"Here comes one now. Lord Derry, I believe?"

Jack assessed the gentleman once they'd been introduced and Katherine was merrily prattling away to his lordship. She was the cleverest coquette, he decided, and Lord Derry was clearly smitten. Jack had no doubt that Katherine could have her pick of any of London's finest once she'd made up her mind. He should be pleased for her, but he had to admit to just the slightest twinge of jealousy. And disappointment that he'd not be around to observe her final brilliant *coup d'etat*. Or rather *coup de matrimony*. He'd have to satisfy himself with hearing about it from his mama when she wrote to him at his far-distant posting across the seas.

"So, what do you think of Lord Derry?" Katherine quizzed him when they were alone once more.

"That you need only to click your fingers and you'll have yourself a rich, titled husband before the season is out."

"I mean, do you think he'd make me a suitable husband?"

Jack shrugged, not enjoying the topic, then sighed as a tall, sartorial-looking fellow with a glossy dark moustache bore down upon them. "I think that you're going to have to repeat your prettily rehearsed performance of before since here comes another potential suitor. You do realise I intend to stick to you like a leech."

"Indeed. I'm certainly not going to turn away only to have your good name besmirched and believe me, this fellow has an expression that suggests he'd like nothing more than to do it."

"That's not very gentlemanly!"

"I'd wager I'm more of a gentleman than Mr Marwick is." Jack wasn't quite sure why he was suddenly becoming so hot under the collar. He took a deep breath and counselled himself to be reasonable. In five days, he'd be off to sea, and he'd probably not see Katherine again for years and when he did, she'd be long married with a brood of children. He tried to put the thought from his head as he extended the requisite courtesies, smiling pleasantly when he'd much rather glower repressively—for all the good that would do—nodding genially as he watched Katherine flirt and simper. Oh, she was good; he had to give her that. Just as Lord Derry had three minutes before, now Mr Marwick looked as if he'd kiss the toes of her neat walking boots if she only asked him.

❧

KATHERINE HADN'T THOUGHT ABOUT HER MOTHER'S PEARL earrings until her mother declared they'd go perfectly with her dove-grey-and-pink evening dress when Katherine presented herself in the drawing room later that night.

"Why don't you run upstairs and fetch them? See if I'm not right," suggested her mother with a wave of her hand, but Katherine was saved from responding when her father asked, "Are you not fast wearying of the endless social round, my dear? Your little sister was asking the very same question in her last letter from the school room. The precocious child suggests she'll find a husband faster than you when her time comes."

Lord Fenton was seated on the sofa beside his wife, the pair the picture of marital harmony as they sipped Madeira. Aunt Antoinette, looking bored, was reclining in a very relaxed fashion, with one daintily-shod slipper upon the ottoman, studying the half-moons of her right hand. She looked up. "Regardless of whether Katherine is or isn't wearying of the social round, tonight is one night she can't cry off since my darling Quamby is hosting the event." She sighed gustily. "I certainly wish *I* could cry off."

Katherine hesitated in the centre of the Aubusson rug. She'd spent a full two hours on her toilette and had come downstairs full of hope for the evening ahead, but now she put her hand to her heart and said, "I'm looking forward to this evening, immensely, but why aren't you, Aunt Antoinette?"

"Monsieur Jervois is unable to attend tonight." Aunt Antoinette pouted.

Katherine didn't miss the warning look her mother sent her sister before she muttered, "Think of your duty to your husband, Antoinette. I'm sorry to say it, but I'm not mourning his broken leg as you are. Tonight you will be the perfect hostess so that Katherine will see how to conduct herself when she is hostess of an event of similar magnitude."

"Unless she runs off with the footman which she may well do if she's allowed to follow her heart—as you've told her so anxiously she must do if she's to avoid the terrible trials our mama put *us* through."

"The trials Mama put me through?" repeated Lady Fenton through gritted teeth, glancing quickly at Katherine before lowering her voice even further to say, "Hush now, Antoinette. You've had too much Madeira, and you know how unguarded you can be when it goes to your head. Katherine is looking to both of us to set an example."

Katherine lowered herself onto the ottoman at her aunt's feet and reached an arm across to pat her mother's knee. "Don't worry, Mama. I shan't run away with the footman, and I'm sorry, Aunt Antoinette, that you're not feeling in high spirits like I am, though I'm quite sure you will be soon when all the handsome young men confuse you for my sister and tell you how beautiful you look tonight."

"What a treasure!" exclaimed her aunt, clapping her hand over Katherine's and glancing up as her son entered the room together with his father and another gentleman. "George, why can't you learn to be so charming? And you too, Quamby? Here I am in a gown that cost you a small fortune and have you paid me one compliment tonight?"

"I'm seeing you wear it for the first time, my dear," the earl defended himself, smiling his usual equable smile nevertheless, as with the aid of his sticks and the shoulder of the very handsome young Greek who'd been his attendant the past year, he lowered himself into his armchair by the fire. Raising his lorgnette to more closely scrutinise his wife, he nodded approvingly. "You do me proud, Lady Quamby. And I believe I shall enjoy your undivided attention tonight as we help to ensure that this is an evening for our niece to remember." He patted the orange curls of his wig as he leaned forward, asking Katherine in conspiratorial tones, "And what young men have taken your fancy during the time you've been in London, my dear? Are you pleased that Young George is back in town, early I believe, following a speedy transaction over a bit of horseflesh? Perhaps you are the reason."

"Oh, don't be ridiculous, Quamby!" muttered Aunt Antoinette. "Katherine can do far better than George. Besides, he's her cousin. They're practically brother and sister."

Katherine shuddered. She couldn't imagine a more misguided statement. Still, she fluttered her eyelashes and, for a bit of fun, said, "You've been missed, Cousin George, since I can rely on you not to bruise my poor toes. Few gentlemen are as light on their feet as you."

It wasn't a wise remark, for she realised later she'd only encouraged George when he claimed the very first dance of the evening, just as she saw both Mr Marwick and Jack advancing with apparently the very same request, from opposite sides of the room. And while it was nice to feel she was so in demand, she rather wished she could have been dancing with Jack so she could regale him with the amusing events that had preceded their arrival.

Flirting with Mr Marwick was very nice too, she decided as he twirled her about the room, putting his lips to her ear and suggesting they might visit an antechamber just beyond the passage.

"And risk losing another pearl earring?" she demanded. "I think you ask too much of me, Mr Marwick?"

"No, no, I wish to *return* your earring to you."

"Then that changes everything!" Katherine declared, smiling at him. "Only, we must be very discreet or"

She blushed, unexpectedly, for she'd nearly spoken rather recklessly.

"Or I'd have an irate papa demanding redress?" He appeared to contemplate the idea, raising his eyes to the ceiling before saying, "I can't say that would be too great a hardship, Miss Fenton. Having known you a full seven days, I think you only grow more charming."

Katherine wasn't quite sure how she felt at such fulsome praise delivered with such clear but veiled desire. Katherine changed the subject. "Oh, there's my cousin, Jack." She hailed him as the music came to an end. "I promised him the next dance," she explained, "as of course you can't possibly dance with me a third time tonight."

"Only if I had certain intentions, that's true. However, I would very much like to secure you for another waltz before the night is through."

Katherine agreed to this, but she couldn't wait to hurl herself into Jack's arms. As soon as she'd extricated herself from Mr Marwick, she told Jack, "I'm so worn out with all this dancing; can't you take me away somewhere quiet instead?"

He seemed quite happy to oblige, and standing by a large

epergne in the centre of the room where there were no other guests, Katherine told him her dilemma regarding the earring.

"He says he has it, but he'll only give it to me if I meet him in the anteroom beyond the passage."

"Unconscionable!" Jack replied with great feeling so that Katherine happily gripped his arm and said, "That's very nice of you to think that, but it *was* my own fault that I lost my earring, and it *was* because I was kissing him, so it's hardly surprising he suggested it." She hesitated. "The only problem is that Mama is being extra vigilant, and I know that Papa would create quite a scene since this is Uncle Quamby's home, so I daren't risk it. I wondered if you'd be so good as to get it from him for me."

Jack shrugged. "I'll try."

"Would you? You see, I need it by tomorrow because Mama said she'd come looking for it. So, if you could just hide it under your pillow, since you're staying here tonight, then I'll know where to fetch it if you go out gaming, or I turn in early and we don't see each other again." Katherine gave his hand a quick squeeze. "You really are so lovely, Jack. I'm going to be so sad to say goodbye to you on Monday."

She smiled sadly up at him. He really was her knight in shining armour, agreeing to fetch her earring from Mr Marwick; saving her from having her toes trodden upon by George.

And he wouldn't even be around to witness the magnificent marriage she intended to make. Perhaps, as a result of her future matrimonial conquest, she might be in a position to aid Jack in climbing the ladder to greater social and financial success.

He certainly deserved it.

CHAPTER 8

Katherine had started off her evening feeling perfectly marvellous about everything. Her maid had done a remarkable twist with her hair, looping it and braiding it and curling it in all the right places. Combined with her new pale-pink silk gown with its gigot sleeves and ankle-length skirt over stiffened linen petticoats, and corset cut in the new style to emphasise her breasts and, of course, minimise her already small waist, she couldn't help preening when Cousin George declared she was the most beautiful girl in the room.

George, as usual, looked ridiculous in a pair of tight-fitting ivory trousers and waist-pinching lavender jacket with exaggerated puffed sleeves, a spotted cravat and high collar, but Katherine made the mistake of responding to his compliment by telling him he looked like a prize prince. Not that it was intended to actually be a compliment, but rather, Katherine had aired the phrase as she idly fanned herself, to see how he'd react to what, really, was a dressed-up way of telling him he looked rather foolish.

Instead, to her initial consternation, he gripped her hand

and tugged her close, so that for a second as he led her onto the dance floor she could feel his moist breath uncomfortably close to her face. "You are a jewel, Katherine," he murmured. "A jewel, and no woman here tonight can hold a candle to you."

After her surprise, Katherine laughed. "Really, George, you don't say things like that to one's cousin."

"One does if they're incomparable, as you are, Katherine. Why, when we were growing up, I used to think you held me in disdain. You and Jack were always dancing about together, leaving me out of the play. Teasing me." His brow puckered.

"But George, you were always sneaking up behind Jack and knocking him flat, then laughing and running away. I don't recall that we left you out of anything that you hadn't already decided you wanted no part of."

"I always wanted to be part of whatever you were doing, Katherine." The music was leisurely, which gave him every opportunity to emphasise his feelings which, clearly, were intense. "I let Jack be my friend *only* so I could be with you. The boy was nothing, coming from the foundling home, but I was magnanimous, do you not remember?"

Katherine couldn't remember a single occasion when George had ever been magnanimous, but she realised it was better not to argue. George was impossible to disagree with for he always became defensive and petulant. And as he was holding her in a waltz hold it was simply better to say, "I'm sure you always meant to be kind."

"And I would be kind to you, Katherine, if you'd let me."

"What?" She blinked in surprise at this unexpected turn in the conversation.

He pressed her closer to him, his eyes bright with an unnatural fervour. It was rather unnerving, and Katherine was very glad to be in the midst of several hundred people who, fortunately, were oblivious to her cousin's passionate outburst.

"I'd revere you like the most precious flower. I'd place you on a pedestal and kiss your slippers. I'd worship you."

"Well, that certainly sounds much pleasanter than tugging my plaits as you were forever doing when we were children, George, but really, I don't want you to revere me or kiss my slippers." Flippancy, she decided, was the best way to tackle this. Ignoring his glower, she went on, "But as we're cousins, we can enjoy all the time we spend together under the same roof while I'm here looking for a husband." She emphasised it ever so slightly to draw the distinction.

"You think I'm too young for a wife"

"Lord, George, of course you are! We're both only eighteen, but I'm here with the express purpose of finding myself a good husband while you're here"

"Because you are!" he cut her off. "Katherine, I know I'm young, but if you'll only wait"

"Really, George, I've never heard anything so ridiculous in my life. At eighteen, you're still a boy! I'm looking for a man!"

She was relieved when the music came to an end and he led her off the dance floor and deposited her with her mama and aunt.

"What's put George in such high dudgeon?" Lady Fenton asked her as George slunk away.

"He wants me to wait until he's old enough to ask me to marry him," Katherine said, "but of course he's got on his high ropes and now is cross with me because I mocked the idea."

Aunt Antoinette took a dainty bite of a sweetmeat which she washed down with champagne, and said with something between a giggle and a hiccup, "I am fond of my son but I like you far too much to wish him upon you as a husband." Her spirits appeared to have returned, and Katherine had noticed she'd spent a good deal of the evening in a secluded corner with one of the young gentlemen who'd been paying Katherine so much attention earlier. It was interesting to note that the men who were ten years older than Katherine and, therefore, ten years younger than her aunt, appeared to be equally complimentary to both ladies. In fact, Katherine had been taking careful notes about the way her aunt behaved. Her mother had expressly counselled her to do so if only to know how *not* to behave, but Katherine had learned a great deal of valuable information from the exercise. Like just what angle she should tilt her head for the most alluring effect in charm. And how to use her fan to the greatest effect. Yes, observing her Aunt Antoinette over these last seven days had been a lesson in coquetry—something the gentlemen very much appreciated.

"Well, I hope he won't be cross with me for long," sighed Katherine, picking up a macaron from a festive tray of them. "I'm sorry to say it, Aunt Antoinette, but George is very trying when he's out of sorts."

"You don't need to persuade me of that. Ah, but here is Jack, and we all know that nothing puts Jack out of humour. In fact, Jack, you were a great restorer of spirits when you were a regular visitor to us, and your mama has told us the same thing, since. You can't know how it will break her heart to see you sail away on Monday."

"But it's a great opportunity," Katherine's mama said, smiling. "It will make a man of you, Jack, and with your fine qualities, I predict you'll not only make your mama and uncle proud, but you'll return a man of great wealth and substance because you're not afraid of hard work."

Katherine was interested to see Jack blush at the praise. "That's kind of you, Lady Fenton."

"And then you can have your pick of any bride you wish," interjected Aunt Antoinette, waving to catch the attention of a footman who was carrying a bottle of champagne. "You'll no longer be the foundling boy who was given a home by generous benefactors, but rather a man of wealth and standing in your own right. That is what I predict."

"A man of wealth and standing," Katherine giggled when she and Jack found themselves alone after their elders had been claimed by their respective husbands. "Doesn't that sound grand?"

Jack stared at the table of half-eaten food. "I've a long way to go before that will happen," he said ruefully. "I have employment to go to where I'll be offered a roof over my head, but other than the belongings I can fit in a couple of trunks, the clothes on my back, and the money I have in my pocket, I'll be penniless."

"But your parents are rich." Katherine patted his arm.

"They are my adoptive parents with many natural children of their own. I don't want to be a further drain on their resources when they've already been so good to me."

"I'm sure you'll find great success, whatever you do, Jack. And when you return, you'll be considered a great catch and will have your choice of bride," she said brightly.

The long, level look Jack sent her made her heart plummet to her feet and her insides go very wobbly. "Ah, but you'll be long married, Katherine," he murmured.

Of course, she had to make light of it, waving her hand carelessly as she said, "Indeed I will. I'm looking for a titled husband at this very moment. One who is both rich and handsome. Lord Derry is the most eligible contender, but Mr Marwick is in line to inherit a viscountcy and I did enjoy kissing him, so perhaps I'll be Lady Marples when you return."

"Lady Marples," he repeated, his former air of gravitas dispelled by a return of his usual pleasant spirits. "I shall await news of your marital conquest with interest. Oh, and I haven't forgotten your earring. Indeed, I consider that my evening's most important mission. If Mr Marwick does not have it on his person, I shall personally go to wherever he does, and bring it back here."

"Oh, Jack, you are my true hero," Katherine told him. And she meant it.

CHAPTER 9

It was two o'clock in the morning when Katherine was taken, forcibly, by her mama, and led to bed.

"Tonight has been a great success, darling," said Lady Fenton, hooking her arm in her daughter's and walking her towards the double doors of the salon, which opened to admit them to the passageway and then the elegant sweeping staircase. "You have garnered a great deal of interest, and it appears you have not been averse to that shown you. Why, there was Lord Derry and Mr Marwick, and then, I could not help but notice Lord Minnow and Mr Sage seemed equally taken."

"You are observant, Mama!" Katherine laughed. "I shall have to be careful."

Her mother patted her cheek. "You behaved with the utmost decorum, I'm glad to say. Not a whisper of scandal to taint your chances, and that's made me very proud."

Chatting companionably, Lady Fenton accompanied Katherine into her daughter's bedchamber so she could help her out of her clothes, as Mary, the maid, had been given the evening off.

"What was your first season like, Mama?" Katherine asked. "Aunt Antoinette has told me often enough you had two."

"No doubt she phrased it somewhat differently. I presume she told you that it took me two seasons to find your darling papa, whereas *she* was fired off during her first—and to an earl, to boot."

Katherine smiled as Lady Fenton undid the buttons at the back of her dress. She liked it when her mama was more relaxed, and, therefore, honest with her—like Aunt Antoinette, though her mama would never tell her all the details Katherine wanted to know and that Aunt Antoinette thought fit to give her.

"Yes, I rather thought that was the case." Her mother turned Katherine around and smiled at her. "But now, tell me about you and what's in your heart, my lovely girl. It's all very well to garner a lot of attention, but you mustn't rush head-long into a romance that doesn't have all the right ingredients so necessary to see you happy twenty years from now. And I'm speaking from experience."

Katherine sighed. "I really want to be happy like you and Papa, but I wish I knew what I should feel right here." She touched her chest, now clad in the new style of corset which her mother began to unlace.

"You'll know, my darling."

"*How* will I know? I mean, I like Mr Marwick as much as I like Lord Derry. And now I think I like Lord Mace and Mr Alexander just as much as both the other two gentlemen. Should I just throw all their names into a hat and choose one?"

Her mother took her hand and sat her on the bed next to her. "You don't have to choose in the first week, darling. You have plenty of time. You're very young. You can wait until next year if you're not sure."

Katherine nodded, not very heartened. She'd wanted to marry in her first season, not be considered a failure amongst the young ladies of her acquaintance who'd found husbands in *their* first season. She wanted to establish her own household and be revered by her husband as an object of...Well, the way George claimed he would revere her, except the last man she'd ever consider as her husband was George.

"You have the entire rest of the season before you need to suffer any sleepless nights," her mother told her from the door after she'd tucked Katherine in, just as she used to when Katherine was a little girl. She was just leaving when, on second thoughts, she stepped back into the room saying, "Oh, and my pearl earring. Where did you say you'd put it, Katherine? I plan to wear those earrings with my dove-grey tomorrow night."

Katherine was glad of the dark to hide her guilty jerk. Adopting a sleepy tone, she said, "They're somewhere in my jewellery box, Mama. I'll give them to you tomorrow."

After waiting a good five minutes to ensure her mama was definitely well away from the wing that housed Katherine's bedroom, Katherine leapt out of bed, threw a shawl over her nightgown, and slipped into the passage.

She was quite confident Jack wouldn't fail her, but she needed her earrings now if she was to sleep a wink.

When there was no answer to her knock, she opened the door and slipped into Jack's room. It was empty and there was nothing under his pillow, so she raised her candle for a quick search, running her gaze over the tallboy and wash-stand without luck.

Disappointed, she went back to her own room again where she remained awake until, about half an hour later, she heard Jack and George in the passage on their way to their respective bedchambers.

When all was silent again, Katherine slipped out of bed

and crept into the passageway, shielding her candle until she reached Jack's room.

For the second time that night, she knocked quietly but, receiving no response, she flung open the door and hurried inside, closing it behind her, before looking up with a gasp.

"Good God, Katherine, don't you ever knock?" Jack exclaimed, reaching for a strip of linen to cover his nakedness.

"I did but there was no answer." Katherine blinked, curious rather than shocked.

"That was probably because I was washing my face and didn't hear you."

She took a few steps forward and put the candle down on the washstand. She'd never seen a man without his clothes and, without embarrassment, she stared at Jack's feet, long and broad, before her gaze travelled up his legs, past his flanks which he'd modestly covered, to his chest, lightly dusted with sandy hair. It was a nice chest, she decided, whether or not it was covered in a well-cut coat. Katherine had enjoyed being pressed against his chest and breathing in the scent of him.

"What are you looking at?"

"You, of course. I don't have any brothers, so I've never seen a man like this." She bit her lip as she seated herself on the edge of his bed. "You look very nice."

"Nice?" He frowned, poised by the wash stand, as if he wasn't sure how to respond.

"Why, Jack. You're not embarrassed are you?" she laughed. "You're never embarrassed about anything. It's only me, you know."

"Yes, and that makes it worse." He glanced away, tossing his wet face cloth onto the stab of marble then taking a few steps into the centre of the room. Away from her. "I don't want you to judge and find me wanting."

"Really?" She liked the fact that he was concerned about her opinion. "I certainly *don't* find you wanting. I really enjoyed it when you kissed me the other day, in case you didn't know it." She straightened. The dim light in the room, combined with the fact he looked so vulnerable and appealing, suddenly made the idea of kissing him again even more desirable.

"Katherine, what are you doing?"

Even Katherine wasn't sure what she was doing. She just knew she wanted to wrap her arms about his waist and press her cheek against his chest.

Which was what she was doing.

"You said you'd get me Mama's pearl earring." She was fascinated by the sound of his heart beating loudly in his chest as she burrowed her face into his warm skin.

"And I was true to my word. I have it in the pocket of my coat." He sounded slightly strangled as he tried to push her away with just a touch of pressure.

But to no avail. Katherine wasn't about to relinquish what she was enjoying too much. "That's good. That's why I'm here, of course. But Jack." She tipped her head up to look at him. His expression was anxious, one light brown curl flopped over his brow, and he appeared, to her mind, quite adorable.

"What? Katherine, you really should leave."

"Can't I stay and chat awhile? We used to talk all the time when we were children."

"But we're not children anymore. And being together like this...might be misconstrued."

"Misconstrued? You mean, if someone thought we were together...kissing...for example?" she asked. She wanted to kiss him again. In fact, the urge to do so was almost overwhelming. She tipped her face, closed her eyes and offered him her lips, expecting to feel the tender brush of his against hers like the last time.

When nothing happened, she opened her eyes and found to her indignation that he was looking with a great deal of desperation at the door.

"I'll lock it," she offered, gliding across the room to turn the key. "There, now you needn't worry."

"Oh yes, I have every need to worry. Katherine, you don't know what trouble you're courting. You say you want me to kiss you again, but do you know what you're asking of me? How difficult—" He broke off.

"Difficult? What's difficult about kissing me? You seemed to enjoy it the last two times we did it."

He made a noise of frustration and knotted the piece of linen more firmly about his waist. "You are an innocent, Katherine. The truth is, so am I, but I just happen to know more than you. And what I do know is that for a start, if we were discovered alone in my bedchamber, with me all but naked, your marital chances would be severely compromised."

Katherine shrugged. "I don't see how that's even a concern. For a start, the door's bolted so no one is going to know we're in your bedchamber together. And second, you didn't seem the least bit concerned the last time you kissed me." Leisurely, she took a step towards him and put her arms about his waist again, pressing her nose into his chest and breathing in. "You smell very nice, Jack. Comforting. And manly. Not at all like Lord Derry who smells of cigarillos. He makes me want to sneeze. So, are you going to kiss me? And if you then feel like doing all those other things you're so worried people will think we're doing, I give you complete liberty to go right ahead and do them."

He unclasped her hands that were laced about his stomach as if stung. "Good God, Katherine; I don't think you even know what you're saying."

Although the look she sent him was knowing and self-contained, the beginnings of a great excitement were now churning in her chest and belly. "I know exactly what I'm saying. I felt some of it when you kissed me, Jack. So I asked Aunt Antoinette, and...she told me everything. It's not only because of Mama's pearl earring that I'm here."

Jack had turned away and was now at the foot of the bed where he'd laid his coat. After fishing in the pocket, he turned, brandishing the earring. "Here you have it. Mr Marwick was not too happy to relinquish it, but I can be a persuasive fellow when I need to be. And now I need to persuade you of what's good for you, which is to leave my bedchamber right this moment and go back to your own bed. Before any damage is done," he added.

But Katherine was not to be dissuaded.

She took the earring with a smile; her eyes fixed level with his chest. "Thank you, Jack." Experimentally, she touched his right nipple and felt it harden. She gave a soft gasp and raised her eyes, gripping his wrist and forcing his hand to cup her breast. "I had the same reaction. Oh, please kiss me, Jack?" she asked urgently. "Please. If I'm to be married, I want to know what to expect, and you're the dearest person in my life. I feel safe with you. And Aunt Antoinette knows everything to make it all right—whatever that means. I just want to know what being married feels like so I can make an informed decision when the time comes. Kiss me, Jack." Again, she tipped up her head. "Just start with one little kiss. Please."

He looked as if he might resist, but when Katherine closed her eyes, it was only a second before Jack's lips were on hers, and she was twining her arms around his neck, pulling him down to her.

Her heart began to race, and blood heated the surface of her skin. Her breath came in short, sharp bursts and, barely breaking the kiss, she dragged him to the bed, scrambling onto the counterpane where he joined her a moment later.

"Katherine." She stopped whatever he was about to say with another kiss, kneeling by his side and bending over him.

His arms reached for her, and he pulled her down so that she was against his side. The candle flickered, then suddenly went out, and they were plunged into darkness with only the feel of their bodies to guide them.

"Katherine, we mustn't do this."

"We must. Aunt Antoinette told me it's an important part of choosing one's future husband."

"But that's not me, Katherine, much as I would like—"

"You would?" she asked, delighted.

"Yes, but I'm going away, and I can't take a wife, and you're in London to choose a husband befitting your station in life. We both know that."

She stroked his cheek, thinking. "But you'd help me if I ever needed help and you could provide it, wouldn't you?"

"Of course I would."

"So that's what I want you to do now. Offer me your help. You're kind and safe and gentle, and I'm asking you to show me what to expect and what to feel so that I'm prepared when I make the hugely important decision regarding my future husband."

"But it won't feel the same, Katherine, so it's not a good enough excuse to do what I would love nothing more than to do with you, but which could ruin you."

"It won't ruin me. Nobody will know."

"There might be...consequences. It's too dangerous."

Jack sounded like he was determined to find an excuse for everything but Katherine was more determined to have her way. Jack had been the most marvellous kisser. That had been very helpful to discover. Now she needed to know about that other, more intimate aspect of marriage and what to expect.

How terrible if she didn't like it. She really had to know before she committed herself to a lifetime of it.

"Aunt Antoinette said she knew how to ensure there weren't consequences, so it's not dangerous. Oh, please, Jack. I do love you, you know."

Katherine had never felt greater excitement in her life as she pinioned Jack beneath her, rolling against his side once she'd established his exact position and that they were not in danger of falling out of bed.

"I love you, too, Katherine." He sounded sad and regretful. "That's why I don't think this is a good idea." He hesitated. "I couldn't bear the idea of hurting the person I love most in the world."

She loved the feel of him, the contours and soft, springy hair of his chest, the responsive nipples beneath her fingertips. And she loved his words. Jack was making her feel like the most precious woman in the world right now.

"You'll hurt me more if you send me away." She'd heard the wavering in his resolve and it fuelled her excitement. Pressing her advantage, she ran her hands over his chest and hips and whispered, *"Please*, Jack. Don't send me away," and when he merely muttered that it appeared he couldn't even if he wanted to, she wriggled out of her long nightgown, which kept getting caught up, and was soon naked and curled into his side, guiding his hand to her breast. "Touch me here," she whispered, before fusing her mouth to his once more. A fierce desire in her lower belly made her squirm, and she was aware of a strange heat and moistness at the juncture of her legs that she'd never felt before. Well, not quite like this.

As his fingertips brushed her skin which had never felt more sensitive, Katherine thought she was going to die of want, though she wasn't sure what was going to happen next.

She continued to kiss him, deeply and lingeringly, and when she drew back, whispered, "What happens now, Jack?

There's more, isn't there?" She squirmed, excited and frustrated, rubbing the toes of her right foot up the length of Jack's leg until he shuddered and whispered she should stop.

"Please, Katherine, I don't want to hurt you." He sounded strangled. "And I can't help you because I've never done this before."

"So you don't know if there's any more to it than this? Any more that married couples do, I mean?"

In the darkness she heard him chuckle. "I know what they do, I've just never done it, myself."

"Then we can learn together." She felt excited and happy. "You're not suggesting I should petition someone with more experience than you, I hope?"

"Lord, no!" He laughed more robustly now, suddenly rising above her and caging her body with his. She could feel that strange hardness of his pressing into her belly, and she thought of the stallion she'd seen covering the mare in their Hampshire home and imagined what Jack must look like in the dark. She wanted to feel that hardness communicate itself to her. Instinct told her that she was ready, and the pain would be minimal. The heat and moistness must account for that.

"So, determined Miss Katherine wants to have her way." Gently, he stroked her hair back from her forehead. Katherine thought she'd burst into flames at his touch. "Last chance, Katherine," he whispered. "I might disappoint you, I might ruin you. I might hurt you. None of those possibilities makes me feel very confident that this is a good idea."

"None of those things will happen," she assured him through gritted teeth, gripping his buttocks and applying pressure that encouraged him to lower himself down upon her.

Into her.

With a soft groan of satisfaction, she relaxed as if to make room for him while he began to move, rhythmically, up and down and as he filled her body, her mind, too, was filled with excitement and satisfaction and pleasure.

She could tell that he was similarly enthralled and she wanted to keep up this wonderful feeling forever. For some time they rocked in wonderful tandem while a strange growing pressure built within Katherine but then Jack gave a sudden cry as he convulsed upon her.

And then was still.

Katherine was confused. Her own body was crying out for more, but Jack had stopped with no warning.

She wriggled beneath him. "Please, keep doing that, Jack."

There was a moment's silence. His body was heavy on hers and he sounded strained as he rolled off her. "Katherine...I can't."

Her disappointment, however, was short-lived as Jack cradled her against his side and kissed her cheeks and eyes and ears. He stroked her hair and she couldn't help wriggling some more, not knowing what to do with the need still writhing within her, though it was diminishing and a lovely glow of closeness was taking its place.

In the darkness, his disembodied voice sounded anxious. "I'm told one gets better with practise. That wasn't what you expected, was it Katherine? I don't know what I expected, either. But are you all right?" He held her almost fiercely. "Was it what you wanted?"

Katherine sighed with pleasure. "I wasn't sure what I wanted, but...it was perfect. And next time it'll be even better."

"Except that you know there can't be a next time, Katherine. There won't be. Ever." She felt his sudden rigidness from his shoulders to his feet as he said it. "We shouldn't have done it now."

Katherine was equally anxious to dispel his fears. "I told

you. Aunt Antoinette knows everything about these things. Please don't concern yourself about me."

"Of course I'm concerned about you, Katherine. I care about you more than I care about anyone. But..." His voice trailed off into the darkness, and there was a bleakness to his tone when he added, "I was referring to me when I talked about not understanding what we might have started..." He took her hand and laid it upon his chest. "What we've done changes everything...here, Katherine. I should have thought about the dangers of that. Being together like this...sharing this closeness...changes everything I feel about you."

"It shouldn't." She tried to sound bolstering when, in fact, she was gaining an inkling about what he meant but seemed unable to articulate. She stared at the ceiling, one part of her revelling in their closeness as he gently stroked her, the other railing over the fact they must soon be parted. "We've always been the best of friends, and this isn't going to change anything."

She could feel his light breath on her cheek as he leaned on his elbow and gently traced the line of her nose. "It's changed everything, and I think you know it." He kissed her lightly then gave her upper arm a squeeze. "And now we're going to have to part. We have to do it now in case we do something unbelievably stupid and fall asleep in the same bed. And then, on Monday, we'll have to part forever."

"Not forever, Jack!" Katherine whispered, close to tears at the thought. "You'll come back one day."

"And you'll be someone else's wife, and who knows but what will have become of me as I strive to make my way in the world." He threw back the covers, sat up suddenly and pulled her across his lap, hugging her tightly. "I'm going to have to give you up to someone else, now, because we both know that I am in no position to take a wife where I'm going."

Suddenly, Katherine was prepared to make that sacrifice. "I *could* go with you, Jack!"

"Perhaps. If you stowed away. And if you were madder than we both know you are." He gave a mirthless laugh. "But you are here to find a husband, not to throw your life away on a fancy. Now, put this on, Katherine." She felt the bundle that was her nightgown pushed into her arms. "You must go to bed and look upon this as some wonderful dream. Sadly, it's as close as I'm ever going to get to my heart's desire."

With tears pricking her eyelids, Katherine drew her nightgown over her head in the darkness, and allowed Jack to steady her as he walked her to the door.

"I hope you're not cross with me, Jack," she whispered before parting.

"Cross with you? Lord, I'd forgive you anything, Katherine. Tonight just made that very clear." He kissed the top of her head. "Now, good night, my dearest. Sweet dreams. I'm not sure how easy I'll sleep after this. Or if I will. And don't forget your earring."

He pressed the pearl into her palm and curled her fingers over it. Then, before she could hurl herself back into his arms, he'd closed the door. Knocking to be readmitted was not practical, but oh how she wanted to throw herself back into his arms and go back to bed with him; to do this all over again and to sleep the whole night through feeling his warmth beside her. And every other night after this.

But what Jack had said was true. The truth was that they were too young to be together.

Which was a tragedy because Katherine wasn't sure she wanted to be with anyone else.

CHAPTER 10

"You're very listless, my dear," Aunt Antoinette remarked as Katherine sat stitching in the drawing room the following morning together with her aunt and Mama.

Katherine just shrugged, but the moment her mama was out of the room, she leaned over to her aunt and whispered, "Please can we take a turn about the rose bushes. Before Mama returns."

Aunt Antoinette wasn't stupid, but nor was she as genial as Katherine had expected her to be when Katherine hinted at what she'd been up to the previous night. No names were mentioned, and if Aunt Antoinette guessed, she said nothing.

Still, her aunt was as anxious as she was unhappy. "It's my fault, isn't it? I fuelled your bravado with tales of my own folly. But I'm a breed apart, Katherine. Your mother and I couldn't be more different, just as you and I could not be more different. Your mama has a heart that revels in the love of one man. I, on the other hand, could never commit myself to one man. Yes, you ought to look shocked for it is not a trait that is tolerated in our society, and were I not married to your Uncle Quamby, I would be spurned—an outcast—for pandering to my proclivities, my eternal quest for novelty. But you, my dear Katherine, need to find a love that will last forever. What you did last night was...pure experimentation. Dangerous! I did not mean to give you licence to behave as you have done before marriage because too much can go wrong."

Katherine tried not to sound tearful as she defended herself. "But you said you had the means to prevent anything going wrong. You *told* me that, and I, therefore, believed you meant that of all my fellow debutantes, I was the most fortunate, as I could find out before marriage if this was the man I wanted to be with for the rest of my life. Because you had the means to ensure I didn't get into trouble."

"Oh, Katherine! That's only part of it. What about the potential damage to your reputation? Not every gentleman is discreet. What if he says something where he ought not, and you are pilloried, your chances of a good marriage ruined?"

Katherine shook her head vigorously. "He'd never do that, Aunt Antoinette. I'd trust him...with my life." She gulped. "And I don't regret doing it because it...made me realise I truly am in love."

"Then that is wonderful news! It's the very reason you came to London." Not once had Aunt Antoinette slowed her graceful promenade, for she was an artisan at remaining graceful at all times, Katherine noted admiringly. She turned her face to Katherine and tilted her head. "Is it Mr Marwick? *Very* soon to be Lord Marples, I've heard tell. I did warn you against him, but if you've already been so foolish as to disregard all my advice, then you have my blessing." She sighed, adding, "And your mama would be pleased to see you settled this season. She does worry, you know."

Katherine wasn't going to tell her aunt that she was in love with Jack. Somehow she sensed that nobody would think that a good thing at all. So she let Aunt Antoinette assume she'd been with Mr Marwick and asked, to hopefully deflect further questions about herself, "Do you mean because of her own troubled season?"

"Oh, she had more than one, as I've told you. Our mama was determined Fanny was to marry Lord Slyther, Mr Marwick's uncle, and you can be assured that when Grandmama visits in two days' time, she'll be most satisfied that you have caught the eye of Mr Marwick."

"Why did Mama not like Lord Slyther?"

"He was not what anyone could consider a...desirable bridegroom...in the physical sense, if you understand, so Fanny begged to be given a final chance to find a potential bridegroom who could offer as much as Lord Slyther in terms of title, address, pin money, and a carriage and two horses for your grandmother. Fortunately, your mama found your dear papa. As you can see, it was the perfect match. And that's what Fanny wants for you. So you like Mr Marwick very much, do you? He makes you happy?"

Katherine bit her lip, then gave a slight nod. She suspected Jack might even be packed off early if there were any suggestion that he and Katherine had formed a closeness that she knew her family would consider unacceptable. Not because they didn't like Jack, but because he had nothing to offer Katherine.

The trouble was, though, that after Katherine had been with Jack, even the sight of Lord Derry and Mr Marwick had the very opposite effect of making her feel happy, highlighting just how deficient they seemed in relation to her childhood friend.

Her lover. She shivered at the thought.

While she hadn't disliked kissing Mr Marwick, Jack's kisses had ignited something magical and joyous inside her.

How could she possibly be satisfied with Mr Marwick as a husband after that?

No, after being with Jack, she knew she'd have to find a suitor who made her feel as wonderful as he made her feel.

The trouble was, she wasn't sure how easy that was going to be.

❧

KATHERINE WAS NOT SURE SHE LIKED THE IDEA OF BEING the object of her venerable grandmother's eagle-eyed scrutiny for the next two days. Lady Brightwell had been critical of her youthful high spirits when she was eight, and no doubt she'd find Katherine equally wayward at nearly eighteen. She certainly would if she knew what was in her heart.

Nevertheless, wayward though Katherine might be, she also tried hard to please.

So, when Lady Brightwell stood in as her chaperone for the evening, Katherine was determined her behaviour would be exemplary.

It had been a day and an evening since she'd seen Jack. He'd gone out of town on business related to his trip away, and Katherine had endured a long and tedious evening the previous night at a ball hosted by one of Lord Quamby's cronies. Mr Marwick and Lord Derry had been in constant attendance, though she'd tried not to dance more than twice with either.

Tonight, she was at the rather flamboyant Lady Primrose's residence, and her grandmother was having a field day criticising every female who crossed their path.

"Much too much bosom on show," the old woman now muttered as a very pretty young lady with a swanlike neck, wearing a gown that seemed like a continuation, in a confection of lace-edged flounces, swept by. Katherine wasn't about to disagree but was glad she was wearing the demure pale-pink-silk her mother had advised her to wear.

Her grandmother turned. "So, my girl, I believe you've caught the fancy of Mr Marwick soon to be Lord Marples. A very fine young man, well connected, with a most impressive moustache. I do approve."

Katherine nodded, just as that gentleman arrived in their midst, bowing with a flourish. "You are looking like an exquisite rose, Miss Fenton," he declared. When he realised Lady Brightwell's identity, he appeared most impressed. "My uncle held you in the greatest esteem, Lady Brightwell." He glanced at Katherine. "Perhaps you do not know that your mama was in fact betrothed to my uncle. Sadly, he died the day before they were due to wed."

Katherine's mouth dropped open. She'd not known the prospective marriage had been quite so perilously close.

His mouth turned up in a look both wry and admiring. "Perhaps that accounts for the more than usual attraction I feel for you." He cleared his voice and glanced at Lady Bright-well. "Though I should not speak so in front of your grand-mother. It's hardly seemly. Beg pardon, ma'am. The Brightwells are known for having this effect on the gentlemen."

Lady Brightwell seemed not to mind in the slightest. "You can say such pretty words and get away with it, any day, young man," she said playfully, flicking her fan at him. "Now, off you go and escort my granddaughter onto the dance floor."

Katherine inclined her head at Mr Marwick and smiled as he squired her into the centre of the throng. He was a good dancer and a charming man, and he knew how to compliment a lady. She heaved in a breath. But there were other equally charming men she had yet to meet. If she only had the desire to.

"May I?"

Her heart ratcheted up with sudden intensity as she recognised Jack's familiar tones, and she beamed with pleasure, not waiting for Mr Marwick to acquiesce, but saying, warmly, "You know Jack is going away the day after tomorrow, sir, so I'm sure you'll not mind."

She didn't wait to see what effect that had on Mr Marwick. She was just aware of a wonderful sense of completeness being in Jack's arms and felt not the slightest embarrassment at the fact that the last time she'd seen him was naked in his bed.

"Lovely as ever, Katherine," he said with a smile, "and the gentlemen are like moths to the flame. You certainly are taking London by storm."

He seemed sad, she was glad to note but said, though the words pained her, "You must be very excited at the prospect of adventure, Jack." She forced a smile. "If I could stow away without spoiling everything for all those who have such hopes and plans for you—and for me—I'd do it."

"Good Lord, Katherine, I'm not sure if you're teasing me or not."

She glanced at her feet. "I mean it. Though, of course, I can say it because it's safe to, can't I?" She gave a rueful grin. "We both know how impossible it would be, but I *can* dream. And that's what I dream about."

"You...do? You dream about running away with me?"

"Yes, but I'd never do it. You couldn't get on in the world with me a drag upon your coattails, and you're too proud to accept success unless it's earned by you. Besides, my parents would disown me, I believe. My grandmother would certainly wash her hands of me."

"I fear we are both in a similar predicament, then."

Katherine gripped his shoulder and pressed herself against him briefly. She wanted to bury her face in his jacket, but of course she couldn't do that here. Desperately, she wished for time alone. "Jack, you're going away tomorrow and I can't bear it," she whispered. "Please let me come and see you tonight. To your room so I can say my final farewell."

He squeezed her hand. "It's too dangerous." There was real sorrow in his eyes as he manoeuvred them past a knot of dancers. "I dare not let you take such a risk."

"May I have the pleasure? Katherine has been in such demand, but I've not had a look-in for two days."

It was George, putting his large and imposing bulk between them so that Jack had no choice but to step aside if he didn't want to have his foot trodden on.

Katherine pretended not to mind. She'd been unwise in her dealings with her cousin before, she realised. George had the power to make her life uncomfortable, and he'd do it if he found an opportunity.

"I'm always happy to dance with a man who knows how to lead," she said demurely, allowing him to spin her about the room, executing some very fancy footwork.

"You're looking especially lovely tonight, Katherine."

"What happened to cuz?" she teased, hoping to ameliorate his earlier displeasure with her. "You always used to call me cousin?"

"As you know, I feel you're more than that. Yes, I know you don't want to hear it but it's the truth. I can't help what's in my heart any more than you can. But we can be friends?"

Katherine couldn't believe it. This was the most mature remark she thought she'd ever heard George make. And she did want to be friends with him.

"Of course we can, George. I'm very fond of you. We've known each other our whole lives so of course we must be friends." She spoke the last word with emphasis. George needed things explained to him more forcefully than other people did, it seemed.

"And we shall both miss Jack. Our time together in

London has been like the days of our childhood, but now he'll be gone for a long time."

Katherine glanced at him to see if there was an undercurrent to his words, but he looked surprisingly guileless. George usually had a furtive look if he were testing her or planning something.

She'd have to be very careful, Katherine decided, but was determined that nothing was going to stop her from being with Jack for his last night on English soil. She'd treasure the memory forever. Nor should her mother be surprised if Katherine returned to London for a second season. She didn't think she had the heart to continue her husband-hunting so soon after her closeness with Jack.

GEORGE RELINQUISHED HIS COUSIN WITH THE USUAL reluctance and churning in his belly. Lord Derry was lined up to dance with her next. No doubt Mr Marwick would follow. He was in line for a viscountcy, so George would eclipse him with an earldom when Quamby fell off his perch.

He just wasn't sure that the title alone would do it. For the whole of George's life, his uncle, George Bramley, had spoken so slightingly of Katherine's mother, Lady Fenton. Common dandelion, climbing and grasping for position, were phrases that came to mind. George used to think he was so much better than Cousin Katherine, but even when they were children, he'd grow fiendishly jealous when she showed a preference for the company of Jack, the foundling. Now Jack was Mr Jack Patmore, adopted son of friends of his parents, and so, in some people's eyes, on a more equal footing in society.

George was glad his old friend was off to the West Indies. If he hadn't been about to make the journey that would take him out of Katherine's orbit permanently, he might not have found it so easy to be polite and accepting of Katherine's predilection for his company.

Of course, Marwick was another kettle of fish, and here he was, bearing down on George now, casting a furtive look over his shoulder at Katherine who was dancing with Lord Derry. When Marwick intercepted George's own gaze he laughed. "She doesn't care for you, George. Not as husband material, if you don't mind my speaking plain, old chap."

George was proud of the way he retained his dignity. "What makes you think that?"

"Because she's going to wed me."

"She said so?" He glanced at Katherine, who looked as enamoured of Lord Derry as any man he'd seen her with. Bile stung the back of his throat but he managed with commendable calm, "She's said nothing. You're lying."

"I won't be if you help me."

"Help you? Good God, why would I do that?"

Marwick grinned, and in that moment George actively hated his moustache. "Because *you* haven't a chance," Marwick replied.

"Sorry, old chap, but I have a much better chance than you. I caught some of your exchange the other evening. You're her cousin; she's fond of you. There's an end to it. Whereas I..." He nodded. "It's in the betting book at White's."

"That you'll marry Katherine?" Of course, George knew wagers were written up all the time, but this seemed somehow shocking. Katherine was the woman he loved.

Marwick nodded. "Two hundred pounds if we're married before the end of the season, a thousand if we elope." He tucked his thumbs into his waistcoat. "Which means that, naturally, we must elope."

"Elope? Good God, you're out of your mind! Why would

Katherine elope with you when she could wed you with all the due pomp and circumstance that would accompany such a union? It's not as if your suit would be frowned upon." George hated to admit this last part, but it was true.

Marwick shrugged again. "No other reason than that there's a great deal more money in it if we elope. A title in the offing doesn't mean a fellow couldn't do with a bit of blunt if he can get it."

Rigid with moral indignation, George asked, "Do you even love her?"

Marwick's features softened, and he actually sounded sincere. "I adore her. The feeling is mutual. Well, it certainly was a few days ago when we enjoyed a little tryst beyond the ballroom."

George clenched his fists as the blood roared to his head. "She's only just been launched. Katherine is discerning, don't you know?"

"Oh, I know it very well. Very unlike her mama, hence the bet which was proposed by someone who obviously felt he had an old score to settle on those grounds."

"Who?"

"Why, your uncle, in fact, old chap. Mr George Bramley. He never could get over the way your aunt Lady Fenton gave him the brush-off. Now, as I've told you, I intend to carry Katherine off as my bride and make her the happiest woman in all England. I have a great incentive to do it soon and do it unconventionally. But I'd be grateful for your help."

George contemplated the matter. He wanted Katherine. He didn't need money. But he wanted respect and if he couldn't have Katherine, he might earn Warwick's respect— and consequently that of his cronies— if he threw his energies into helping secure Marwick's desires.

He bit his lip. He didn't want to hurt Katherine but she'd made clear how little she cared about *him*. So, despite a certain warring of his conscience, George inclined his head. "A wager? Yes, a wager will get the ball rolling. And you need results, soon?" He sighed. It was wrong but if Katherine had kissed Marwick, she might as well marry him. She'd made it clear she was not going to marry George. "I'll make sure it's a wager the like of which Boodles Betting book has never seen before," he muttered.

CHAPTER 11

Jack opened the door with a mixture of apprehension and the greatest pleasure. He'd wanted Katherine to come. Desperately. Yet he knew that if she were discovered, they'd both pay a high price. Katherine's, though, would be higher. He'd be leaving in the morning and sailing on the high tide the following day to a strange land, the beginning of an adventure whose pull had been so strong. Until the past two days.

Falling in love had been decidedly inconvenient. Hearts and feelings would have to be denied but Katherine was right. One last night of stolen moments would be a memory they'd carry forever. It would sustain Jack through all the loneliness and toil and discomforts he fully anticipated would be thrown at him as he made his way in the world.

"Oh Jack, I'm going to miss you so!" Katherine cried, before he'd fully opened the opened the door but already she was hurling herself into his arms.

Quickly, he closed the door behind them and drew her towards the bed. They didn't have long, and he wanted all the closeness they could get. It wasn't only about making love—

the wicked by-product of their need for each other—but about everything. Every last whisper, caress, wistful yearnings, and whisperings. He wanted to soak it all in so he would have it forever, to treasure.

"Not as much as I'm going to miss you," he murmured, scooping her up and placing her on the counterpane before joining her.

Curled up in her fine linen nightgown, she looked like a dark-haired angel.

"Blow out the candle and kiss me," she begged, pulling at the ribbon beneath her chin.

"I'd rather see you." He touched her cheek, then slowly traced his finger along her jawline and down her neck.

She contemplated this a moment then said, "Face the wall so I can wriggle under the covers. That way I can decide what you see." She giggled, and when he turned back, she was sitting primly up in bed with the covers drawn up to her chin. "If you kiss me, I shall let you see just a little more."

Jack needed no prompting. He reached forward to take her in his arms and kissed her soundly, then drew back.

"Oh Jack, why stop?" Despite the disappointment in her tone, the hint of a smile hovered around her mouth. She dropped the covers, revealing two beautifully formed white breasts, tipped with the tiniest pink rosebuds. Jack thought he'd never seen anything so exquisite.

"You can touch, if you want to," she encouraged, smiling to see his hesitation. "Oh yes, please do *that*." For Jack had done more than just touch. That had only ignited the need to move forward and kiss first one, then the other. And then, when he sensed how much it seemed to inflame her enthusiasm, he concentrated on just the nipple, rolling it around on his tongue and suckling, just a little, loving the way it made her squirm as she gave little squeaks of pleasure. Naturally, this was having a huge effect on him, but he was more interested in what it was doing to Katherine. He'd been led to believe that women took a more restrained attitude to bedroom activities. Clearly, Katherine didn't, and he understood that their previous, first time, had not been as wonderful for her, from a physical point of view, as it had been for him. Tonight, he was determined, would be different.

When at last Katherine could take no more—and neither could he—she begged him to join her beneath the covers where they stroked and fondled each other between and during kisses.

So this would be what he'd be missing for the rest of his life. It was torture to discover something truly wonderful only to lose it.

"I could wait for you, Jack," she suggested when they were sated, clasped in each other's arms, staring at the ceiling in the darkness.

"For four years? I don't think that's practical, Katherine."

"So, you don't want me to wait for you?" She sounded hurt.

"I want you to live your life to the full and not go into a spinsterish decline on my account." The words made him feel too old for his years, but they were true. He reached for the candle and raised it so he could see her better. Her eyes were luminous and her lips moist and swollen from kissing him. Pain washed over him as he whispered, putting down the candle and cuddling beside her again, "I don't want to subject you to the fate of the wives of explorers who disappear to the other side of the world, perhaps never to return."

She gasped and put her head on his chest. "You will come back, won't you, Jack?"

"It's my intention. But I don't know when." He felt sad. "You know I can't take a wife, but if I could, I'd take you."

She nodded, staring at her fingernails. "I'd not burden

you, Jack."

"Lord, it would be no burden. But for some of the time I'll be in single quarters. I'd not be allowed a wife and nor would I have the means to keep one. And I'll be travelling constantly, at least for the first year or two. Yes, I know of fellows who pledge marriage for their return, but you can do so much better than me. We've only had a week to rekindle our friendship"

"More than just friendship!"

"Yes, of course, more than that." Jack bit back the words that sprang to his lips. He'd not be complicit in encouraging declarations of love that would in turn burden Katherine. She was so full of vitality, and if she could love him with such enthusiasm, and so quickly, he felt that spirit should be channelled to worthier causes. Not that he didn't consider himself deserving. It's just that their time was not right. Katherine was seventeen years old, and about to be launched into the adult world to find a husband and establish her own household. They'd been childhood friends, and they'd found love—inconveniently, he acknowledged this reluctantly—but it was not a love that had a future.

She was tearful as he walked with her towards the bedroom door. He held the candle aloft and bent to kiss the wetness from her cheeks.

"If you change your mind and want me to come with you, I'd do it, Jack," she declared.

She was lovely. So impulsive and sincere. It would, he feared, get her into a great deal of trouble in her lifetime. Katherine had always been impulsive. But with her spirit, she'd find happiness with someone else. He hoped his greatest regret wouldn't be losing her.

But at least he'd leave with the sweetness of her loving on his skin and the knowledge she had the world at her feet.

For what greater gift could he give her than her freedom?

CHAPTER 12

Katherine tried not to cry as she accompanied her mother and aunt to the lobby of Quamby's London townhouse. Pausing on the landing, she saw Jack below, bent over his trunk, checking the leather straps that secured it were fastened firmly. With the back of his neck exposed, he seemed frighteningly vulnerable. Would he be safe when he was gone? What dangers would he encounter?

Of course, her fears would not be shared by him. Katherine knew how much this adventure meant to Jack. Before their friendship had developed into unexpected love, he'd talked endlessly of his excitement at leaving the cold and familiar climes of their homeland to make his own way in the world. And to make his own fortune.

When he looked up suddenly, she blinked rapidly to remove any trace of her fear or sadness. It was the least she could do: show how much she endorsed this wonderful next phase of his life.

So, in heroic terms, she bounced down the last of the stairs, nearly colliding with Aunt Antoinette who was rounding the corner with Lord Quamby leaning heavily on his sticks.

"Oh Jack, you're going to have the time of your life!" she cried, hugging his back impulsively. Dressed up as cousinly enthusiasm, she could feel him close against her for these extra few seconds. When the time came for that final farewell, she must be careful not to cling.

He straightened unexpectedly, gripping her shoulders to stop her stumbling backwards, a genuine smile of so many emotions crossing his face. Of course, he couldn't hide the fact that he was itching for adventure. Katherine wouldn't have expected him to. But she caught the fleeting concern, wariness, consciousness of what they were to each other.

And told herself it was enough.

"Be careful, won't you?" she went on, turning to her mama. "Jack must write and tell us the exciting things he's been up to. If I were a man, I'd go adventuring too! Not stay obediently at home doing what I'm told."

"You sound like you want to behave just like your mama did before she was snared by the worthy Fenton," remarked Lord Quamby with a twinkle in his eye.

Aunt Antoinette's mouth quirked. "But you're not a man, Katherine, so you have no choice but to remain obediently at home, though no doubt that's why you can't wait to spread your wings and have your own household. Like you so rightly said when you first came to London, marriage is the only way to be independent. And it's the only way to behave as one *wants* without society's disapproving eye coming down upon one's shoulders. Am I not right, my darling Quamby?"

"As always, my dear," the earl responded as the pair exchanged a look.

Katherine again wondered at the foundations of their irregular marriage. Her mama had been evasive when she'd brought it up. She sighed inwardly. With so many things grown-ups didn't tell their children, it seemed the only way to find out was to get married oneself.

However, she was very glad she knew what to expect regarding physical relations between a man and a woman. Loving Jack had made her realise how magical it was to be united with the 'right' one. Tears welled up behind her eyes and she forced them back. She'd have to throw herself into revelry in the hope of cauterising the pain if she wasn't to become a nun instead. Regardless, she didn't think she'd find herself married in her first season.

The carriage drew up in front of the house as George appeared in the hallway to offer his own farewell. "Safe travels, Jack," he said, shaking his friend's hand and clapping him on the back. "Write, won't you? I want to hear what adventures you get up to."

Katherine was about to use her last bit of cheeriness to endorse this, but then Lord Fenton and Cousin George Bramley arrived and the men all clustered about, exchanging male talk, and Katherine felt excluded. And lost.

Two footmen arrived to take Jack's trunk, and then Jack was standing on the threshold of the wide-open double doors, and Katherine could see the carriage door open, ready to receive him.

She didn't think she could bear it. She was too aware of her mama beside her to rush forward and impulsively embrace Jack yet again, this time clinging as if her life depended on keeping him close. If it had been like the old days when they were simply good friends, she'd have done it, but she was too self-conscious of displaying any emotion that would give them away. So, she simply remained in line, awaiting her turn as Jack farewelled each of her relatives with either a handshake or an embrace.

He hesitated when he came to her, glancing at her mama on her right and her Aunt Antoinette on her left.

"Look after my favourite proxy cousin," he told them, putting his hand on Katherine's shoulder.

Katherine tried not to close her eyes and crook her neck so she could rest her cheek upon it. She blinked back the tears. "I'm going to miss you, Jack," she said hoarsely.

"You'll have too much fun to miss me for long."

"That's right, Katherine," said Aunt Antoinette in bolstering tones. "Because looking after you means, in part, ensuring you settle upon a man worthy to be a husband of whom Jack would be sure to approve."

"I already have," Katherine whispered, so softly she was sure only Jack could hear, except that Aunt Antoinette looked sharply at her.

Jack squeezed her shoulder. "I look forward to hearing all about it, Katherine," he said, just as if he was the old Jack with just the right words for everyone and Katherine was just his friend. He looked away to address her mother. "When I lie awake beneath the Southern Cross, it will give me comfort to think of Katherine, happy and well placed with a good husband, which is, of course, the reason she's in London," he added meaningfully.

Katherine's mama laughed. "I think you might find the news already awaiting you when you reach Kingston. In case Katherine hasn't told you, there are several likely contenders already."

"What makes you say that, Mama!" Katherine cried more hotly than was warranted for everyone looked rather strangely at her.

"I'm sure it's no secret that Mr Marwick is most taken, and your Aunt Antoinette suggested you returned his interest." Lady Fenton sounded almost defensive. "Now, come along, Katherine, this is Jack's send-off. We can talk about *you*, later."

It took a great deal of willpower for Katherine not to

flounce off or to rebuke her mother, which she rarely did besides. But of all the things for Jack to hear upon leaving. It was enough to break her heart.

Which is what she felt was happening as she collapsed on her bed once Jack had well and truly departed. It was not ten o'clock in the morning, but she drew the blinds as if the night had gathered upon her dreams and she was in the deepest mourning, and wept until she fell asleep.

ANOTHER BALL TO CONTEMPLATE, ANOTHER LONG, TEDIOUS evening to endure.

How different Katherine felt about the social whirl now that Jack was gone. And it had been only hours!

After she'd washed her face and put on a walking dress to take some fresh air in the large, beautifully landscaped gardens that surrounded the Earl of Quamby's London residence, she happened upon Aunt Antoinette seated on a curved garden seat in a little arbour. As soon as Katherine rounded the corner, the gentleman with whom her aunt appeared to be engaged in earnest conversation, and she was sure they'd been holding hands, leapt to his feet, offered a cursory bow, and disappeared amongst the trees.

Aunt Antoinette smiled at the look on Katherine's face and patted the seat beside her on the garden bench.

"Don't be shocked, Katherine. As a married woman who has provided my husband with the required heir, I have licence to follow my heart. Dear besotted Raoul feeds my vanity and is quite unsuitable for the role of anything other than what we might have referred to in my younger days as a cicisbeo. But he is necessary to my happiness. You will learn such things are permissible, with discretion, if you are unfortunate enough to contract a marriage that isn't a match of hearts."

"A cicisbeo?" repeated Katherine, sinking down onto the cushion beside her aunt. She felt unaccountably shocked, though of course she knew her aunt enjoyed the company of men not her husband.

Aunt Antoinette stroked her fine pigskin gloves and looked reflective. "Marriage is not always what one expects it will be, though young women today are given greater licence to follow their hearts and inclination than they were in my day, and certainly in your grandmother's era before romantic love was given the acceptability it's gained today." She tucked a curl behind her niece's ear and added, "However, it appears you've done your best to ensure you know well and truly what to expect of the man you're considering to be your husband— in all respects. Your mother would be scandalised, and I'm not sure I entirely approve but I daresay I am to blame."

Katherine seized her unexpected chance. "It's true what you have to say, Aunt and..." Nervously she plucked at her skirts. "Which reminds me...well, could I have more of what you gave me the other day? Those Saint Anne's Lace seeds?"

"Why, Katherine, what does this mean?" Aunt Antoinette frowned. "You need to reassure me that you're in love. You're not like me. You favour your mother in matters of the heart. There was only one man for her, and she was determined to have him at any cost. You're not...taking this newfound knowledge of yours and experimenting—"

"Heavens, no!" Katherine felt her cheeks flaming. "Oh Aunt, there is only one man I love. And I love him, truly, deeply, but I fear—" She broke off.

"Come, Katherine; tell me." Her aunt smiled in sympathy. "You fear your parents may not approve? That they would consider him an unsuitable match?"

Sadly, Katherine nodded, wavering as to whether to

confide in Aunt Antoinette. A flare of hope took hold as she contemplated whether her bold and adventurous aunt might go so far as to suggest how Katherine could indeed pursue Jack in a way that their families would consider appropriate, and that wouldn't hinder Jack's ambitions. Wildly, she wondered if perhaps she could become a governess in a family near to where Jack would be residing for the first year.

"Katherine!"

They looked up as Lady Fenton advanced, smiling.

"Katherine, darling, Mary was wondering where you were in order to dress your hair before she starts work on mine." Lady Fenton gave a long-suffering sigh. "The fashions in hair today take twice as long as they did in my day, and I'm not sure I like them half as much." She stroked her daughter's cheek. "You, of course, look charming whatever the prevailing style and I'm sure you'll be as great a success tonight as you have been to date." Her look clouded. "There are many fine gentlemen other than the ones you've already met from whom you can take your pick. Please don't be exclusive, my dear. Why, there are weeks before the season winds down, and you've only just begun."

"Katherine declares her heart is already engaged," Aunt Antoinette said with a smile that made Katherine squirm. Oh Lord, she couldn't reveal Jack as the one, and she was very much afraid she'd blurt something inappropriate or even a lie. Her mother always seemed to catch her out in those.

"I really have to hurry if I'm to be ready for tonight," she mumbled, rising and hurrying away, leaving her mother and aunt staring after her.

Fanny had become deeply troubled by her daughter's odd behaviour the last few days. She frowned and bit her lip. "You don't suppose it's Mr Marwick who's captured her heart, do you?" she asked, taking a seat by her sister.

Antoinette smiled. "I can't think who else it could be?

He's been very particular in his attentions, and Katherine seems to have been besotted from the evening she met him." She put her head closer and said in confidential tones, "In fact, they shared a kiss in the corridor at Lady Maxwell's which, if I recall correctly, was within a very short time of their meeting."

"A kiss? Well, as long as it was only a kiss," Fanny said, distractedly, thinking of her *far* worse behaviour when she was determined to snare her darling Fenton. Behaviour that might land Katherine in greater trouble than it had Fanny. Fanny, after all, knew that Fenton was lauded as an honourable gentleman and would make the most perfect husband. Indeed, he had fulfilled every aspiration Fanny had ever had.

"Fanny, I know you don't like the idea because of his relationship to your late Lord Slyther, but he's a fine catch. The future Lord Marples."

Fanny nibbled the tip of her little finger. "I know, I know. Oh Antoinette!" she blurted out. "I do hope Katherine hasn't lost her heart to him for I've heard some very concerning things about Mr Marwick lately."

"Rumours? Why, what gentleman of any interest doesn't have some scandal attached to them?"

"Please don't sound so sceptical. This is my daughter's happiness we're talking about."

Antoinette inclined her head and looked suitably contrite. "Very well, tell me what you've heard."

"It's only rumour at this stage; I do admit that. You see, I heard that Mr Marwick is not in fact as plump in the pocket as he would have others believe."

Antoinette looked scandalised. "You'd stop your daughter marrying a man she loved because he didn't have a fat enough pocketbook? Really, Fanny, I can't say that I'm not utterly appalled you would behave with as much cavalier disregard for your daughter's happiness as...well, our own mother."

Fanny knew she deserved her sister's censure to a degree, but there was more that niggled. "Please don't accuse me of being anything like our mother," she begged. "Of course, I can't but hope that Katherine will make a match that is worthy of her. She could attract a man of substance *and* charm. Why, she could have anyone she wants, I do believe. I've just heard that Mr Marwick is something of a buccaneer. Also, that he's been associated with a number of women—"

"A man in his position is bound to attract interest from the feminine sex."

"Yes, yes, I know that. But he's fond of gaming and he's not terribly successful, I've heard. He's lost a great deal of money, lately, in fact—"

"I'm fond of gaming too, my dear. Most men are fond of gaming. It's what a young man of his class with too much leisure *does*. He just needs a good woman—a clever, engaging wife—to exert the right influence over him."

Fanny rose. There was no point in arguing with Antoinette when her opinion was made up as it certainly was in this case. And perhaps she was right. Perhaps Fanny was putting rumour ahead of her daughter's happiness—simply because she thought Katherine could do better than Mr Marwick.

CHAPTER 13

Katherine stared disconsolately at the couples in the centre of the room. Strange how just days ago this was what her whole life revolved around. Having fun, dancing with handsome, eligible men. She'd thought it was the pinnacle of life's adventure.

Tonight, she'd danced with three candidates who, a week ago, would have perfectly fitted her marital criteria—and that of her mama and grandmother. Lord Derry was charming and funny; Mr Marwick was dashing in a rather dangerous, exciting way, and Mr Ludwig was poetic, dreamy and very, very rich. All had excellent credentials, came from good families, and seemed to think Katherine utterly delightful.

Yet, her heart was with Jack right now. She wondered where he was. A storm had blown up off the coast, she'd been told, and the weather here in London had deteriorated rapidly. Gusts of wind and rain had hampered their preparations and arrival, and her slippers had been wet when she'd been announced in the grand ballroom of Lady Derby's London townhouse. While sipping lemonade, she'd been told by her grandmother that the storm was travelling south, and it was unlikely any ships would depart from Southampton for another two days.

Katherine wondered if Jack was thinking of her as he whiled away his time in some seaside tavern, no doubt checking the long lists he'd made regarding his intended travels. He was an organised young man who knew what he wanted out of life. Adventure, yes, but he was not a regular buccaneer; Katherine knew that very well. She sniffed, determined to keep the tears at bay. She'd get over her first love. And she'd marry well. It was what they'd both agreed must happen, though they'd pledged always to be friends.

"Do you have something in your eye, my dear? Here, let me look." It was Mr Marwick, in a solicitous mood, or else wanting an excuse to get closer, for as he bent his head to peer into her eyes, his own were filled with collusion.

"Perhaps you ought to attend to that tiny rip in your skirt that I fear is likely to trip you up in a more energetic polka," he suggested.

Of course, it was code that Katherine might like to meet him in the corridor for a quick kiss to follow the single kiss she'd received from someone other than Jack.

Her body revolted at the thought. She didn't want to kiss Mr Marwick when her thoughts were entirely taken up by Jack, but she also needed to jolt herself out of what could become a dangerous malaise. Jack would think of her for a few days, but the moment a pretty girl crossed his path in some far-flung part of the world, Katherine would be forgotten. That was the way men were. At least, it helped to tell herself that. And perhaps Katherine ought to try and take a leaf out of their book if her heart wasn't to become a mushy, difficult thing to manage as she waltzed from ball to ball.

So, nodding slightly, first to his suggestion, and then to his follow-up that she depart just before the end of the next dance, so there was no danger of her becoming engaged by someone asking her to partner him in the next waltz, Katherine bit her lip and prepared to be wicked.

Yet, why was it wicked to see if she liked a man enough to make him her husband? It seemed a contradiction. She knew that if she and Jack had been caught doing so much worse, she'd have had to marry him. She'd have been happy to have done so, but she'd not for the world spoil his chances of adventure, knowing his need to prove himself on his own merits.

"Mama, I'm going to the mending room. I'll be back shortly."

Her mother barely acknowledged her. She was in animated discussion with her mother and sister, so Katherine glided through the crowd, and no sooner was she behind a concealing curtain than she was whisked into a pair of strong arms and Mr Marwick's mouth was upon hers.

It wasn't unpleasant, but it had neither the magic of Jack's kisses that made her heart melt, and nor did it have the novelty of the illicit edge that had made kissing Mr Marwick the first time so exciting.

When it seemed like he might extend his amorousness, Katherine pushed herself out of his embrace with carefully calculated modesty. "It's very dangerous, and I really must return. Mama keeps a close eye on me."

"Your mama would not approve of me?"

"Oh, it's not that! I'm quite sure she would."

"Has she said anything to suggest that my suit would not be well received?"

Katherine was shocked. Was he hinting that already he was considering marriage? Katherine was not at all sure that she liked the idea of marriage to Mr Marwick. She directed him a considering look. He certainly was handsome. His dark, oily locks were carefully coiffured, and his side whiskers were very impressive.

But really, Jack's boyish charm was far more to her taste. The more she thought about it, the more she could imagine running away with Jack to the other side of the world with just a trunk between them. And now that Katherine knew there were ways not to keep adding to their family they'd be free for the first few important years.

The realisation that she'd not yet sourced the Queen Anne's Lace seeds she needed from her Aunt Antoinette made her gasp, but Mr Marwick misinterpreted it for excitement at his veiled allusion to a shared future.

"You are an exquisite creature, Miss Fenton."

He really did look as if he were enchanted by her, and naturally, Katherine's vanity was fed. "You are very kind, Mr Marwick," she murmured as she took the arm he offered.

"And did you enjoy kissing me?" he asked, just before they reentered the ballroom.

"Very much," she assured him, smiling as she thought of Jack.

"And do you like adventures, Miss Fenton?"

She was surprised at the odd question. "I adore adventures, Mr Marwick." What a marvellous adventure it would be if Jack suddenly appeared and begged her to run away with him. She would, too!

But then her grandmother was by her side; her normally pinched mouth drawn up as she greeted Mr Marwick like an old friend.

"You are nothing like your uncle," she told him, "and yet I hear he was a dashing youth in his day. Very nearly married Katherine's mother, did you know?"

"Oh, I'm very well aware of it." Mr Marwick raised an eyebrow at Katherine and stroked his plush moustache. "A tragedy his untimely death precluded that though, of course, I'm delighted, otherwise I'd not be squiring your lovely granddaughter about."

"She is lovely, isn't she?" Lady Brightwell's assessing gaze travelled from Katherine's burning cheeks to Mr Marwick's smug confidence. She gave Katherine's arm a squeeze. "You enjoy yourself, my dear. I'm sure Mr Marwick will take very good care of you."

Katherine was relieved to be deposited back with her mother and aunt, and even more relieved when it was proposed that they should leave early in case the weather grew worse.

Pleading exhaustion when they arrived home, she went straight to her bedchamber and sat on the bed, staring into the dancing flames of the small fire her maid had stoked up in anticipation of her return.

With every passing moment, Jack was going further from her. She'd thought she was big enough and noble enough to be happy for him, but the truth was that she longed to be away from here. She'd suffer any privation to be with Jack, she decided.

Balls and fine clothes were all very well, but the real substance of life was sharing adventures with a kindred spirit.

Half an hour later when she was about to undress for bed, Mary entered the room bearing an envelope with Katherine's name on it.

"It were handed in at the kitchen, miss, wiv directions it come straight to ye," the girl said. "I'm sure it ain't proper, but I won't say anyfink if yer don't want me ter."

Katherine grinned and handed her sixpence. "There you are, Mary. That's for your silence. I'm sure there's nothing improper about it at all. No doubt one of the gentlemen I met tonight wishes to go walking with me tomorrow."

In this genuinely sanguine mood, she dismissed Mary after she'd helped her off with her ballgown and into her night clothes. Taking a seat at her writing desk, she slit the envelope and pulled out the elegant piece of paper with its hastily scrawled message. And her heartbeat grew more rapid as her eyes scanned the following lines:

"Dearest Katherine,
You said you loved adventure, and so I'm proposing the greatest adventure of both our lives.
Run away with me! Tonight, when it's possible, and I have a carriage awaiting! Let spontaneity and whatever is in your heart right now dictate your actions, for if you sleep on the idea, a more composed view of your future will ensure that you behave with a propriety that may be at odds with the future happiness of both of us.
If you look outside your window, you'll see a post-chaise. It'll be there for the next three hours. Three hours to enable you to prepare; to take what you need to take, or as a potent symbol of possibility if it takes longer to persuade you of the merits of my proposal.
Tonight, as I stared into the dark night and listened to the storm, my heart was full of—"

SHE BROKE OFF READING AS THE DOOR OPENED AND HER mother entered the room, her night attire covered by a beautiful, blue-and-gold silk dressing gown. "Katherine, my love. I thought you'd be in bed by now."

Katherine tried to regulate the pounding of her heart. "I couldn't sleep, Mama," she lied, clasping her hands behind her back to hide the letter.

"In that case, now would be a good time to have a little chat." Her mother looked distracted as she moved forward, presumably to sit on the bed.

"About what, Mama?"

"About Mr Marwick." Her mother held out her hand to take Katherine's. Katherine crumpled the letter in her palm, but when she saw her mother was about to take that very hand, she unfurled it, letting the letter drop. A gust of wind through the partly open window rustled the several letters on Katherine's writing desk, lifting one and sending it across the short distance towards the fireplace.

"Quick! Catch it!" said her mother, taking a step towards Katherine, about to bend down, but not as quickly as Katherine who whisked up the letter she'd been writing to a school friend just as she saw flames lick the corner of the note she'd just received.

"Katherine, there's another one. Quickly!" Her mother reached across her to seize Jack's note, but Katherine stayed her hand. "It was a discarded draft," she said, looking at the crumpled parchment. She'd read all that was necessary, and so it was better that it be reduced to cinders.

If Jack wanted Katherine to elope with him, Katherine didn't need three hours to make up her mind. No, Katherine was prepared to cross stormy oceans to be with him because she loved him. Loved him too much to be a burden if he needed to do his adventuring alone, but enough to cross oceans to join him if that's what he wanted.

"Katherine, I've heard talk surrounding Mr Marwick that I think you should know."

"Please, Mama, I'm very tired." Katherine sat heavily on the bed and rubbed her eyes. "Can we talk about this in the morning?"

Lady Fenton looked troubled, then sighed. "I'm sure it can, my dear." She wrapped her dressing gown more closely about her, rose, and walked to the door.

"Mama..." Katherine hesitated, unsure how to progress but bolstered by her mother's sympathetic and enquiring look when she turned. "How did you know you were in love with Papa? I mean, you surely had other suitors who were just as eligible."

Lady Fenton put her hand to her heart. "How did I know? I just did. Just as I knew no one else would do, now that I'd met him. Don't worry, my dear. You have plenty of time. Be patient, and the same will happen to you."

Tentatively, Katherine asked, "Would you have crossed oceans to be with Papa? Even if he *hadn't* been rich?"

Her mother looked indecisive. "Fortunately, it didn't come to that, my darling. Now, go to sleep. We'll talk in the morning."

The door closed behind her and Katherine covered her face with her hands, joy and thrilling anticipation coursing through her. Jack wanted her as much as she wanted him.

The storm which had stayed his progress, halted his spontaneity, and had him holed up in some tavern in Southampton, had given Jack enough time to realise he couldn't live without Katherine.

And Katherine had been granted a second chance to forge ahead and take a chance to be with the love of her life.

Her mother knew how tumultuous and desperate true love could be. Surely she'd forgive Katherine?

❦

THE MOMENT HER MOTHER'S FOOTSTEPS HAD DIED AWAY, Katherine tore off her nightgown and changed into her most practical travelling dress. Then she seized the carpetbag beneath her bed, and began cramming into it everything she would need for the next three days as well as all her jewellery. This she could sell or pawn for the necessities to sustain her until they reached dry land.

Jack hadn't needed much and nor did Katherine. A week in London had buoyed her up with all the social excitement to last a lifetime. Jack had taught her what was important: true, honest feeling, and there was not much of that, she'd discovered, as she'd waltzed from one ball to another. Her time in the social sphere would come, and she'd embrace it when it did. Jack would go far; she knew he would. His adoptive parents had connections, and when Jack had proved himself and returned home with a fortune he'd earned by his own toil, he'd be given the appropriate welcome. Katherine would be forgiven, and her new life on English soil in a few years' time would be all the richer for having followed a purer path when she'd been given the chance.

It was squally and blustery as she tiptoed out of the house, giving the scullery maid who was half asleep on a pallet in front of the kitchen fire sixpence for keeping quiet until morning.

Then, with her breath coming in short, jerky gasps, she dashed across the cobbled road and into the waiting carriage, the coachman jumping down from the box to help her in and to tuck a rug about her knees, saying, "Me master'll be glad yer chose to come. Now, 'ave some rest, fer it'll be three hours on the road, I'm guessin'."

Yes, three hours to Southampton would be right, thought Katherine, putting her head against the soft cushion that had been provided for her comfort, and telling herself she should get the rest she needed while she could, because there'd be plenty of adventure ahead of her during the next phase of her life.

But she knew she could not sleep a wink. Not with the knowledge that Jack would open the carriage door when she reached her destination, take her into his arms, and tell her how proud of her he was that she wanted to be an adventurer with him.

BUT SHE DID SLEEP. ALTHOUGH THE RAIN WAS ULFALTERING

and the night was dark, the carriage rocked at a steady pace over the cobbled streets of London and then onto a good, flat road. The motion was calming and rhythmic, and since Katherine couldn't see anything in the dark, her excitement was soon lulled into a state of happy calm, until her eyes closed and her mind took her to the faraway places she and Jack would explore.

"Wake up, miss!"

A rush of cold air swept into the carriage, together with the rough though not unfriendly rousing of the coachman.

Rubbing her eyes and sitting up, Katherine saw she was in the stableyard of an inn. A lantern was raised to light her way, and she took the hand she was offered, struggling out onto the hay-strewn cobbles. She raised her face to the sky and tried to breathe in the smell of the sea, but the most prominent aroma was that of horse manure.

"This way, miss." The matronly voice identified herself as the tavern keeper's wife before she led Katherine through the courtyard and up a short flight of stairs, and into the warm tavern. "Yer gennulman friend is waitin' fer yer in the private parlour. Follow me."

Barely able to contain her excitement, Katherine hurried after the woman. By the time she'd reached the end of the corridor and the door was thrown open, she thought she might collapse with it.

Joyously, she burst into the room, ready to throw herself into the arms of her beloved Jack.

But it was not Jack who stood by the fire, smiling his welcome.

In shock, Katherine blinked several times, her mind trying to assimilate the strange reality that instead of Jack, striding towards her as if she'd made him the happiest man on Earth, it was Mr Marwick.

"My dearest Katherine," he cried, enfolding her in his

arms. "I truly wasn't sure if you'd come. In fact, it has been in the greatest trepidation that I've waited these past hours, wondering if you'd act on the daring note I sent you, or whether you'd simply crumple it up and consign it to the flames. But you have come!"

The fire crackled; the lamp flickered in the dim, comfortably furnished room while outside the wind howled. Like Katherine felt like doing as her jaw dropped, and she allowed herself to be kissed on the head and finally on the lips, at which point she drew back her face.

"Of course, you're feeling vulnerable, and so I must assure you that until we are married, I shall behave in the most gentlemanly fashion." He put his hand to his chest. "Upon my honour, I pledge that not until my ring is on your finger will I do anything unseemly. Have no fear that I will besmirch your reputation."

Except that Katherine knew it was besmirched already. The mere fact of being alone with any man overnight, regardless of where each slept, would damn her in the eyes of the world.

Terror, uncertainty, and finally dumb grief gripped her as he led her to a blue-velvet sofa and handed her a brandy. Dear Lord, she needed that to dull her senses. So, Jack hadn't written the note begging her to elope with him? Apparently not. Which meant he'd not thought of her at all with his new world taken up by excitement and adventure.

Meanwhile, Katherine had behaved like the most foolish of impetuous misses who ever got hung out to dry. She hadn't even got so far as to read who'd signed the note before she'd crumpled it in the fire and set off on this madcap fool's errand.

"Don't look so fearful, my dear. Of course, you've had a long journey and clearly not enough sleep." Mr Marwick seated himself next to her and patted her hand. "I promise to look after you, always, my dearest Katherine. I promise I'll reward you forever for trusting in me like this."

Katherine considered how wise it was to confess her error. It was possible he'd not take kindly to learning that she'd intended eloping with another for, in truth, Katherine had no idea what kind of man Mr Marwick really was.

She just knew that she had to keep the peace, keep her virtue, and hope that her family came to her rescue so that the whole affair could be hushed up and she'd not find herself bound to Mr Marwick for life.

She was surprised when he laughed suddenly, a sound both full of glee but tinged with sympathy. "You poor child. You look quite dazed. I'll have Mrs. Tate take you to your room for the night, and then we shall continue to Scotland where we can be married by the afternoon. Then you will be mine—forever!" He reached over and pressed his lips softly against hers.. "I knew from the first moment you agreed to kiss me with such touching alacrity that we were bound together forever."

CHAPTER 14

"Antoinette! I can't find Katherine! I'm sure she's not slept in her bed, and Mary knows something—I can tell—but she won't say."

A terrible dread washed over Antoinette, who guiltily put on her dressing gown and hurried to her niece's bedchamber in Fanny's wake. It was she who discovered Katherine's note beneath the pillow, and tearing it open, read it quickly.

She dropped the hastily scrawled missive and sat heavily on the bed. "She's eloped!" She put her hands to her face and heaved in a breath while her sister gasped, stooping to snatch the discarded note, crying out as she read it, "She's run away to be with the love of her life. That's all she says! That, and that she'll explain everything in a much longer, detailed letter when she reaches her destination."

"And where might that be? Oh, Fanny, she's more like you were than either of us supposed!"

"But I never eloped!" Fanny ran her fingers through her already disordered hair. "This is ruinous. It's Mr Marwick, of course. She knew I was going to tell her of my concerns about him last night, but she didn't want to listen." Fanny began to cry and Antoinette, feeling a little spark of pride for Katherine's boldness in following her heart, but also sympathy for her sister, for, in truth, she agreed nevertheless that Katherine could have done better, patted Fanny on the shoulder and bade her sit down on a chair by the fire.

Antoinette sat on the arm of the chair. "Katherine suspected, perhaps, you'd not have sanctioned her marriage to Mr Marwick, and in a fit of adolescent bravado, she's taken her future into her own hands. Please don't cry, Fanny. I know how much she loves him and that's all that counts, in my book."

"But I'm not convinced he'll make her happy. He's the first man who danced with her when she came to London, other than Jack. Why, I'd have preferred it if she'd married Jack instead of some man on the make as I know Mr Marwick is. He's already run through one fortune. I don't want her to align herself with some reprobate worse than our father."

"Come now, Fanny; your imagination is running away with you." Antoinette tried to sound brighter than she felt. "There are few reprobates quite as bad as our father was. We came to London with no reputation to speak of, and we were very lucky to make the marriages we did. But Katherine will be protected by the Fenton name."

"And the Fenton fortune," Fanny muttered, dabbing her eyes with her handkerchief.

"Come now; Freddy Marwick is not a fortune hunter. Allow Katherine the latitude you took when you were her age. Katherine is *in love*. You've always said you'd never be like our mama when it came time to your daughters falling in love."

Fanny sat up, clutching the note to her chest, staring out of the window as if she hadn't heard Antoinette. "Mary must be made to talk. She knows more than she's saying, and if we set out, now, there may still be time to prevent this disastrous union. She'll not have reached the border if she's going by carriage. Fenton can go on horseback and bring her back." Brightened by the fact she had a plan, Fanny rose and began to pace. "Poor Katherine has no idea what marriage is truly like. She'll be horrified by what this man wants her to do with him. Childish, romantic love of the heart is one thing, but a lifetime of bedroom delights with Mr Marwick is another matter altogether. No, we have to bring her back! We can hush everything up."

Antoinette shook her head. She too was filled with sorrow, but she had to persuade her sister of the truth. "Do you think Katherine would have gone so far as to elope only to change her mind within a few hours? No, Katherine is in love. She confessed as much to me. In fact—" She stopped, reconsidering whether to continue.

"What?"

Tact was needed to divulge the extent of Katherine's misdemeanours however, as it reinforced the fact that Katherine had truly lost her heart. Antoinette went on, "Katherine is a girl who falls fast and hard, like you, Fanny. She asked me to explain how love and families work, and I did, and so she decided it would be wise to see if she loved Mr Marwick in the...biblical sense before she said yes to being his wife."

"And what did you do, Antoinette?" Fanny's eyes were wild in her pale, anxious face. "Oh, dear Lord, you *encouraged* her to lose her virtue?"

"I gave her something to take as a precaution against the consequences of losing her virtue which, I might add, was only so she could see if Mr Marwick was the man she wanted to spend the rest of her life with."

Fanny dabbed her eyes and looked at her sister, shaking her head. "Katherine truly did that? She's eloped with Mr

Marwick after carrying on in this way for the past week?" She gave a little shuddering cry. "I never would have believed it of her. And I truly would not have picked Mr Marwick as the man to sweep her off her feet."

"Well, he has," Antoinette said decidedly. "And Katherine has sealed her own fate, but she's happy I assure you. She was all aglow when she spoke about him. And if you're going to be true to your word and not interfere when it comes to letting her follow her heart, then you must just wait for them to return after saying their vows upon the blacksmith's anvil over the border, and then announce the happy news to all the world. I think you'll be glad you listened to me, for once, Fanny. I am, as you know, rather adept at successfully navigating potentially ruinous romantic liaisons."

Fanny stood up and walked to the window. Antoinette had made some disastrous romantic decisions in her life. Perhaps the worst was when she'd allowed herself to be seduced by George Bramley, which had resulted in the birth of Young George. What should have been ruinous had instead been astonishingly fortuitous after Lord Quamby, needing an heir and happy to accept the bastard son of his nephew, had married the now-pregnant Antoinette.

Although this had been more serendipitous than calculated good fortune, Antoinette did have a point in that Katherine had always known her own mind. Since coming to London, she'd been so happy, which suggested she'd fallen in love almost immediately.

The last thing Fanny wanted was to estrange her daughter by being the coldhearted and manipulative creature her own mother had been.

"I still can't accept that this is the right decision for Katherine's happiness, Antoinette," she sighed, turning back to her sister. "But if it's what Katherine wants, then I shan't dispatch Fenton on a fleet-footed horse to drag my daughter home. If she wants to marry Freddy Marwick this badly, then I'll accept her decision with good grace. The simple fact she's eloped indicates the depth of her love for him, as she was clearly quite terrified that we'd not sanction his suit in view of the rumours flying around concerning his recent gaming losses. Perhaps Katherine will reform him."

❧

KATHERINE WOKE TO THE SOUND OF THE MAID IN HER room stoking up the fire. She felt exhausted and disoriented, and when the girl opened the windows, letting in a rush of air that was not salt-laden, she nearly wept. She should have been at a seaside tavern, with Jack, about to embark upon the adventure of their lives.

Instead, Mr Marwick awaited her downstairs. Well, she had to tell him. Not the truth, perhaps, as she was depending upon his goodwill to get her safely home again. But she would tell him that a night's reflection had made her realise her desire to marry respectably; that it would devastate her parents if she slunk away in the dark of the night when she could have had a grand ceremony with all her relatives in attendance; that she'd acted with much too much haste. Yes, that ought to satisfy him.

But she wouldn't go down yet. No, a few more hours just might be enough time for her distraught family to discover her whereabouts. If her father were to burst into the tavern to drag her home, she'd be saved any awkwardness and, perhaps, anger, from Mr Marwick and then she could put this whole unfortunate episode behind her.

Feeling slightly lighter of spirit, she finished her breakfast from the tray brought to her room, slept several hours longer, then went downstairs, arriving at the doorway to the private parlour at the same moment as her prospective groom.

It was three in the afternoon, and he was looking anxious though his eyes lit up when he saw her. "My darling Katherine, I wasn't sure if you'd changed your mind. I've been pacing the corridor by your room for hours." He hurried forwards and gripped her hands, bringing them up to his lips. "Dare I hope that you are fired up at the prospect of spending the rest of your life in my care?" He lowered his head, murmuring against her lips, "I do swear I'll be the gentlest and most considerate of husbands, my angel."

Katherine let him kiss her briefly. She felt awkward and unsure how she would broach the very difficult subject before her, but an excited cry from further up the passage made them break away abruptly.

"Mr Marwick?" The shocked recognition was followed by a pause before the large and venerable society hostess whom Katherine remembered well from descriptions given to her by her mother, followed up her original question with, "Miss *Fenton?*"

Mr Marwick chuckled as he took Katherine's hand and led her towards the Countess of Lexington. "Lady Lexington, may I present my new wife, Mrs Marwick, no longer Miss Fenton. Yes, we've been wicked; we've just eloped, but we hope society will forgive us as it did your very own niece last year when she hastened across the border with a man who has now been welcomed into the family."

Lady Lexington hesitated as she was joined by the earl, their three daughters, and respective husbands. And then suddenly the passage seemed filled with half of London society offering Katherine and Freddy their best wishes.

And amidst their gaiety and well wishes, Katherine knew that her fate was sealed.

PART II

Seven Years Later

Jack stood on the stern of the *SS Eglinton*, and watched the shores of his homeland grow from a tiny speck in the distance, to discernible landmarks while he worked to suppress his excitement. A new phase of his life was about to begin, and after years of toil, travelling, a generous mentor and clever investments, he was returning to the land that had always occupied his heart, a self-made man with a substantial fortune.

A new decade had begun, and he foresaw the forties as heralding an exciting era of innovation and prosperity for the British people. Trade routes were opening up, and that could only mean exciting and hitherto unthought-of opportunities for those with energy and an eye to the future like himself.

So much had changed since Jack had first journeyed to foreign shores on the *Hugh Lindsay*. After a year in the West Indies, Jack had travelled to Bombay where he'd worked in various capacities these past six years. When he'd been taken under the wing of the astute but kindly Zebediah Worthington, three years before, Jack's fortunes had soared.

Now Jack was returning to England a prosperous

merchant. He'd purchased an estate to please the worthy bride he'd chosen. The only daughter of his mentor, Odette had arrived in Bombay the previous year to visit her father and had left with him to return to England three months earlier.

Strange, then, that Jack's thoughts should be occupied so much by Katherine.

When he'd left England, it had been the same. He'd thought more about the girl he loved during the long crossing than he had about the prospect of adventure and success. He'd not expected to feel such a sense of loss; as if the aching void could never be adequately filled now that he'd discovered what made him feel whole. He'd thought of writing to Katherine to beg her to join him if she felt as he did. He wanted to tell her that if she loved him, they'd find a way to make it work.

What a green boy he'd been. He turned up the collar of his coat and wiped his spray-wet eyes with his sleeve. He'd wanted adventure, and he'd longed for Katherine's spirited company but he'd been right to know that the two were quite incompatible.

When the first letter from his mother had caught up with him three months after his departure, it had contained the news that Katherine had eloped with Freddy Marwick within a day of Jack sailing away. Before he'd boarded the boat even. That had wounded his pride more than he'd ever admit.

All the hours that the howling wind had delayed the ship sailing, Jack had paced the small chamber of his Southampton tavern with only one wish: to see Katherine burst through the door, begging him to take her with him.

And he could have. The captain, as it turned out, was travelling with his wife and three small children whose nurse-maid had abandoned them on the eve of their departure. Katherine could have fulfilled the role had fate played into their hands. That is, if she'd been reckless enough to follow her heart and had chosen to elope with Jack rather than with the already established Marwick, now Lord Marples.

Instead, she'd channelled her adventurous spirit into other directions, and following her marriage to Marwick, produced one child at last count.

Well, he hoped she was happy. His mother's last letter, received eight months previously, for Jack had been on the move, hinted at some cloud over Lord Marples's reputation, but no doubt he'd overridden that. Freddy Marwick had money, position, and benefactors.

Jack was proud of the fact that his own success hadn't been secured by family connections. His adoptive father was a gentleman, but with no considerable fortune or influence, and he had his natural children to worry about. Patmore Farm was prosperous, but it was no grand estate like the one over which Katherine would now have dominion.

Jack had always been conscious of his good fortune in being elevated from the foundling home. He knew nothing about his natural parents. There was nothing he could know; no information on record, meaning he must be extra enterprising in making his own way in the world.

But soon Jack would have his own family. When the *Eglantine* reached shore before the sun set, he'd be greeted by the lovely daughter of the man to whom he owed so much— the young woman who was to become his wife in six weeks.

Jack had not taken much notice of Odette Worthington when she'd first arrived but after her father had fallen ill, he'd found himself increasingly called upon to squire Odette around Bombay in her father's stead, with Zebediah Worthington's sanction.

Almost without Jack realising it, an understanding appeared to have been accepted by old Mr Worthington and his daughter that intimated marriage. Six months before, with a great sense of inevitability, Jack had made a formal proposal that had been accepted.

Now, within hours, he'd be greeted by his bride-to-be and conveyed back to the London townhouse in which she lived with her ailing father.

It certainly wasn't an unpleasing prospect. Odette was lively and engaging. In fact, she had all the attributes he'd have looked for in a wife, had he been looking. But perhaps it was better this way. Odette seemed delighted by the arrangement. In the last two postal deliveries, he'd received an accumulated six gushing letters from her.

He tried to remember what she looked like as he leant over the railing and closed his eyes against the spray. Instead, he saw Katherine's face, impish and lively, the dimples in her cheeks popping out when she smiled at him, the sparkle in her eyes when she caught his gaze upon her, the limpid, dreamy look that came over her when he held her in his arms.

But Katherine was out of reach now. Her family would have grown, and she'd be weighed down by the cares and responsibilities of being, no doubt, one of London's notable society matrons. He could well envisage Katherine excelling in whatever role she undertook and, as Lord Marples's wife, she was no doubt immersed in charitable activities while smoothing the way for her husband's career to climb.

Giving himself a mental shake, he forced his mind back to Odette. He supposed it was not surprising that he couldn't remember the colour of her eyes, whereas every time he saw a sapphire, he was reminded of Katherine's and the way they'd sparkle as she was about to impart some secret piece of information or amusing *on dit*.

Of course, it wasn't surprising since he'd only known Odette for the three months she'd spent in Bombay with her father, while he'd known Katherine much longer than that. Not as an adult, of course, but from childhood. That would explain why his memory was so sharp with respect to his childhood friend and not so much with regard to the woman he'd marry. One didn't marry childhood friends who eloped the very same day that the fellow she *had* professed to love was sailing off to new adventures.

Of course, he'd make a joke of it, when they met once more. He couldn't tell her how wounded he'd been at the time. Boyish pride; nothing more.

Odette. That's where his future was. With the lovely, russet-haired young woman who'd lost her slipper when descending the stairs of Government House to her carriage. When a street urchin had snatched it up then disappeared, Jack had chivalrously swept her into his arms and carried her to her conveyance. What more romantic start to a lifelong union could there be for a man like Jack, a romantic at heart?

Nevertheless, he *was* looking forward to seeing Katherine once more, and seeing through his own eyes how the last seven years had changed her.

❧

IT WAS NOT A PLAN THAT WON APPROVAL FROM HIS intended, he learned, after their mutually tender welcome and lingering embrace. And truly, it was lovely to hold a soft, beautiful woman in his arms, and to kiss her and know that his marital path was set. Jack was not a philanderer with a roving eye, so the occasional dalliances over the past few years had always been unsatisfactory due to the discovery he was not with a woman whose acquaintance he wished to further in the direction of marriage.

Now he would be married before the end of the summer, and he'd install Odette in the handsome townhouse in Cavendish Square he'd purchased; though now he'd accompanied her, with her aunt in tow, back to her father's townhouse immediately after their reunion at the docks.

"I think it's very unwise, dearest," Odette was saying, as she curled her soft little hand about his. He was seated on the arm of the sofa on which she'd ensconced herself; her flounced skirts taking up most of the available seating. But he preferred it like this. Odette's aunt had discreetly taken up position in a dark corner where she was bent over her tatting while Odette's father rested in his darkened room upstairs.

"Of course, I'm not jealous that you'd wish to see a female friend you've known since childhood, but I do think you should bide your time. For the sake of what people will say about me *and* her."

Odette had spent more than an hour pressed up against Jack in the chaise that had transported them to London, her happy chatter and clear enjoyment at being allowed so close to him resonating with Jack. She was witty and informed and, he thought, quite the perfect choice, putting aside the few occasions during his last months in Bombay where he'd wondered if this engagement had been a little rushed and peremptory.

"Bide my time?" he queried plucking at the knee of his trousers, newly made up for him at London's most exclusive tailor. How things had changed. Jack had money; all of it acquired through his own hard work and shrewdness. "I haven't seen Katherine in seven years. If she hears I'm in London and haven't seen her, she'll be offended." A thought occurred to him. "You don't imagine her husband will be jealous? Is that it?"

"It's because she *has* no husband that I think you should bide your time."

Jack blinked.

"Darling, she can't be that good a friend if you didn't know she was widowed seven months ago." Odette laughed at his shock. "So it's certainly not good form to entertain a male caller, regardless of how long you've known each other." Odette tapped him playfully on the nose with her fan and tickled his ear, about to change the subject, Jack felt sure.

"Widowed? No, I didn't know," he said, feeling unaccountably unsettled by the news, though he couldn't quite decide why for he'd never liked Marwick particularly, and had thought him definitely not good enough for Katherine.

"Well, she is, and the fact that she's wallowing in this terrible scandal right now, means I think it could be misconstrued if you call on Lady Marples at this time."

"Scandal?"

Odette raised her eyebrows. "She's mired in it! Goodness, Jack, you tell me she's an old friend but you know nothing about her, it seems."

"Well, I didn't know anything about a scandal," Jack muttered. Dismay churned in his stomach. Poor Katherine.

"Her husband was hardly a gentleman, though that was no excuse for what she did. Ouch, Jack. You're holding my hand much too tightly."

Jack released his grip and ran his fingers around the rim of his shirt collar, which suddenly seemed too tight.

"What did she do?"

"Some say it was taking a lover that killed Lord Marples. But that's just a rumour."

This was getting a little too much for Jack. He wanted to prise every last bit of information from Odette that he could, and he wasn't sure if she was testing him over his interest in Katherine which he had to admit was considerable.

"I thought innocent young ladies like you didn't discuss such matters," he remarked more mildly than he felt.

"In six weeks, I shall be a worldly married lady, and I believe it entirely appropriate to start testing my wings, so to speak. To tell you the truth, I'm just repeating what I heard my aunt whispering to Mrs Gunning the other night, and I wanted to see how you'd respond. Are you shocked? Disappointed? Or are you not surprised? After all, Lady Marples scandalised everyone by eloping with Lord Marples, whom she must have known her parents would have forbidden her to marry, even though everyone put on as good a show about being accepting about it and Lord Fenton even paid off some of Lord Marples's debts."

"My mama wrote nothing about this, and she's a friend of Katherine's parents, Lord and Lady Fenton."

Odette raised her hand to cup Jack's cheek. "I'm sure she had much more important things to talk about than Lord Marples's gaming debts. He lost the most enormous sum of money not long before he eloped with your friend, Katherine. She must have been quite madly in love with him if she was prepared to embark upon married life in such dire circumstances, for do you know that the creditors came from all over, until he couldn't take it anymore and ran away, before members of his family came to his rescue and started paying them off so he and Lady Marples weren't starving in the streets. Finally, it seems, Lord Fenton parted with a small fortune so his daughter could hold her head up in society. Though that took some time, I'm told. But let's not talk about these wicked people with whom we have nothing in common, for you, Jack, are clever and cautious and wouldn't dream of acting with the kind of haste that makes such a mess of things. Which is why you're my ideal husband, and now that I see that Aunt Sharp has nodded off, won't you kiss me again?"

BY THE END OF THE EVENING, JACK COULD ALMOST BELIEVE he was the happiest man alive. Odette's delight at seeing him after their months apart was touching and gratifying, and it was only with the slightest effort he managed to whip up the enthusiasm required as he shared with her the musings of their future together.

He was a little surprised she thought his townhouse needed such complete refurbishment when he took her there to show it off. He'd bought it partly because he was fond of the old-fashioned panelling and wall colourings, but if redecorating to Odette's taste would make her as happy as she said it would, then he certainly had the funds to gratify her wishes.

So, as the hours ticked by, and he responded to her happy chatter, he found himself thinking only a little of Katherine. Odette didn't wish him to call on her, but in a couple of days when Odette could be wholly reassured of his affections, Jack intended to broach the subject of a visit, once again. Regardless of Odette's feelings, he wanted to see how Katherine did these days.

If nothing else, he owed a pilgrimage to honour the intense flame that, nevertheless, had burned itself out—certainly in *her* heart—the moment he'd left the country.

CHAPTER 16

Katherine heard the clock strike five o' clock. In four hours she *would* go out.

Furtively, she took in her reflection in the long, wide mirror above the mantelpiece as she attempted a confident sashay from the wall to the window.

It was hard to appear confident when she no longer had a roof over her head. Freddy's death seven months ago from a sudden fever had seen the creditors take everything that wasn't nailed to the floor. The ancestral home, which had not been entailed, had long since been sold.

Still, living under her aunt and uncle's roof in London as a scandal-ridden impecunious widow, was preferable to existing in a hovel never sure of what mood her husband would be in when he woke up.

Which, fortunately, had not generally coincided with her waking hours; she'd made sure of that.

At the sound of footsteps in the passage, she nervously patted her ringlets and tugged at her décolletage before sinking demurely onto the gold chintz sofa. She would weather the inevitable altercation with dignity, she told herself, as she clenched her hands into fists while feigning a pleasant smile to greet the arrivals the moment they walked through the door.

The reaction was no less scandalised than she'd expected.

"Katherine! You're not going out wearing crimson when you should be in mourning and eschewing worldly delights for at least another four months, darling," her mother admonished her, sweeping across the room and facing her squarely.

"It's deep rose, not crimson." Katherine had been practising an easy unaffectedness she was far from feeling, but still her voice shook. "Besides, it's not as if Freddy deserves me to mourn him a day more than... Well, I think I've been punished long enough, and I'm sure nobody at Lady Garwood's ball will be counting the months."

"Oh, but they will, Katherine," her mother countered, biting her lip and taking a seat beside Katherine. She patted her arm as if trying to work up the courage to tell her something. "Katherine, I know things have not been...easy for you these last years, but I truly believe that if you behave yourself with decorum, obey the rules and avoid scrutiny, all will be forgotten, and you'll have a second chance at being happy."

Katherine bristled. "It's not my fault matters were misconstrued. I'm blameless, Mama, I told you!"

"I'm sure we both believe you, Katherine." Antoinette tapped her fingertips on the mantelpiece. "But society is not so forgiving."

Her mother, usually so carefree, looked imploring. "Please, Katherine, I think it's unwise for you to go out in public. And certainly not wearing a gown like that."

Katherine took a deep breath and bit her lip to try and keep her anger under control. "Aunt Antoinette gets away with far worse than I've ever done."

"Katherine!" Although her mother was quick to her sister's defence, it was Antoinette who called for peace.

"What Katherine says is perfectly true," she said mildly. "But Katherine, I'm well protected being married to Quamby. The earl has weathered society's opprobrium, and now that I've done my duty and provided him with an heir, I'm given greater licence than might otherwise be the case."

"So, if I'd just given Freddy a son I'd be forgiven for taking a lover?" Katherine took a shuddering breath and squeezed her eyes shut, afraid the tears might spill. "I could be more reconciled to the impossible situation I find myself in if I truly *were* guilty of taking a lover." She swallowed and dashed away a tear with the back of her hand. "I don't expect you to believe me, but Lord Derry took advantage of my distress, and now everyone believes I was willingly in his arms only days after Freddy was in his grave. And suddenly word was all over town that Derry and I had been lovers on and off since my reckless elopement."

Lady Fenton put her arm about Katherine's shoulders, but Katherine was too agitated for such consoling. She knew she had the sympathy of both her aunt and her sister, but they were not society. And it was society that counted.

"Katherine, I believe you, and even if you were guilty as charged I'd forgive you, knowing Freddy as I did," her mother said. "But please, promise you'll do as we ask?"

"I'll change my dress, if that's what you mean," Katherine muttered.

Aunt Antoinette threw up her hands. "Surely you can wait just a little longer! Why is tonight so special?"

That was something Katherine was not about to divulge. She'd worked hard to keep her feelings to herself when they'd told her—casually and as if it would be of little interest to her—that Jack had returned.

The fact he hadn't seen her in three days was eating Katherine alive. Why had he not rushed, posthaste, to visit? Regardless of everything that had happened to each of them in the intervening seven years, they were bound to each other by more than just childhood friendship.

All Katherine could think about was Jack, and that she was free, and that, in all her seven years of hateful marriage, the only reason she'd never been tempted to stray from her husband was because...

Well, what was the point if she couldn't have Jack?

So, dressed in drab mourning, no doubt completely washed out by the deadness of the colour which matched the way Katherine was used to feeling inside, she boldly attended Lady Garwood's ball, alone, defying both her mother and aunt, and no doubt titillating society.

She didn't care. What did anything matter these days?

But when she found herself completely abandoned amidst the gaiety, Katherine realised she'd made a grave miscalculation. Handsomely garbed guests nodded stiffly in recognition before passing on, condemnation clear in their thin smiles. She saw clusters laughing, eyes darting in her direction, but never received an offer of refreshment or enquiry as to how she fared.

This was not the place to come face to face with Jack. Widows did not attend society balls, especially when they needed to restore their reputations. It was just as her mother and aunt had warned her only now it was too late. Her impetuosity had again got the better of her. She tried to ward off the shudder of despair that would reveal her weakness and vulnerability. Would she never learn?

"Lady Marples, why, it really *is* you?"

She turned at the delight in the gentleman's voice and recoiled inside to see Lord Derry smiling at her. Of course, she had to smile back. Furthermore, she could hardly refuse the offer of his crooked arm. No one else was making any effort to lessen her social embarrassment. No, clearly the rumours regarding her dealings with this man had found fertile ground. Her ostracism couldn't be more apparent.

"This is a bold move on your part, Katherine." His voice was unsettlingly close; the pressure of his fingers on her arm a more intimate gesture than made her comfortable. "Widowhood suits you as little as I suspected, Katherine, which, I suppose, explains why you're here. I admire your bravery, and I hope you'll let me reward you for it."

Before Katherine could express her real feelings, either through a look, or to more thoroughly repulse him, she was startled by a greeting so warm and sincere it took her right back to the days when she was at the start of her journey into womanhood and so full of confidence she'd find happiness.

"Katherine?"

She swung round at the familiar tone, her heart beating wildly. "Jack?" She hoped her joy wasn't too transparent. Or her astonishment when she took in his altered bearing. This was not the eager stripling who'd won her heart when they were both little more than children. This was a broad-shouldered, handsome young man dressed impeccably in evening clothes with an air of confidence that made him a striking presence.

Clearly, Lord Derry didn't recognise Jack, though admittedly their paths might have crossed only once or twice. Nevertheless, there was a frisson suggesting rivalry that Katherine was very aware of as the introductions were made with great politeness.

"Lord Derry?" Katherine noticed the interest with which Jack repeated his lordship's name, and immediately wished she could reassure him that any rumours he might have heard linking Katherine with the gentleman who was squiring her this evening were untrue. *Could* he have heard something? He'd only been in the country three days but news travelled.

Instead, she said, "I barely recognised you, Jack. I hope you had a good journey."

His warm smile continued. It gave her hope, as did the fact he appeared to be alone. "Ah, Katherine, it was just one of so many journeys, but if it's the last for a long while I shan't be sorry. I've done what I set out to do, and I've returned, to the country of my birth, and where it's my intention to remain for a long time."

"You've been lucky to have found the success you have," said Lord Derry, immediately feigning concern that he might have been misconstrued. "I meant that with the greatest respect, I assure you. But I had not known you knew Katherine." There was a proprietorial tone to his remark, which sent anger snaking up her spine. How dare Lord Derry pretend he had any claim on her.

"We knew each other as children." Before Katherine could elaborate, a graceful, russet-haired young woman resplendent in gold-and-green lace-edged flounces glided up to Jack and, in the most familiar manner, slipped her hand into the crook of his arm.

"I'm sorry I was delayed, dearest. You know what a terrible talker Mrs Glassop can be," she murmured to him before presenting her brightest smile to the rest of them in anticipation of being introduced.

Katherine tried to keep her own in place, but as she was introduced to Miss Worthington who was displaying such supreme confidence in Jack's affections, she thought she'd like to run her fingernails down her alabaster skin as she wailed her despair.

Not even when Freddy had admitted that money had been his greatest motivation in marrying her had the spear of devastation cut so lethally; certainly not when he'd taken the first of his many mistresses. And most definitely not when Freddy had died from the sudden fever. Katherine had thought his untimely death would release her, but immediately there was fresh scandal, and whereas she'd only been implicated by association with Freddy, now society's opprobrium was directed at her, as if Katherine were as duplicitous and guilty of all the wrongdoing that had plagued Freddy's scandal-ridden life.

"I had not known congratulations were in order, Jack," Katherine murmured, trying to keep her voice steady. "When is the happy day?"

"Six weeks from now," she was happily informed by the transparently joyous Miss Worthington. "Jack and I met when he was working for Papa in India. We were fortunate to enjoy some of the exoticism of the Far East, but I'm very content to be setting up house back in England. Aren't you, dearest?"

She had to repeat her question, Katherine noticed, as Jack seemed quite focussed on looking at Katherine. She felt her cheeks warm and her heart race. He did love her. He *did*.

"And Lady Marples, my condolences on your loss, though I'm glad to hear you've found comfort with Lord Derry."

Katherine tried not to gasp her indignation aloud. Was Miss Worthington sneering at her? She glanced from Jack to Lord Derry, who patted Katherine's hand saying, "I was an admirer of Miss Fenton's, as she was seven years ago before her marriage to Lord Marples, and I remain an admirer." The warmth in his insinuating tone as he stroked her hand made her squirm with embarrassment. Carefully, she withdrew from any physical contact, but the assessing way Miss Worthington's gaze followed the surreptitious gesture made her feel ill.

Jack, on the other hand, was smiling at her as if he saw only the Katherine of his youth.

"You must call on us, Katherine. My mother is in town and would, I know, be delighted to see you again, though you could hardly miss her. Though perhaps you've already seen her as she's a regular visitor to Lord Quamby's, and on just as friendly terms with your dear mama and aunt as she ever was."

Katherine noticed that this was not well received by Miss Worthington, though why her pretty little mouth should turn down at such news suggested she saw Katherine as a threat. Good!

But the truth was, Katherine was far from the bright and eager young woman so full of hope that Jack had once admired. Katherine had fallen far in the eyes of society whereas Miss Worthington was, as her name suggested, entirely worthy of the attentions of a handsome, and now very wealthy young man such as Jack was.

Katherine nodded.

"And you have a child, I hear?" Jack asked. "Or perhaps more than one? News is so slow to arrive. I had not known of your bereavement before tonight."

Double bereavement, Katherine thought, silently. She didn't know how to respond and was saved from answering by Lord Derry squeezing her hand and saying, "Since you'll have every opportunity to catch up on old news at a future date, might I claim this next dance, Katherine?"

Stricken, Katherine said, "I can't possibly dance, Lord Derry. No, I must go home. Immediately."

"Quite right, quite right, my dear. It's so hard to remember you're a widow, truly. In that case, let us go. Good evening, Miss Worthington. Mr Patmore."

If she could have, Katherine would have picked up her skirts, dashed across the ballroom and jumped in the first hackney carriage to pass by, thereby publicly severing the impression that there was anything between Lord Derry and

herself. But she'd scandalised the guests here tonight sufficiently by appearing in mourning and then being so much in
Lord Derry's company; as if she were snubbing her nose at
the whole world, not least her husband's memory.

She glanced over her shoulder and saw that Jack was
looking after her, similarly twisting his neck, though Miss
Worthington was chattering to him and clearly intended to
have him all to herself.

And Katherine realised with sinking inevitability that she
probably would.

CHAPTER 17

It was hard to be the mother of a daughter who was so unhappy which made it even more of a pleasure to greet an old friend.

Fanny rose as the parlourmaid announced Mrs Patmore. "Eliza, my dear, I can't believe it's been more than a year. But you've been in London four days without calling," she added with mock severity. "Though I understand the reason all too well." She drew Eliza to the sofa and pulled the rope to order refreshment as her friend took a seat opposite her. "Katherine tells me Jack has grown from a stripling into the most splendid young man. You must be so proud of his achievements. But my goodness you must have missed him. Seven years is a long time."

Eliza, who rarely showed emotion, dabbed at her eyes with a fine lawn handkerchief and smiled through her tears. "I should be used to it. After all, it was almost seven years between being forced to give him up as an infant to the foundling home to recognising him when I visited Quamby House."

The women shared a colluding look. What a happy

circumstance it had been when Fanny and Antoinette's matchmaking had pushed Eliza into the orbit of charming, honourable Rufus Patmore. At the time, she'd been intent on marrying the Brightwell sisters' cousin, odious George Bramley, only because he lived at Quamby House where Jack was a regular visitor, a playmate of Young George's.

"I'm sure you never thought it would be seven years before he'd return again as a young man. I can't wait to see how he's changed. Katherine said I'd recognise him as Jack, but that to see him was to see Jack as the best man he could ever have become, and that's praise indeed, coming from her." Fanny sighed. "Poor Katherine. Widowed at only twenty-four."

Eliza reached over to pat Fanny's hand. "It's more than that though, isn't it? You intimated as much in your letter. For the sake of our long friendship, I won't pretend nothing is wrong when it is. You can confide in me, and if there's anything I can do to help, I will."

Fanny smiled at her kindness. While she and Antoinette were close, they did not always agree on the best course regarding Fanny's headstrong daughter.

Eliza did not often come to town, so her distance from the gossiping ton was some comfort. She sighed. "Katherine seemed to have the world at her feet when she was launched. She had such a genuine desire for a true and lasting happiness that I was prepared to be indulgent when she made her choice." She twisted the black-and-yellow cotton print of her simple gown between her fingers and went on, "I believe she could have made a wonderful match." It wasn't often Fanny allowed emotion to get the better of her, but she had difficulty going on, and it was Eliza who supplied, "Except that her head was turned by Lord Marples before she'd properly found her feet and might have made a wiser decision. Oh, my dear Fanny, I know only too well how easily that can happen."

Fanny nodded. "I know you do, Eliza. And you know that I, too, was in a situation very similar, only, I was the lucky one of the three of us. I set my cap at Fenton, and I threw caution to the wind and...success and happiness were my rewards rather than...repercussions and a life of disappointment. You also followed the impulses of your youthful heart, but while you were not as fortunate as I was in the first instance..." she said with a smile, referring to Eliza's youthful indiscretion with Jack's father, "Jack was your compensation, for despite the pain of being parted from him, you had the joy of winning him back through the love and goodness of admirable Rufus Patmore. I'm surprised Jack left you again for so long, knowing how much pain it would cause you in view of your first forced separation."

Eliza sent Fanny a level look then lowered her head. "Jack knows nothing of that," she murmured.

Fanny truly was shocked. "You've never told Jack you're his natural mother?"

Eliza shook her head. "I never wanted him to learn of my shame. That I was an unwed mother, a disgrace, and he was born out of wedlock. Even to be the child of poor farmers would be better than that."

"So, Jack still believes he's just the foundling boy taken in by the kindly Patmores for no other reason than charity?"

"Fanny, please don't put it that way!" Eliza cried. "I can't tell you the agony I've gone through over this. Rufus said it must be my decision as to whether Jack was told the truth. There've been a few occasions over the years that I've nearly told him but..." She took a deep breath. "Jack has always been such an upstanding, honourable young man; such a stickler for observing the highest of morals. I was terrified I would forever be tarnished in his eyes for...giving birth to a bastard." She'd dropped her voice so it was hard for Fanny to hear. "I don't know if it contributed to him going away. The fact that he believed, and still believes, that he's not our natural son. He said he was determined that he would make his way in the world on his own merits, with no financial backing from Rufus."

"Oh, Eliza." Fanny squeezed her friend's hands. "That's a hard thing to live with."

"When I waved him off at the docks, I knew I'd made a mistake. But it was too late."

"Then tell him."

Eliza nodded. "I shall…when the time is right."

"I hope that's sooner rather than later," said Fanny. "And Rufus and Jack…they are still on good terms?"

"Tremendous!" Eliza smiled. "Jack has always looked up to Rufus and was so determined to make him proud. Which he has done. Jack is the greatest comfort to both of us and the most wonderful of brothers to the younger ones who all adore him, though, of course, Theodosia doesn't remember him because she was only a baby when he left. And perhaps it's because I was too involved with a new baby that I failed to read Jack's mood, though nothing would have changed his mind about going. Even falling in love."

"Jack fell in love before he left? Did he know Miss Worthington then?"

It was Antoinette who asked the question, her eyes gleaming as she breezed into the room and took a seat opposite her sister and friend. She was dressed for walking and Fanny noticed there were leaves in her elaborately coiffured hair. No doubt her sister had been indulging in the attentions of her latest lover. "Do tell! Who was he in love with?" Antoinette's eyes sparkled and Fanny reflected that her sister had never truly had her heart broken. Loving men, collectively, seemed enough for her.

"Perhaps Katherine knows," Antoinette went on. "She and Jack have always been such good friends. And on that subject, do tell me Jack's going to visit Katherine and try and cheer her up. She's taken this business about Lord Derry very hard."

"Lord Derry?" Eliza's brow creased, and Fanny felt her daughter's embarrassment personally.

"He's the reason I'm so concerned about Katherine as I hinted in my letter." Fanny looked sadly at her friend. "Katherine's name has been linked with Lord Derry in a...romantic sense, though she strenuously insists that the rumours are unfounded and there's been no wrongdoing on her part." She sighed. "Poor Katherine seems to have lurched from one disaster to another ever since that ill-advised marriage of hers." She glanced at Antoinette, who had the grace to look slightly chastened, for Fanny still found it hard to forgive her sister for aiding and abetting Katherine's youthful infatuation before she'd properly come to know the man.

Antoinette looked past Fanny's censorious look and said, "At least Katherine has darling Diana to dote on. She's such a comfort and so grown up for her six years. So, regardless of the gossip that Katherine and Lord Derry were carrying on a clandestine romance while Lord Marples still lived"

"Antoinette, how dare you!" Fanny exclaimed.

Antoinette shrugged. "I'm not saying it's true. I'm just saying what everyone else is saying, whether or not they believe it, and that is that Lord Derry provided Katherine with the kind of comfort her husband certainly did not when he was losing a king's ransom at the gaming tables and consorting with a line-up of unsuitable women. But, as always, the woman is blamed."

The sound of a door banging and loud, masculine footsteps had them all turning as George, flinging himself through the door, said, "Oh, Mama, you really are too much!"

"And you, Young George, have no right to speak to your

mother so rudely," Antoinette rebuked her tall, bulky son who was now striding towards the sideboard. "Use your manners. You've not seen Mrs Patmore for more than a year, and I don't believe you've called on Jack, either, when you were once such firm friends."

"Indeed I have, Mama. Mrs Patmore." He bowed, rising with a satisfied smile. "I met Jack and his intended at the theatre last night and might I say how charming I found Miss Worthington. The pair of them were simply smelling of April and May, as they say."

Eliza settled back in her chair, a look of contentment overlaying her previous concern. "I can't tell you how relieved I am that he's found himself the perfect wife. Jack always had such impossibly high standards. I think he was seeking a goddess of purity."

She realised her error when Antoinette giggled, adding hastily, "That's not that I don't think Miss Worthington a creature who clearly combines purity in addition to the natural traits of liveliness that his original angel might have lacked." Her smile broadened as she took in Fanny's quirked mouth. "I'm very well satisfied," she finished.

"Well, I'm glad to hear it," said Fanny. "Now we just have to find someone who'll make Katherine happy. When the time is right," she added with an arch look. "She has at least another four months to wait before she can decently wed." Remembering George was in their midst and perhaps such free talk was unwise, she glanced up at him. While she'd never much cared for her sister's son, he didn't seem vengeful and malicious in the same way as his supposed uncle, George Bramley. He and Katherine and Jack had played together as children—not always harmoniously, but well enough. And George had developed a real fondness for Katherine in adulthood which was comforting, even if Katherine didn't return his feelings. At least she had someone looking to her interests.

George, intercepting her look, nodded. "Don't worry, Aunt; I'll watch over Katherine."

And despite his oily face and resemblance to the man who had sired him, that odious George Bramley whom Fanny knew would love any opportunity to bring her—and her daughter—down, she felt she had no choice but to believe him. George, she decided as she looked at him again, was harmless. As the future Earl of Quamby, he had no concerns when it came to money. His position and comfort were uncontested, and he would find any number of women only too delighted to fulfil the position of the future Countess of Quamby.

Having George's patronage, Fanny decided, could only be in Katherine's best interests now that Katherine was a widow again and in need of a man to smooth the way for her, given the latest scandal with Lord Derry.

CHAPTER 18

Jack had been in England a week, and he was uncomfortably aware of the fact he still hadn't called on Katherine at home. Each time he declared to Odette that it was his duty to his old friend to find out how she did and nominated a time or date, Odette would remind him of some competing social event to which they'd been invited, half of which he was sure she'd just fabricated.

But Odette was so vibrant and full of loving energy, and he certainly didn't want to disappoint her again; not when he'd been back in the country such a short time. Women's tears were not something he was used to, so he'd not known what to do when, two days earlier, Odette had stared at him as if he'd announced he was going to Outer Mongolia when, in fact, he'd simply told her he intended going to Boodles where he proposed to be a member with the sponsorship of Lord Dingley. First her lip had trembled, then she'd covered her face with her hands and sunk onto the sofa, choking on sobs as she'd declared that such talk signalled the beginning of the end; that Jack obviously intended to no sooner wed her than he'd be off drinking and gaming with the men, and she'd be abandoned to while away her evenings alone when she'd only just got her darling Jack back.

This evening was surprised, however, when Odette reminded him they'd been invited to call in on Ladies Fenton and Quamby. Disappointed, he countered that they'd be abed at such a late hour.

"No, they won't. They'll be in the midst of Lady Quamby's birthday feast."

"I can't call uninvited if there's a family celebration," Jack told her.

"We were invited, don't you remember?" Odette put her hand on his wrist and said sweetly, "Only, we already had tickets to the opera tonight."

Jack was absolutely certain he'd not have turned down an opportunity to attend a Quamby family event which would include Katherine, who was not seen much in society, but he said nothing. Even if he *had* already secured tickets to the opera. Perhaps he'd simply not been attending properly to Odette's chatter. She chattered a lot about social events, and he'd found it was easier to allow her to direct their social activities when she had so much to organise in the lead-up to their wedding. His mother had advised him that Odette was quite capable of making the right decisions as to who they should or shouldn't 'know'.

Jack was pleased at how much his mother approved of his new wife-to-be. It certainly made life more harmonious, and it was in his nature to desire harmony first, which inevitably led to domestic comfort in all spheres.

As he looked down at her glossy russet hair decorated with pearls, then was met by her limpid loving gaze as they waited on the doorstep to be admitted to Lord Quamby's, he made a point of reminding himself that she was indeed the perfect wife.

Two steps behind was Odette's spinster cousin, who, in

her early thirties, could have been an elder sister and who was quite happy to stand in as chaperone when Odette's aunt was disinclined. As the cousin allowed them great licence, which included kisses and cuddles, Jack knew he really was very fortunate when it came to his future. He'd been regaled many a horror story of men finding themselves saddled with harpies or frigid misses no sooner than the knot was tied. After so many years of being alone, Jack knew when to count his blessings.

"Jack! What an unexpected pleasure!" Lady Fenton and her sister greeted him in the drawing room as they were clearly enjoying the aftermath of a small party.

All the men were there: the old earl, deep in conversation with a handsome young man, deeply tanned and clearly not from England, joined by Lord Fenton. Young George was instantly at his side, offering him and Odette refreshment, with Lord Derry in his wake.

Jack had heard from Odette who'd heard it from others that Lord Derry was simply waiting for Katherine to have been widowed a sufficiently decent time before he became her new husband. And Katherine, who was obviously as headstrong as ever if she'd been prepared to defy society by appearing at a ball in widow's weeds, clearly held a candle to the tall, handsome viscount. Just as she had to Freddy Marwick...and to Jack before him.

Nevertheless, Jack would have liked to hear her thoughts on marriage, directly. He could envisage her characteristically pert and humorous response to any question that suggested her behaviour was less than exemplary.

So he was disappointed to hear that Katherine had already turned in for the night.

Odette, who'd wanted only to look in quickly, looked suddenly very comfortable as she was brought into discussion by Lady Fenton. Jack, alone for a moment, was just contemplating the fact that good manners require that he join Lord Derry and George by the sideboard on the far end of the room when, to his right, he noticed the door slowly open.

His heartbeat accelerated as he thought perhaps Katherine had heard he was in the house and had come to look in, but instead of seeing Katherine's lively face emerge at shoulder level, a pert, bright-eyed miniature emerged at thigh level.

The little girl cast a furtive look around the room before she widened her eyes at Jack, then smiled, putting her finger to her lips.

"Don't tell anyone," she whispered. "I'm supposed to be in bed."

"Of course you are," Jack whispered back. "Little girls are supposed to be in bed long before midnight."

"I'm not a little girl," she countered. "I'm six. I'm Oh, drat! Aunt Antoinette's seen me!"

"Diana! Naughty child, you should be fast asleep!" said Aunt Antoinette fondly, leaving her husband's side and coming across to Jack, putting out her hand to take her niece's.

No one else in the room seemed to have noticed them. "Come along now. And Jack, I'm sorry Katherine wasn't here to see you. She'll be disappointed. I know she was hoping you'd call on her, but she understands how busy you've been. She just feels rather dreary having to languish in widow's weeds when everyone else is having fun."

Lady Quamby's words didn't conjure up an image of Katherine actively pining for her late husband, and Jack felt a frisson of satisfaction at the knowledge.

"I'm sorry I missed her, too," he said. "I only saw her for two minutes at Lady Garwood's ball the other night."

Antoinette clicked her tongue. "Katherine's as naughty as her daughter. I told her she ought not to have gone. It's done nothing for her reputation, which was completely ruined by that dreadful husband of hers. I know I'm not one to talk, but I'm also a great deal older and in very different circumstances. Now, if you'll excuse me, I'll take Diana back to bed." She hesitated, half through the door, and then added as she noticed Jack's aloneness, "Perhaps you'd be interested to see the painting Lord Marples commissioned of Katherine just before his untimely death. It's a very good likeness and it's hanging in the library just up the corridor. Take the candle on the sideboard there and follow me."

Jack, who had no desire to join George and Lord Derry, was more than happy to slip out of the room in Antoinette's wake bearing the single candlestick.

Obediently, he followed the older woman and the child until Lady Quamby pointed to a door on her right. "It's through there," she said. "I'd be interested in your opinion. I think the painting is too regal, but Lord Marples thought it depicted her as just the wife he wanted her to be. Modest and obedient."

Not the way Jack thought of Katherine. He entered the dark room, closed the door behind him and took a few steps into the centre to contemplate the painting. It was enormous, located above the mantelpiece and, indeed, regal. He thought Katherine's expression was wistful, and was suddenly brought to mind of the times he'd find her contemplating some outlandish plan. The moment she'd turn at the sound of his footsteps her natural liveliness would flood her countenance, and she'd grip his hands and describe some fiendish activity in which to embroil George, or else a wonderful adventure into which she'd roped Cook who would have prepared a basket of cakes and pies so they could be out all day.

Raising his candle higher as a great wave of wistfulness enveloped him, he was suddenly conscious of movement.

Then the partly opened window rattled in the breeze, and his light went out.

He stood still a few moments, enjoying the darkness and the silence while his thoughts continued in the direction they'd happily been dwelling upon—Katherine.

Returning to London and seeing her so changed had been confusing. He wished he'd had the opportunity to quiz her on the speed with which she'd eloped with Marwick. Surely she knew it would be wounding to Jack, regardless of the fact they both had released any hold one had over the other.

Jack wouldn't have pledged himself so quickly to another, and he was surprised Katherine had.

Still, there was no accounting for the way in which the heart worked; he knew that well enough. The passion he felt for Katherine was dangerous; destined to end in disaster—her impetuosity and his pride would make poor bedfellows. How often had he tried to convince himself of this over the past seven years?

But Odette's pliant nature and willingness to please was everything a husband could wish for.

Wasn't it?

A gentle breeze was blowing papers from a writing desk. He could hear but not see, and took a step towards the window, colliding with a solid bulk that suddenly materialised in the very centre of the room.

It was a person—a woman he ascertained from her gasp and the slight shoulders he gripped to steady both of them.

But as he breathed in the scent of peonies, and his hands contoured the familiar collarbone and then, without realising what he was doing, the swanlike neck, he knew exactly who she was.

He did not drop his hands. Rather, he tightened his grip. Tightened it as, unthinkingly, he drew her against him; then, just as unthinkingly, dipped his head. In the darkness, robbed of vision, he had no idea what he was doing or what to expect, but when his mouth encountered a pair of soft, pliant, delicate lips flowering beneath his own, it was only natural to take matters in the same direction they'd been going before his travels seven years before.

She melted against him, and gently he contoured the silken softness of her hair before he cupped the back of her head and deepened the kiss.

Her arms twined behind his neck as she pressed her delicate, beautifully formed body against his then softly breathed out—a sound of contentment, which made every nerve and fibre of his being tense with anticipation.

This was what love was. The heady intoxication that made a man so ready to become, without thought or reason, a slave to his desires. For seven years, Jack had been a slave to duty, honour, and toil, but in this moment, he'd have sacrificed everything to extend the dreamlike, mystical wonder of rediscovering what it was like to be utterly in thrall to a being so much more precious than life itself.

Jack drew Katherine more firmly against him as the flame within him exploded, and his mind was alive only to the sensations evoked by touching her face, her hair, her exquisite, achingly familiar body.

Wrapped in each other's arms, they orbited in a dark, mystical, magical solar system, where sensory exploration was the only reality in the absence of sight.

Then sound became the chatter in the corridor, and the door was thrown open, light seeping into the room as a sconce of candles was held high.

"Goodness!"

He wasn't sure who said it. It could have been Katherine, Odette, or either of the Brightwell sisters.

Struck dumb by guilt and embarrassment, Jack could only admire Katherine's composure as she blinked sleepily, saying,

"Good Lord, was that you, Jack? I stumbled when the candle went out. Did you know, I'd fallen asleep on the sofa here after we had tea, Mama. And that was hours ago!"

She rubbed her eyes and smiled at everyone before self-consciously tidying her hair. "I must look a fright. But Jack! It's so good to see you again. And Miss Worthington, you look perfectly lovely in rose pink. Where have you been to this evening? The opera, perhaps?"

"Shall we repair to the living room?" Lady Fenton asked. At least she didn't look at Jack as if he were the devil incarnate. He was very conscious of Lord Derry's glower and George and Odette's tempered suspicion. But, of course Katherine's explanation was perfectly logical—he thought so anyway, though perhaps that was because he wasn't thinking as clearly as he had been before the kiss. Nevertheless, Odette, fortunately, was soon in fine spirits, clinging to his arm as they went back to the warm, brightly lit room he'd quit only moments before.

Everything felt like a dream. Like he'd been tugged back to the past; his body responding to the lingering reminder of that kiss like a drowning man clings to the rock that is his salvation.

Except that such a notion was ridiculous. *Odette* was his salvation. Katherine was his friend. The friend he thought he loved until she'd demonstrated through her own actions that expediency and impulse trumped everything, including love, in the face of an enforced separation.

❧

KATHERINE WISHED THAT THE EXODUS FROM THE LIBRARY included Lord Derry, and that she could again be subsumed by the darkness she'd enjoyed before she'd been interrupted.

So beautifully, joyously, interrupted. It truly had been like a dream, literally falling into the arms of the man she loved.

This was very clear to her now. She always had loved Jack, but she'd married the wrong man. She was free now, but Jack was not.

And yet, how could he have responded to her with such ardour if he didn't share her feelings? He wasn't married to Odette *yet*.

In the few seconds it took Lord Derry to cross the room from having seen the others out of it, Katherine reflected on every nuanced expression that had crossed Jack's face during the seconds he was exposed by the light. Surprise, wonder, delight. Hope. Yes, there'd been hope before Miss Worthington had extinguished it with that proprietorial little hand of hers clutching his arm and drawing him back into her orbit.

But what had come before was more telling. He had clung to Katherine with the ardour of a man who suddenly realises he's found what he'd lost. Jack realised in those few seconds in the dark what he really had lost. Katherine was sure of it.

Hope now fluttered in her breast. She needed to speak with him, alone, frankly. While there was time.

"My dear Katherine, so we are alone at last." Lord Derry strode across the Aubusson carpet and gripped her shoulders. An unwelcome, proprietorial grip; unlike Jack's. His gaze was smouldering, his nostrils flaring as if something was bottled up inside, ready to be released into smiling goodwill at the merest sign from Katherine. Or perhaps, no sign at all. He wanted her. He'd wanted her for seven years, and now he thought she'd be his.

But he was wrong. She could be no one but Jack's. Tonight had made that clearer than anything had before.

When she said nothing, he went on, his tone dropping suggestively, "I was told you'd repaired to your room and were sleeping. I wish I'd known you'd fallen asleep here. It would have made the past hour I've spent in inanities with your cousin a great deal more pleasurable. And then you were interrupted by that interloper."

"Jack?" She was indignant he'd call Jack an interloper.

"Is that his name? I'd forgotten. A foundling made good. But now we have a few moments together, and I think the time has come to establish the understanding we have and make plans accordingly."

Katherine stiffened. "With all due respect, Lord Derry, we do not have an understanding."

He tilted his head, a frisson of temper marring the warmth of his expression before he was again all smiles. Clearly, Katherine was like a filly who needed to be properly managed. Lord Derry was very fond of using his love of horses to make such analogies though, in truth, he wasn't a bad man. He wasn't a philanderer or a drunkard or a gambler like Freddy had been.

"In a few months, your year of mourning will be at an end and you can respectably remarry." He drew her closer. "I want to reassure you that I'm not just playing with your affections, my dear. I want to make it very clear that it's an honourable marriage I have in mind." He cleared his throat. "Just in case you feared my notions may have been less gentlemanly, though there's no reason why we cannot enjoy a little more licence if the ultimate intent is respectable matrimony."

Katherine stepped back and broke his grip. "I'm sorry, Lord Derry, but we have no understanding," she repeated.

She was glad of the proximity of her family in the drawing room just along the passageway, for the spasm of displeasure that crossed his face was not one she'd have felt comfortable with managing had she been alone. "If I have led you to believe otherwise, then it is regrettable; however, I have no wish to marry you."

He would have pulled her back to him except that Katherine was too nimble, gliding out of his reach and opening the door that protected her from any further unwelcome advances by the sound of voices issuing into the room from further up the passage.

With a cultivated smile, she made her way back to the drawing room, self-conscious enough that she did not seek out Jack, but rather allowed herself to be waylaid by George, who assiduously looked to her comfort by brandishing a glass of claret.

Grateful, she sank onto the sofa and he took up position beside her, saying, "My dear Katherine, you look flushed. You're not coming down with something, I hope. I fear falling asleep in the library is not a good sign of your health."

Except that falling asleep was the best thing Katherine could have done. Her body was singing. Jack would never have taken her in his arms and kissed her had he known she was there. She slanted a look across at him. Odette was chattering, rapidly and with great enthusiasm and vivacity as was her wont, Katherine realised. And Jack was staring at her—mesmerised as Odette no doubt thought him, only Katherine knew that look too well: boredom, a glazed, interested look he was able to plaster on his face so that his thoughts could travel their own way. No, Jack did not love Odette like he loved Katherine. But he needed to be given the chance to act on his real feelings. Did he know that he loved her? Surely, their kiss had made it clear?

Odette was a fierce opponent, and Katherine needed to gauge the opposition.

When the opportunity arose, she swapped places with George, artfully introducing a topic that enabled Katherine to engage Odette in interested conversation while the men discussed their latest horseflesh. And on this topic, Jack was a master. A horse had brought his adoptive parents together, and he'd had many a faithful mount when in Bombay. The moment he made mention of his latest steed the men huddled closer.

"Who will win the Lancashire Derby?" asked Lord Derry, with a nod to Jack's superior knowledge in that field.

Meanwhile, Katherine was on the sofa beside Odette now, and she asked, "I believe you met Jack in Bombay. When did you travel over?" Odette might be in love with him, but she did not have the devotion of a lifetime behind her. There were less than six weeks to their wedding and Katherine's mission was a difficult one, but she had to use whatever she had at her disposal to tip the balance in her favour.

She hoped Odette didn't notice the way her gaze slid to Jack's face. She loved his animation. His expression was so malleable, unlike many men's. Freddy had had a few stock expressions she'd come to know well: boredom, avarice, lust, and discontent. But Jack seemed to pulse with life. She'd forgotten that about him. Perhaps because she'd taken it for granted that men displayed enthusiasm on topics of importance. Freddy had found little that he considered of importance unless it was lining his pockets with another ill-fated venture, or showing Katherine he was master. Not that he was overtly cruel, and never physically. He just had a habit of being cynical and dismissive about most of what Katherine cared about.

Miss Worthington tipped back her swanlike neck and fluttered her eyelashes at the ceiling before swivelling her glance back to meet Katherine, hesitating en route to take in Jack.

So, she was more vigilant than she'd like others to realise. Katherine would have to remember that.

"My father worked for the East India Company, and he took Jack on in the early days when Jack was just a lowly clerk. I loved him then, too," she said, artlessly. "And you?"

She might have been asking if Katherine loved him too, but Katherine merely said, "Jack visited the home of my uncle, Earl Quamby, when we were children, to be playmate to my cousin George. In those days, George could be a fiend to us both, though Jack seemed to know how to manage him." She dressed it up lightly. "Jack and I became allies, and I was sad to see him leave for so long, but now he's home I hope we'll see more of you both." What else could she be but welcoming? It was the only way to ensure Odette was not on her guard where Katherine was concerned.

For she needed to be.

She glanced over at Jack at the very moment he glanced in her direction. Something in his look made her heart still, but she was on parade. Odette's instincts would be easily aroused, and even one unguarded look could be enough to destroy any further chance of Katherine gaining access to Jack, either alone or with his betrothed.

So Katherine tossed her head, in an attempt to deflect the look, and clasped Odette's wrist warmly, saying, "My aunt is having a house party next weekend and Jack's parents will be there, so of course you and Jack are invited."

She was relieved when the party broke up shortly after Odette had accepted. Exhausted by the nervous energy she'd expended in appearing unaffected when every nuanced look at or by Jack made her heart pound and her palms clammy, she nodded to the remaining gentlemen after Jack and Odette and her chaperone had departed.

"If you'll excuse me, I shall retire for the night." She barely smiled in Lord Derry's direction, though she was sure she must have as she passed through the door. It would be a mistake to set up his bristles but, really, he was suddenly of so little consequence, she barely gave him a thought as she trod lightly up the passageway, her heart singing as she relived, again and again, the kiss in the darkness she'd shared with Jack.

❧

KATHERINE WOULD HAVE DONE WELL TO HAVE CONSIDERED Lord Derry's feelings a little more. He was positively seething as he accepted a brandy from George after the rest of the household had retired.

"It's your cousin," he responded after George asked him why he was looking so hangdog. "She says we have no agreement."

"No agreement? Why, she's going to marry you, old fellow. Her reputation depends upon it."

"Apparently not." Lord Derry began to pace, the contents of his glass sloshing against the side before he downed the drink in one go before pouring another. "By God, I've waited a long time. Seven years! And now she's going to slip out of my fingers."

George shrugged. "Sometimes one has to accept a hopeless cause. Not worth the trouble, I'd say."

Lord Derry's nostrils flared as he glared at George. He must have consumed a great deal for he was not usually prone to such agitation. "I don't admit defeat so easily." His breathing was rapid. "There must be some way to persuade her." He glanced up suddenly. "You don't suppose there's someone else?"

"Not that I've heard of." George refilled Derry's glass. "Come along, old chap. No need to get all maudlin. You'll find another girl with spirit who'll suit you even better."

"I don't want another. I want Katherine. And I want to vanquish that damned spirit of hers!" He closed his eyes and his shoulders slumped. "That's not true. I want to make her happy. I know I can."

George patted his shoulder. "I'm sure you can. And you will."

"Katherine is devoted to her parents." Derry sounded gloomier than ever. "Despite the fact Freddy left her with nothing except debts, she has her parents' support, so she has no need to get married."

George nodded, considering. "But Katherine is...impulsive. Wayward. Katherine needs bringing into line. Devoted, her family may be, but they think it, too. A discontented widow is more of a wild card than an impulsive debutante who's still under the authority of her parent."

He went on. "As a widow, Katherine answers only to herself. She can do what she wants to please herself and there's not a damned thing her family can do about it."

"But you're family. Or at least, you're the son of that aunt she's so devoted to. Surely you can help me?"

George felt a rare jolt of pleasure at the hopeful, interested look Derry was directing at him. As if George had sway and influence.

Yes, Derry was looking to him to influence matters. Just as Marwick had all those years ago.

He rolled his shoulders. George still felt guilty at interfering to make the terms of the wager in Boodles Better book so attractive for encouraging an elopement between Marwick and Katherine but Katherine had *kissed* Marwick. George knew she had. And almost straight afterwards she'd made clear her aversion to doing anything similar with George so she might as well have married Marwick if she was so willing to trade her favours, he'd thought at the time.

But he was sorry Marwick had turned out such a blackguard. Sorry for Katherine. He truly was.

Derry was a different piece altogether. He was a decent chap and he clearly thought a great deal of George's ability to set wheels in motion.

He puffed out his chest. "Yes, she takes what my dear mama has to say very seriously but there is someone else, I believe, who might have greater influence in seeing Katherine sensibly married."

A wonderful thought had just come to him. A drift of memory when his mother had recounted Katherine's dismay at the fact the late Freddy Marwick had given his own mother such an influential role in her granddaughter, Diana's upbringing.

As far as George could tell, Lady Hale had shown not the slightest interest in her granddaughter. But that was because Lady Hale had no interest in anyone other than herself. George had heard Katherine say this often.

Derry's attention had drifted. His eyes looked glazed and his shoulders slumped. "It's no good," he muttered. "I can hardly force Katherine if she has no wish to wed me."

"What about the money Freddy borrowed?"

Derry shrugged. "Lord, I'm not the blackguard Freddy was! He made her beg and I couldn't resist her. I can afford to lose what I lent him and I'd not press her on that. Blackmail? That's not my game."

"Didn't mean to suggest blackmail as your only recourse, old chap," George assured him while the cogs in his brain were working along these very tracks.

George wouldn't resort to blackmail, either.

But Lady Hale just might.

CHAPTER 19

There was a lightness in Katherine's step that she hadn't felt for years as she entered the conservatory where her aunt, her mother and Mrs Patmore, Jack's adoptive mother, were having tea the following morning.

Katherine had heard that her aunt and mother had initially disliked Eliza Patmore, but then she'd rescued Katherine and her cousins, and Jack, from drowning. At the time, Eliza Patmore had been betrothed to Young George's disreputable uncle, George Bramley, until they'd persuaded her of the merits of marrying handsome Mr Rufus Patmore. At least, that was the story Katherine remembered having heard.

And now she was standing before that still very lovely looking woman with her sculpted blonde hair and perfect bone structure, hoping with all her might that she might one day call her mother-in-law. There was a delicate line to navigate, but surely if Katherine's heart and Jack's were as one, they could finally be together—just as they were meant to be all those years ago?

"Ah, Katherine, we were just talking about you," her mother said, patting the seat beside her in invitation. "I'm glad you seem finally to be emerging from your gloom of the past few days. Of course you must mourn your husband, but common sense must guide you."

She was referring to the disastrous evening at Lady Garwood's when Katherine had appeared in widow's weeds, learned that Jack was betrothed to another, and had her own reputation sullied by Lord Derry's overly familiar attentions.

She pushed back her shoulders and smiled brightly. All could be overcome. Jack just needed to know how Katherine felt about him, and then he could admit that his feelings matched hers and he'd do the honourable thing towards Odette—which would be *not* to marry her if his heart was elsewhere engaged.

"Of course, Mama. Perhaps I'm happier now that Jack has returned." There, she would use subtlety where she could over the next few days to make her feelings clear for Jack, and that way, there'd be no surprises or horror when Jack and Odette's betrothal was dissolved, and Katherine became his new bride-to-be. It might have happened seven years ago if Katherine had been as wise as she was now.

"That holds true for all of us," Mrs Patmore said with a smile. "I could never have imagined my darling boy leaving us for so long."

"Or coming back with a bride," said Katherine, preparing her next line. "Or rather, bride-to-be. However, I wonder if..." She was about to suggest an element of doubt over Odette's qualification if only in terms of there being a contender for Jack's affections. No, Katherine would not be underhand, of course. But she had to win. She and Jack loved each other. It was only right that they be together, and while she didn't like the thought of being the cause of Miss Worthington's disappointed hopes, all was fair and love and war, didn't they say?

"Ah, poor Miss Worthington; I hear her father's health took a turn for the worse last night," said Aunt Antoinette, shaking her head. "I doubt they'll manage to the house party next weekend."

"I'm sure Mr Worthington will be better by then," Katherine said brightly, sitting down and not willing to entertain the thought of there being a reason why Jack mightn't be able to spend a full three days under this roof. The very idea of being alone with him made her skin prickle with anticipation.

"Oh no, my dear, Mr Worthington is not expected to improve. Did you know he's dying?" Fanny's mother looked suitably gloomy. "There's even been talk of bringing forward Jack and Miss Worthington's nuptials in case he doesn't make their currently proposed date."

"No!" Katherine couldn't help herself as she brought her hands up to her face with a gasp.

The others looked at her oddly as she turned her head away to hide her tears. This couldn't be. Miss Worthington's father couldn't be dying? Jack's most noble sentiments would be brought to the fore. Willingly or not, he would accept his role as Miss Worthington's support and protector, a role that would be of added importance considering this was the man who'd helped him make his fortune in the business world.

"I'm sorry to hear it," she said shakily, searching for something with which to deflect the conversation and coming up with, "Has anyone seen Diana? Miss Nibble was looking for her to do her lessons, but the naughty girl has run off again."

"Well, she's not nearly as naughty as you were at her age, Katherine, but in fact, she's with her grandmother." Lady Fenton smiled at her daughter. "I thought you knew. They're in the drawing room."

"Which is why you're all here?" Katherine countered with raised eyebrows, to which Aunt Antoinette said blithely, "Of course. The dowager really is the most dreadful woman, and as she seemed happy enough to enjoy only Diana's company, I didn't see why we should have to suffer hers and be polite. She rarely is."

Katherine felt a frisson of dislike at the mere mention of her mother-in-law with whom she'd never enjoyed good relations.

"She came here unannounced?" She knew that Freddy's mother disliked her, though the dowager had been a more regular visitor during the past couple of months, calling on Diana and taking her on outings about which Diana complained endlessly afterwards.

"I didn't think I needed to announce my intention of seeing my own granddaughter," came a stentorian voice from just outside the passage before the thin, humpbacked dowager appeared, a gimlet light in the gaze she settled on Katherine.

When she'd been respectfully greeted by the others, and taken to a seat by Katherine, the old lady commandeered the conversation as was her wont.

"That child is running wild. Why, I found her hiding under a chair when I was in the very same room, calling three times for her!" She glared at Katherine as if she thought it her fault. Which she clearly did as her next sentence was, "Diana needs discipline. She needs a father. Yes, I know my son has been dead less than a year, but the rumours flying about suggest you have a replacement already lined up. No need to blush, my girl. I've known you seven years, so I know what I'm talking about. You're a girl who needs a husband with a firm hand."

"Lady Hale!" It was Katherine's mother who leaned forward to object. This was going too far, clearly. But superior age and the pretence of deafness in this instance had the dowager ignoring Fanny to continue, pointing her gnarled forefinger at Katherine. "You and Lord Derry. Yes, it's a scandal, but it'll be more of a scandal if you don't enter into an honest union with him the moment you're free to do so."

Katherine, whose growing horror could no longer be curtailed, said sharply, "I will not be dictated to!" She stood and pointed at the door. "You have no right to come here and tell me what to do, Lady Hale. You spent seven years doing that when Freddy and I were married, but now I'm my own mistress, and I like it!"

It gave her great pleasure to see the old woman's demeanour slip, if only for a minute. Then the trembling mouth was replaced by a sneer as she sat hunched on her chair like an old toad in purple, the two grey ringlets that hung on each side of her lined, pinched face quivering with indignation.

Katherine stabbed her finger at the door once more. "Please leave if you can only carp and criticise."

"Katherine!" Fanny's mother looked mortified. Aunt Antoinette looked rather excited by the exchange, but clearly, Mrs Patmore was deeply shocked. Katherine didn't care. Lady Hale had been a poisonous influence on her marriage with Freddy. If she didn't think Katherine good enough, it was time for the old lady to go.

"Your house?" Lady Hale transferred her scornful look from Katherine to the rest of the company. "I'm not sure what Lady Quamby thinks of such a grasping statement."

But darling Antoinette simply said mildly, "Katherine's grown up in this house, so I'm happy for her to refer to it as her house." She patted a golden twist of hair then waved a languid gloved hand in the direction of the door. "Good afternoon, Lady Hale. Is your carriage waiting? If not, I'll order mine round to convey you wherever you might wish to go."

Fanny turned on her sister when Lady Hale had made her

furious exit. "Antoinette, what were you thinking? You went too far—like Katherine!"

Katherine was shaking. She sat down, but a terrible pounding in her head made her feel ill and tearful. First, she'd learned that Jack's wedding might be brought forward for the legitimate reason of Miss Worthington's father's illness, and then Lady Hale had aired those terrible, *untrue* rumours about having an improper liaison with Lord Derry.

She raised her head just as Diana put her head around the door, her lips pressed together before the little girl exhaled. "Is it safe? Has she gone?"

"That's no way to speak of your grandmother," Katherine said tiredly. No one would believe her if she even tried to voice her innocence over the old woman's unfounded allegations.

Mrs Patmore, who was glancing between the women and young Diana, patted the arm of her chair. "Yes, she's gone. Why don't you come and sit by me so I can tidy your hair, Diana." She seemed to realise the tumultuous emotions the rest of them were going through. Katherine had always liked Jack's adoptive mother. She thought the story of how she had been united with her charming husband, Rufus Patmore, a lovely one.

Diana, who fortunately had taken a shine to Mrs Patmore, trailed across the room and sat beside her while Katherine glanced between her mother and aunt. Both seemed to have plenty they wanted to say but felt they could not. Katherine opened her mouth to speak but was cut short by their visitor's stifled gasp, before Mrs Patmore shook her head to allay their concerns.

"Such a terrible knot in Diana's beautiful hair," she murmured. "Perhaps I should take her for a walk and leave the rest of you to talk."

"Well, Katherine, that was quite a show you put on,"

Fanny's mother remarked as the door closed behind the pair and she picked up the cold tea she'd been drinking. She didn't sound too chastening, Katherine thought, surprised. When she looked up, her mother's eyes were twinkling at her over the teacup. "You did well to put that old termagant in her place."

"*You* certainly weren't going to do it," Aunt Antoinette said with patent disgust. "Really, Fanny, I was disappointed. Have you lost all your spirit?"

"Certainly not. You just forget I have more tact than you, Antoinette, and that sometimes caution and tact go further than blurting out your outrage and indignation or playing up to something as thoughtlessly as you do."

"Well, of all the insults to throw in my face," Antoinette bridled before conceding, "Though there is a little truth in what you say. But when one is a countess, one can rather do as one pleases. And it has pleased me to do a great many things that others—including you, Fanny, and certainly you, Katherine—could not get away with." She reached for a piece of caraway seed cake and fixed Katherine with a beady stare. "What *is* this business over you and Lord Derry? I fear there is something in what that sour old crab apple of a mother-in-law has to say about giving the world the impression you're a bit flirty if you don't marry Lord Derry. I rather thought you liked him."

"I've always liked him well enough—in fact, a great deal more than Freddy—but not enough to make him my husband!" Katherine sucked in a breath and clenched her fists. "If I've been on terms that appear too friendly, that's only because he's helped me at my lowest ebb when I've needed it such as..." Her voice shook. "When Freddy locked the doors upon me after a night of gambling, and I had nowhere to go, and Derry happened to be passing and came to my rescue. I never meant to give him ideas about marriage!"

Antoinette sighed. "About Freddy, he deserves to be writhing in the flames of Hell right now. But about your feeling, or lack of, for Derry, it's a pity. He's pleasant enough and he's a handsome man, and he has money—which you need, badly, my dear. And he has no son to inherit, so you really would be making a fine match."

"Not if my heart were engaged elsewhere!" Katherine cried.

"Oh Katherine, you never said!" Her mother looked both concerned and hopeful. "Are you saying your heart *is* engaged?"

Katherine stood abruptly and turned to look out of the window. "I've loved him for so long but...marriage between us is not possible." She couldn't risk their questions. It was a relief to unburden herself, but she dare not be drawn on the truth. Jack's love was forbidden. They all knew how committed he was to marrying Miss Worthington; that the wedding was barely five weeks away. She'd only be an object of pity if she blurted that out.

Her mother put her hand on her wrist, and her eyes were so kind as she drew back her daughter's attention that Katherine nearly gave in on the spot. But no, she wasn't ready. She wiped her eyes with the back of her hand. "I think I'll go for a walk," she said. "Thank you for understanding. And for understanding that I'm not yet ready to talk about it."

"Oh dear," Fanny said when her daughter had gone. "I hope Katherine doesn't do something rash—again."

"I rather hope she will—if it makes her happy," countered Antoinette.

CHAPTER 20

Jack had taken the unconventional approach to Quamby House, cutting across the back garden having slipped through a hole in the hedge after being visited by quite an outrageously impulsive plan to see his...mother. Yes, he'd come purely to see his mother whom he was sure would be visiting her friends, Ladies Fenton and Quamby.

Katherine was unlikely to be there, so, as there was no reason to concern Odette with that faint possibility, he hadn't thought it warranted mentioning. Besides, Odette had various fittings with the dressmaker and had been in a fluster as to certain important decisions regarding the merits of lace or beading.

Jack didn't mind that Odette liked to know what he was doing at all times. With her father so ill, she really only had Jack to look to. She'd depend upon him for the rest of their lives, so the fact he could be her rock in a stormy sea now, when her father's illness was draining her, meant a great deal to him.

Jack liked to help and be needed. He was a man who did

not shirk from life's challenges. He was *not* a man like his father who would abandon those who depended upon him. The challenge of finding that his heart was not dancing to the tune of moral necessity disturbed him deeply. That kiss in the darkness with Katherine had been more than unsettling. It had tilted him off his moral axis. He should never have kissed her in the first place. Even now, three days later, he wondered what he'd been thinking. He hadn't. He'd just done what had seemed the most natural, pleasurable thing in the world, and now he couldn't get Katherine out of his mind.

It was a good thing she was about to become betrothed to Lord Derry. Jack would ensure their paths would not cross until he was thoroughly immersed in the role he'd not undertaken lightly: to be a good husband and a good father.

Yes, the moment he was a father to the children he and Odette would have, he knew his heart would act in line with the moral fibre of his being. Nothing and no one would tempt him from being the most devoted and loyal husband and father.

When, to his surprise, he saw his mother and a small figure he took to be Diana, strolling across the lawn in his direction, he was both pleased and disappointed. His intention had been purely to see his mother—of course—and now he *could* do so without fear of running into Katherine. And that was a very good thing. A very good thing, he told himself. For then he could answer all of Odette's questions about what he'd done that day with complete transparency.

"Why, Jack, this is the most wonderful surprise!" his mother greeted him when she was close enough to identify him and had appeared round the bend of the gravel path that bordered the small stream. She bent down to the little girl. "Diana, you remember Jack, don't you?"

Diana politely executed a little curtsey saying she did, and appeared to lose concentration before swinging her head back to him and asking with a frown, "Are you the Jack my mummy talks about?"

"I don't know. Does she talk about a Jack?"

"Yes. She said one day her best friend Jack would come back. I've never met any other Jacks. Are you that Jack?"

"That's right. I came to visit your mama as soon as I came back to London."

Diana nodded. A butterfly had caught her attention but she swung round to correct him. "Not right after. She was waiting."

Jack looked awkwardly at his mother who in turn sent an interested look back in his direction. "You were always thick as thieves when you were Diana's age—or a little older," she said with a smile, adding to Diana, "Jack and your mama played together when they were seven years old. That's a year older than you are now. But they've not seen each other for a long time because Jack went away across the sea."

Diana nodded as she wobbled a front tooth. "Across the sea," she repeated, staring at the ducks that paddled over the surface of the nearby ornamental lake. She glanced up at Jack. "Mama was always looking through the window. When I asked her what she was looking at she always said: *across the sea*."

Of course, that meant nothing, Jack told himself, and if he imagined there was the slightest connection to Katherine telling an inquisitive child she was merely looking 'across the sea' it hardly meant Katherine had been looking for *him*.

Yet, something niggled in his chest. The way Katherine *had* looked at him in the brief seconds when the room had been flooded with light as the others had interrupted their unconventional reunion suggested so many possibilities.

He shook his head to clear it while his mother said, "And now Jack is home, and he's going to get married. You know what that means, don't you?" Her tone was indulgent but Diana answered sadly, "Poor Jack."

Startled, Jack and his mother exchanged looks before Diana said brightly, "I can see Thomas over there! I must go and say hello."

Without waiting for a response, the little girl took off towards an old man balanced on a ladder clipping the hedge that bordered the kitchen garden.

His mother turned and laid a hand upon Jack's arm. "I think Katherine was very pleased to see you. I hope she approves of Odette."

"I hope *you* do, Mama," Jack said, awkwardly, to deflect the subject. "After all, we are to be married in little over a month—or earlier depending on her father's health. The decision is hers to make after she visits him this afternoon."

"Would Odette really want to bring the date forward when all the preparations are made and her wedding dress will not be finished?"

"I think that her preference is for the grand ceremony in her lavish finery, Mama, but she is very attached to her papa and wants him to witness her happy day."

"And your happy day, Jack. I never thought you'd meet someone who reached the high standards you set for yourself and everyone else. Odette must be a paragon of virtue, a true angel. She is certainly very pretty, and from what I can tell, her nature is sweet and pliant."

"Oh, she can be headstrong too, Mama. Like Katherine, she knows what she wants." He looked away, fearing he'd said too much but his mother pressed him.

"You know a lot about Katherine when you didn't spend too much time with her in your adult years. I suppose the time as children cemented a very brotherly relationship in you towards her."

Jack looked over the trees towards the house and both

dreaded and longed to find Katherine ensconced within. Just a few minutes in her company, sharing an amusing story or laughing at nothing in particular suddenly seemed like the tonic he needed. Then he told himself that Odette's intensity and need to have him near her all the time was natural due to what she was going through with regard to her father's precarious health.

"Katherine was everything to me when I'd been abandoned and had no one." It was not often he spoke of those early days, but it was as much to explain the strength of feeling he'd developed towards Katherine as a very young child as to answer his mother's question.

Immediately repentant, he gripped his mother's hand. "But you and Uncle Rufus took me in when there was no reason in the world you should do that for a boy whose parentage you knew nothing of. I could be the son of criminals, yet you found the goodness in your heart to give me a home."

"Criminals? Surely you've never thought that, Jack!"

"Did it never occur to you, Mama? I thought of it constantly. What if my soul was stained with the blood of my father's victims and the same blackness was within me, waiting to come out?" He smiled and touched her cheek when she gasped. "Please, don't look so distressed. No one knows the truth of who left me in a basket in front of the foundling home, but it was only natural for the imaginative boy I was to think the worst."

"Was it, Jack?"

Again, Jack laughed to lighten the situation. "I didn't mean to distress you, Mother. But you can see that my confusion about my place in the world meant I was easiest with a friend the same age who did not judge and speculate about what kind of boy I was or the kind of man I'd become. Katherine simply liked to sit up in trees with me and plot devious mischief to avenge herself against George. She was kind and thoughtful, too. Even when I was seven. She knew I was hungry most of the days I was at the foundling home, so she stole from the kitchen on my behalf, though, truth to tell, Cook was more than generous. She'd send me back with a basket of cake or scones to feed the other children." He smiled. It gave him a warm feeling to recall this rare bright spot of his childhood. Before Eliza and Rufus Patmore had adopted him.

"Ah, Mother, your eyes are moist. I didn't mean to upset you."

She shook her head. "Please go on, Jack. You were only eighteen when you left to become a man, determined to make your way in the world through your own efforts. I was proud of you then, but I can't tell you how proud I am of you today. As Odette must be."

"Odette doesn't like me to talk of the fact I'm adopted. She'd rather no one knew."

"She should be proud of you for having become a man of substance through your own efforts."

"Trade, Mama?"

"The East India Company is hardly trade. It's what made her father the wealthy man he is today."

"Ideally, I'd be landed gentry, like Uncle Rufus, and have inherited my pile. Still, it's not stopped her wanting to be my wife. I was afraid of her reaction when I told her, but it seems she'd set her cap at me long before. It was a shock she digested." Quickly, before his mother could speak, he changed the subject. "And Katherine will always be my friend, Mother. Early friendship lasts forever. I hope she'll be happy with Lord Derry. They knew one another before she married Freddy Marwick as he was then." Jack grinned, remembering those early churnings of adolescent jealousy even though he and Katherine had both discussed the impossibility of their being together. "I disapproved of Marwick *and* Derry and I told her so, though who was I to offer my opinion? I didn't think she'd be happy with either. Lord, it was a great blow to hear she'd eloped with Marwick the very day I set sail for the West Indies."

"You felt...*wounded?*"

"I know, I know." He sighed. He certainly didn't want to be too transparent, yet talking about it made him realise how *much* it had rankled. "I had no right to feel anything, did I? Just as I have no right to feel anything now that she's soon to wed Lord Derry, from all accounts."

"Of course not, as you have been betrothed to Odette for the past six months," his mother said pointedly.

It was the salutary reminder he needed, and briskly, he nodded, patting her on the arm as he said, "Indeed I am. And soon I will be the happiest husband in England."

He wished his mother hadn't looked with such doubt upon him as she responded, "I hope so, Jack. I truly hope so."

For it simply reinforced his own doubts about this marriage, and the knowledge there was no way out now.

But why that should trouble him, he had no idea. He repeated the old mantra silently. Odette was the ideal wife: pretty, lively, loving. Yes, devoted. Sometimes, he felt, *too* devoted.

Fanny looked up in surprise as the drawing room door was thrust open and her friend, who'd left not long beforehand, returned from her walk, saying, "Katherine's not here, is she? No? That's good."

"My dear Eliza, what is it? You look quite discomposed, which is not at all like you."

Concerned, Fanny rose and plumped up a cushion on the chair opposite her before deciding it was as good a time as any for a glass of something more fortifying than tea.

"This morning, you may have noticed, I was suddenly deeply unsettled by an unexpected discovery, and when I took Diana for a walk in order to prove that my suspicions were groundless, I met Jack, who only confirmed them." Eliza fanned herself while waving away the claret that Fanny had poured.

"Eliza, you're talking in riddles!"

Fanny wished her brother Bertram hadn't chosen that moment to enter the room. Eliza had been about to divulge something of great importance, but she'd hardly do that with her indiscreet and bumbling brother in attendance.

"Oh, I'll have Eliza's if she doesn't want it." Bertram plucked the glass from Fanny's hand and went to lean against the mantelpiece. As usual, his collar was too high and stiff—Bertram thought it made him look important—and his checked trousers on the garish side. Bertram had always embraced fashion as if he couldn't decide whether he was a gentleman or wanted to join the theatre. "So, what was this you were telling my sisters about your unsettling discovery, Eliza? It's about Katherine, eh? You've heard the rumours, then? Been swirling around for years only seems I was the last to know. In fact, it was only when I stumbled upon it first hand, written in ink for all the world to see, that anyone spilled the beans. Small fry it was, though, compared to the other biz that's going on these days. Long time ago, besides."

"Lord Bertram, now you're the one talking in riddles!" Antoinette exclaimed while Fanny leapt up and snatched back the glass of claret her brother was about to toss back, promising to reinstate it only if he explained himself.

He managed to look blank while directing an unfocused look of longing at the glass Fanny was waving in front of his nose. "I thought I explained myself very clearly. We were talking about Katherine and those rumours."

"Vile whispers." It pained Fanny even to utter the words. "But hardly anything new. If people believe Katherine's association with Lord Derry should compel her to marry him, then they've got nothing much else with which to trouble themselves. Derry helped her when Freddy proved himself such a wastrel of a husband, but there was absolutely nothing inappropriate in it. Katherine tells me so, and I believe her. She says she doesn't want to marry Lord Derry, now, and she never did."

"I wish she'd take my advice that it's in her interests to marry a rich and besotted gentleman this time," Antoinette interrupted. "I'll have another word to her. Don't I know how much easier life is married to a rich man who'll give you the moon."

"You're very different to Katherine, and besides, she won't listen," Fanny said tightly. "Katherine's heart is elsewhere engaged. Apparently, she's been in love with a gentleman she won't name—though I will tell you it's not Lord Derry—for years."

Eliza made a small noise like a gasp while Bertram, seized back the glass from Fanny's hand. "I'm not talking about *those* rumours," he said after he'd tossed back the contents, I'm talking about the wager I saw written up in Boodles Betting Book dating back seven years. Lord, no one told me at the time, though I believe I was elsewhere, making my mark in the world."

"Boodles Betting Book!" Fanny exclaimed, horrified. "What was written up about my daughter? Goodness, Bertram, but you can be vexing. Will you just come out with it?"

Bertram looked offended as he pulled out his snuffbox before deciding on more fortification and going towards the brandy decanter that stood upon the sideboard. "Seems that someone we know quite well," he said with a pointed look at Antoinette, "wagered that young Katherine would elope on a certain day in June seven years ago. I then saw Lord Derry wager that she *wouldn't*—with a sizeable payout to go to the son of yours truly here," he claimed, with a flourish of his hand in Antoinette's direction "if she did! And we all know she did."

Antoinette jerked forward, crying indignantly, "Are you accusing my George of having a hand in Katherine's elope-ment? What, exactly, *are* you saying, Bertram?"

"Lord, ain't it obvious?" Bertram looked vexed. "I've said it clear as daylight. Your George mightn't have written up the *original* wager, for it was George Bramley who did that, but he embellished it and he had a vested interest in ensuring your Katherine," he said, directing a look at Fanny, "eloped on June the 9th. And she did."

"Of course she did, because she was madly in love with Freddy Marwick!" cried Antoinette, quite riled up. "George has done nothing wrong."

Bertram chewed his lip thoughtfully before agreeing. "Dare say he did the right thing in case she had second thoughts, since, as the next wager has it, if she was delivered of a girl within nine months, five hundred was to be paid out to the chap closest to the day and a thousand in the case of a boy. But that's by the bye. Can't remember who wagered that, besides."

"My poor Katherine," Fanny whispered, distraught. "How vile people can be." And yet she knew better than anyone, and from experience, the answer to that question. She also knew that Katherine's flirtations in the first fortnight of her coming-out had made her vulnerable to such poor treatment by the rakes and reprobates who caroused and made wagers at Boodles.

"But she did not suffer from the rumours, and that's what's important," Antoinette reminded them, though she didn't look as airily unconcerned as usual. "And if her choice in husband and to, in fact, elope was not wise, it's not as if she was pressured into a marriage not of her choosing, as our grandparents and even parents, were."

"But I'm not so sure it was of her choosing."

Fanny was no less surprised than Antoinette and Bertram, who turned to look at Eliza. After all, what could their friend know about the state of Katherine's heart seven years before?

Eliza looked stricken as she shook her head, unable to continue for the moment and Antoinette said, "I hate to say this but..." She stopped and looked at Bertram. "Bertram, I'd like you to leave the room now, for you've said all you need to.

We'll consult you if necessary on what steps we can take to mitigate further scandal—if we decide more scandal could ensue."

Bertram looked at his timepiece and shrugged. "Time to be off, besides. I daresay there'll be more entertainment to be had at Boodles, and I'll do my bit to ensure my niece's reputation remains as blemish-free as it ought. Not that it's particularly blemish-free right now, but I have a fondness for the girl, and I'll do what's right by her as her uncle. She doesn't deserve what people say of her."

Now Fanny really felt like weeping though it was Antoinette who said, "Just conduct yourself with caution, Bertram. You ever were one for getting more than just yourself into scrapes."

"And hasn't everything turned out for the best when I've had a hand in it?" he asked, pinching his nose. "Why, think of young Thea, who never would have married Grayling if it hadn't been for me. And you, too, Eliza, have a great deal to be glad about as a result of me knowing what was what when you were intent on marrying that reprobate, George Bramley."

Fanny shooed him out and turned to Antoinette, whose words filled her with dread. Eliza had clearly decided not to expand upon what she'd been about to say, nor respond to Bertram, but Antoinette seemed very keen to impart her thoughts.

She twisted a ringlet around her finger and moved forward in her seat. "As we all know, Katherine met Freddy Marwick the first night she came to London. I thought she'd lost her heart a little too readily, and even *I* was scandalised when she quizzed me on the kinds of attentions a wife would be subjected to from a husband."

Fanny felt unaccountably awkward, despite that fact she'd been far from innocent when she'd married Fenton. It seemed so different in the case of one's own daughter. She also felt a little disturbed that Katherine had chosen to consult Antoinette rather than her own mother on matters relating to marital relations.

A little stiffly, she said, "I'm sure I explained what I needed to in preparation. At the time, I had no idea Katherine's head or heart had been turned by anyone. And I certainly didn't want to furnish her with too much knowledge that might not be...appropriate."

"Lord, is that Fanny Brightwell, my own scandalous sister talking?" Antoinette threw up her hands. "What have you turned into? Mother Goose? Why, no wonder Katherine consulted me, then, on a safe means to test her selection of a potential husband."

Eliza reddened, and Fanny said, "You're going too far, Antoinette, to air this publicly. Nor had you any right to be so...accommodating. No wonder Katherine eloped if her head was filled with ideas of romance and desire and all those other things you love to talk about."

"I said exactly the right thing: the truth. And I was at pains to reassure her that she had carte blanche to decide upon her own husband. I reminded her of how fortunate she was to be able to choose for herself, unlike us, and she was very pliant."

Fanny tried to cast her mind back seven years. Had she misread the situation at the time? "Katherine seemed very levelheaded. Eloping was out of character for her. But obviously, Young George had a great incentive to ensure that she did, no doubt pressured by Marwick, since we all know now that he'd lost a fortune at the tables just days before and needed a rich wife who was in ignorance of his pecuniary difficulties."

"No need to look so fiercely at me!" said Antoinette indignantly. "I knew nothing of this wager and George's involvement until tonight. And nor should you rail over what was inevitable if Katherine was in love with Freddy."

"But what if it wasn't *Freddy* that Katherine was in love with?"

Fanny stopped what she was about to say to frown in Eliza's direction, for it seemed her friend had a great deal of knowledge of what was going on seven years before.

"Eliza, I'm sorry to say it but she eloped with Freddy of her own free will. You're not suggesting he kidnapped her. I think Katherine might have said something to us at the time if not in the intervening years."

Eliza's brow was creased. She bit her lip and fidgeted in a way Katherine had never seen. Eliza was always the picture of restraint. "What if..." Eliza stopped and shook her head, suddenly reluctant to continue until Fanny encouraged her with a wave of her hand.

"What if she meant to elope with *Jack*?"

"Jack?"

The sisters repeated the name in one single shocked syllable.

"Please, before you think me completely mad, just think back to their time together. They were always friends—"

"Yes, friends. I don't mean to offend you, Eliza, but I really don't think Katherine harboured romantic feelings for Jack," Fanny said awkwardly.

"You're not offending me," Eliza said. "I'm just thinking over what I saw just now with the possibility that seven years ago, Katherine had planned to run away with Jack, only for some inexplicable reason, she ran away with Mr Marwick." She shook her head to stay the inevitable responses. "And the reason I say that is because just half an hour ago, I saw for the first time that Diana has a tiny sixth finger. It's barely noticeable—not nearly so noticeable as Jack's—but you can't deny that's what it is. Such a rare anomaly, deformity, call it what you will, runs in families." She hesitated then shrugged. "I really don't know what to think except that it is a possibility."

The stunned silence that followed was broken by Antoinette. "Oh, my! That is indeed a possibility!" Fanny had rarely seen her sister looking so distressed. "I remember, all those years ago, Katherine making some veiled hint about the man she was...experimenting with."

"Lord, Antoinette, do watch what you say!" muttered Fanny. "There are enough rumours swirling about Katherine without you adding to them!"

"I'm teasing out Eliza's suggestion of what could really have happened, not endorsing any rumours," her sister responded, offended. "And I do recall that the allusions Katherine made to the gentleman she'd fallen in love with did not equate with Freddy, though I dismissed that at the time. I think she was using Freddy as a...decoy."

"And Diana was born exactly nine months later, with a tiny sixth finger." Eliza put her head in her hands before looking up. "But why would she elope with Freddy? It doesn't make sense." She appeared to be thinking before she added. "What I do think, however, is that Katherine was in love with Jack seven years ago, and I think—no, I *know*, that Jack is in love with Katherine right now."

"He can't be. He's marrying Miss Worthington." Bertram had just reentered the room with these bold words as he pulled on his gloves. "And we all know he won't cry off at this late stage. Can't, really, if he's the sort to worry about his honour and reputation and all that. Which we all know he is."

"Yes, I think you're right, Eliza," said Fanny bleakly. "I think Katherine's in love with Jack, though I have no idea whether she was in love with him seven years ago since she chose to marry Freddy." She looked sorrowfully at her friend and siblings. "Oh, my poor child. Her marriage to Freddy was a disaster. And she's been so unhappy these last seven years. Yet just when happiness might be within reach, it turns out that Jack now is about to become unavailable."

"We'll just have to make him available," said Bertram matter-of-factly as he picked up his silver-topped cane and was greeted by the inevitable scorn of his sisters. Undismayed, he continued, "We need to find someone who'll sweep Miss Worthington off her feet in order to free Jack up for Katherine."

"So easy, Bertram," Antoinette mocked. "Jack and Odette are due to wed in a little over four weeks and Odette is, as is plain to see, quite besotted."

Eliza nodded gloomily. "She has her claws well and truly sunk, and she knows how to play on Jack's highly tuned sense of honour."

Fanny was surprised. "I thought you liked Miss Worthington."

"Very much. And I'd think her the perfect daughter-in-law if I were convinced Jack was in love with her and nobody else, for then he'd not begrudge dancing to her tune. Believe me, Miss Worthington may look very sweet and pliable on the surface, but there's a ruthlessness beneath that soft veneer. She will always get what she wants, and she wants Jack, regardless of what Jack wants."

"Then we must make her want someone else," said Antoinette.

"Derry thought her a proper bit o' frock."

"And what's that supposed to mean?" Fanny rounded on him. Bertram's sanguine approach irritated her for her daughter's happiness was at stake. Matters were serious. "I suppose you mean Odette caught his eye, but then, so did Katherine all those years ago. And Katherine has associated with him sufficiently intimately to lend credence to baseless rumours, it appears. It'll be a scandal if Katherine doesn't marry Derry, and that, I believe, is what she may have to do if she is to be welcomed warmly by society. Which she does. If she doesn't, she'll be a social pariah, regardless of the fact the rumours linking her to Derry are baseless."

Bertram hesitated in the doorway and shook his head sadly. "Am I the only one with inspired ideas. Why, you and Antoinette were considered queens of your craft when you brought Eliza and her beloved Rufus Patmore together."

"Queens of our craft?" cried Antoinette, delighted. "Why Bertram, that is clever and I like it very much. And Fanny, what he says is true. You've turned into a proper curmudgeon. What happened to the bold sister I once knew who did not shy away from taking the risks needed to ensure the happy outcome desired? Would you really wish Katherine to enter another marriage not of her choosing just to be accepted by society?"

"Of course I wouldn't, but right now I can't see an alternative. Katherine is miserable and has been for a very long time. She wishes to be welcomed by society, but she won't be if she doesn't marry Derry. And I hardly think even the boldest scheme is going to succeed in making Miss Worthington miraculously fall in love with Lord Derry, of all people, or anyone else. Besides, Lord Derry has wanted Katherine for his wife for more than seven years. Meanwhile, Odette Worthington is determined to wed Jack...in four weeks!"

"Yes, the odds are stacked against us and we are working against the clock," agreed Antoinette. "But making Miss Worthington fall in love with Derry is what must be arranged." She nodded, thoughtfully, as if they were all agreed on a plan which Fanny had just outlined as being totally unworkable, if not outrageous.

"I'll start by influencing Derry." Bertram rested his cane against the back of the sofa and went to the sideboard to pour himself another drink. "Remember that you're looking at the clever fellow who masterminded dear Thea and Grayling's very successful romance."

"Which nearly sent Aunt Brightwell to the moon in a balloon when matters got totally out of hand," Fanny reminded him.

"But matters didn't," Bertram countered cheerfully, raising his glass then tossing back the contents. "So, with such a stellar past experience to buck us up, you can rest assured that I will soon have matters well in hand as regards Derry and Miss Worthington." The grin he fixed upon his sisters softened as he turned his attention to Eliza. "No need to look so concerned, my dear girl; they don't call me dependable Bertram for nothing."

CHAPTER 22

Katherine eyed the deep-blue-and-gold flounced gown longingly. It was so nearly time to put aside her mourning. And tonight's entertainment was to be held at Quamby House. So, surely she could wear the exquisite confection that she'd just had made in preparation for the moment she could fling off her mourning forever.

She'd spent money she didn't have, but her father had been generous. She knew it was taking advantage of that generosity to outlay such a proportion of what he'd made over to her in order to survive, but deporting herself like a lady was tantamount to survival.

"Dare I put that on, Mary?" she asked her maid who'd just entered the room. She'd not have bothered to ask the question if it had been Millicent, her previous lady's maid, a severe middle-aged woman secured for her by her mother-in-law seven years ago.

But Millicent had died of the scarlet fever while visiting her village and Katherine had been thrilled to have her own choice of retainer.

Mary pressed her lips together but her eyes shone. "Ooh,

Miss, if yer dare ter wear it, I'll dare to fix yer hair so's at all the gennulmen won't be able ter look at anyone else but ye."

"That's not the idea at all, Mary," said Katherine. "Besides, there's only one I want to do that."

"Lord Derry?" asked Mary matter-of-factly as she went to Katherine's dressing table and started selecting pins and hair pieces.

"Not Lord Derry," Katherine said under her breath, not expecting Mary to jerk her head up and look at her with surprise. Only when Katherine demanded that she must explain her response did Mary say reluctantly, "The talk is that ye'll wed Lord Derry jest as soon as yer cast aside yer mournin'."

"Well, I'm casting aside my mourning—temporarily—tonight, but I have no intention of wedding Lord Derry either tonight, tomorrow, or any other day."

Mary looked uncertain which again had Katherine saying, "Come on, out with it! There's something you've heard that you don't want me to hear, I gather."

"Jest that the servants were sayin' the talk is yer 'ave no choice but ter marry Lord Derry."

"No choice? Why have I no choice? Come on, Mary, tell me!"

But Katherine knew it already. Her reputation was so tarnished by her association with the handsome, smitten, and very attentive Lord Derry, she had little alternative but to marry him if she were to reenter the echelons of society that had barred first Freddy and then both of them. And Katherine knew very well that her daughter's future depended upon society's acceptance.

"Ain't me place, ma'am," Mary said in a small voice, and Katherine let it be, silent as Mary helped her dress in the new gown she'd decided she'd wear, regardless of the scandal. There wasn't much worse she could do, after all.

TONIGHT, KATHERINE FOUND HERSELF UNACCOUNTABLY nervous to venture over the threshold of what was really her second home. No, that wasn't true. She knew very well why she was nervous. Tonight she'd see Jack playing the attentive husband-to-be and know that he was forever out of bounds. He'd not give up Odette for her. Katherine had missed her chance—if she'd ever had a chance. Timing and circumstance had not favoured either of them.

"Katherine, what a charming picture you present—a symphony in sea green. Or is the colour a variation on blue?" Earl Quamby, leaning on the shoulder of his young Mediterranean companion, hobbled a few steps towards her and kissed her hand.

"It's called teal," said Katherine, glad of a welcome from the person least likely to condemn her for her decision to eschew mourning. "It's a colour combination using a clever technique."

"Well, a clever technique, plan, or device it was to arrive as a treat to the eyes, rather than a sight to conjure up a hunched-up crow as you would have appeared had you worn the dreadful black bombazine affair you turned up in last time I saw you."

"Mama will be displeased. I should be wearing full mourning for months yet."

"But you're *not* mourning, are you?" Lord Quamby squeezed her hand and gave her a knowing look.

"I never mourned him, Uncle," Katherine said, not even feeling the slightest guilt, positioning herself on his other side so she could help him to a chair.

"He didn't deserve you, did he, my dear? A good thing he's gone is what I say. A bloodsucker he was. Took your youth and innocence and then sucked you dry and your father for all he could get out of him to pay for his vices."

Katherine didn't want to go over the past. Her mouth was suddenly dry for she'd glimpsed Jack in the crowd. She was able to look at him as he had his back to her, but the moment he turned in her direction, she darted her attention back to her uncle.

"Someone caught your fancy, eh?" Lord Quamby said perceptively as, with a great deal of laboured breathing, he lowered himself onto a blue velvet Chippendale chair. "And why not? A pretty young woman like you? You're a vision, Katherine, with the world at your feet. Don't go marrying Lord Derry if you don't want to, just because everyone says you have to. I've never listened to good advice."

"You're the Earl of Quamby, and a man," Katherine said softly, for she could speak to her uncle candidly. It was one of the reasons he'd been such an important member of the family to which she belonged.

"They are advantages." He looked kind and a little sad, too. Then he whispered, "But sometimes a chance can pay off, Katherine. Even if the risks are truly terrible. We get few chances at happiness."

"Katherine! You look—" Her mother stopped abruptly, the smile turning to a look of worry as Katherine rose from her uncle's side.

"You were going to compliment me, weren't you, Mama, until you remembered I'm flouting convention and you disapprove," Katherine bristled.

"It's the fact society will disapprove that concerns me, darling," said Lady Fenton, nodding at her brother-in-law and drawing her daughter to an alcove so they couldn't be overheard by an interested group of guests standing nearby. "Katherine, believe me, I want you to be happy. I know it's been hard for you, but you must curb your impulsiveness."

She might have softened the rebuke in the next sentence only suddenly Jack was at her mother's side, with Odette clinging to his arm, and Katherine had no choice but to turn her attention to the man who set her pulses racing and manage a cordial nod at his intended.

"You're looking lovely this evening, Miss Worthington," she complimented her. "I hope your father's health has improved."

"Thank you. Indeed it has, much to everyone's relief. I'd feared I might have to bring forward our nuptials, but the date remains. My dressmaker was very pleased." Miss Worthington directed a happy smile at Jack who responded in kind.

Katherine turned her head away, only to find Lord Derry leaving his conversation with her Uncle Bertram and advancing upon them. Her heart suddenly seemed very heavy.

Gritting her teeth as she prepared to be invited to partner him in the waltz that was about to begin, she was surprised and relieved when, after the necessary formalities, he bowed before Miss Worthington and offered her his arm.

"I hope Mr Patmore won't object if I squire his fair maiden onto the polished boards," he asked. "I've heard she's an excellent dancer. Learned to dance with the best of them in India, eh?"

Suddenly, Katherine found herself alone with Jack, her mother having slid away, too. Unaccountably awkward, her body thrummed with possibility when Jack raised his eyebrows and asked, "Would you like to dance, Katherine? Or is that not allowed when you're in mourning? Not that anyone would know it." His eyes twinkled.

"Do you disapprove, like everyone else?"

"I'd never disapprove of you, Katherine," he told her, patting her hand as she rested it on his arm and he led her towards the floor.

"You're the only one, then."

"I've probably known you longer than anyone. Except your own family, of course. And I know there's not an ounce of malice or unkindness in you." He put one hand about her waist and took her other hand for the waltz hold before they both stepped onto the dance floor.

"I haven't danced for so long I'd forgotten how much I enjoyed it," Katherine gasped as he twirled her about, though she realised it was as much her companion that accounted for her pleasure. A frisson of sadness enveloped her prompting Jack to ask, concerned, "I didn't step on your toe, did I?"

"I wouldn't have cared if you did," Katherine laughed, determined not to spoil the moment.

"Then why did you suddenly look as if you were gripped by pain?"

"I didn't."

"I wouldn't have accused you if you hadn't. You can't pretend with me, Katherine. I know you too well."

She glanced up at him, suddenly serious. "All right then. It's because you're going to marry Odette Worthington, and I'll never see you again."

He hesitated as if weighing up what to say. She thought he'd say what convention might have decreed: that of course they'd see each other again. Instead, he said, solemnly, "I'm obligated to marry Odette. You know that, Katherine."

"Just as I'm obligated to marry Lord Derry. Do you think that?"

"I don't think you should feel obligated to do anything you don't want to, Katherine. You *can* cry off. Yes, you'll suffer for it, and no doubt you're weighing up whether the consequences are worth it." He looked away briefly before bringing his troubled gaze back to her. "I *can't* cry off. I'm a gentleman, and a gentleman has a code of honour that dictates every sphere of his life. Perhaps you'd be called shameless; perhaps you'd be shunned if you didn't marry Derry. But I would be branded a cad, no longer a gentleman, if I were to break off with Odette now, a month before our wedding and with her father so ill. And..." His voice trailed off. "I would break her heart."

Just as you are breaking mine, Katherine thought, though his words thrilled her for the fact they said so much of his true feelings.

"Did you miss me, Jack?" she whispered.

Light flared in his eyes, which dulled as Derry and Odette brushed past them in a swirl of lavender taffeta and black suiting.

"I missed you, Katherine. I missed you when I left. Desperately. But we both knew a future was impossible. You weren't about to throw in your lot with me in some mad, impulsive declaration that your heart had taken leave of your senses. I knew that..." He frowned, and Katherine bit down on the impulse to say the words that would give the lie to his long-held belief. Words that would also throw into turmoil his basis of honour. The transluscent blue of his steady, earnest gaze sent need skittering through her—the need for him; the need that he know the truth...

The need that he be protected from a truth that would only imprison him between two impossible choices.

"Do you have any regrets?" She straightened her spine.

Again, he met her look, squarely. "A gentleman would not have taken what you offered so generously," he said softly. "But I was a young man in love—with you, *and* the adventure I was about to embark upon. A gentleman was what I was determined to be...on my own merits. I do not regret our time together, for it sustained me through so much. But if I had my time again, I would have behaved more gallantly, Katherine."

Katherine tightened her grip on his hand. "I wouldn't

have changed any of it, Jack. The week before you left was the happiest of my life."

"And mine, Katherine—"

"If I may intrude." It was Derry, tall and commanding, reminding Jack what was his. What he believed was his. Without a word, Katherine transferred her hand to his forearm as he led her off the dance floor and Odette took her place.

"I trust you enjoyed conversing with the future Mrs Patmore," Katherine said lightly, shaken, exultant, unsettled over her conversation with Jack. "She looked in a talkative mood."

"Were you jealous?"

"What a question!" Katherine knew she shouldn't have snapped out the words.

He stopped and stared down at her, storm clouds and sorrow in his gaze. "I'd never cause you grief or harm, intentionally, Katherine. Unlike Freddy. You know I'd be a good husband."

"It's too early for words like that," Katherine said tightly.

"Anyone who didn't know the truth would have no idea you were a widow. Surely I could be forgiven for taking the same licence you do."

Katherine sighed. "It was churlish of me. You confuse me, Derry. I'm sorry. But tell me, what did Miss Worthington speak of?"

"Her father, her life in India, her desire for a home in England, her love of theatre—"

Katherine put up her hand to stay him. "I should have asked if there was anything Miss Worthington did *not* speak about!"

"She certainly was a good deal more talkative than you, Katherine." He raised one eyebrow as if challenging Katherine to make a spirited defence.

Which she might have if she'd cared.

Instead, she looked longingly at Jack's back and wondered what he and Miss Worthington talked about during the many hours they spent together.

And if Jack ever spoke about what was really important to him.

***

"Did you hear what I said, Fanny? You really aren't paying attention, are you?" Antoinette grumbled, causing her sister to at last transfer her attention away from the dance floor.

"I've been watching Katherine's face while she's been speaking to Jack, and it's breaking my heart. She's in love with him, Antoinette! Why did I not see what was right under my nose? And she can't have him!"

"She's going to have him," Antoinette vowed, breathing through her nose. "Bertram!" She hailed her brother. "I saw you talking to Lord Derry. What did you instruct him?"

"Unlike you, Antoinette, I do not instruct. I use the art of subtlety to achieve my ends." Bertram's irrepressible grin stretched his mouth wide as he joined them. Bertram always seemed so pleased with himself, Fanny thought in exasperation. Like as not, he'd make things worse.

"And how did you subtly convey your desire that he make Miss Worthington fall in love with him?"

"Lord, now you're being ridiculous, Antoinette!" he grumbled. "I merely commented that I'd overheard Miss Worthington telling a friend that of all the gentlemen in the room, she considered Lord Derry far and away the most handsome."

Fanny darted a glance at Lord Derry who was now talking to Katherine, and noticed that his gaze occasionally rose above her shoulder to settle upon Miss Worthington who was talking in her usual animated fashion to Jack. She was about to compliment her brother on his strategy, when a slight rearrangement of the room caused the betrothed pair to be pushed into their orbit and Fanny seized her chance, clapping her hand upon Odette's shoulder.

"I'm going to steal away your intended if you have no objection, Jack. Your mother has been looking for you and is by the long windows. So, Odette," she went on when Jack had obediently headed towards Eliza, "how are you finding life in London with your intended and so much to organise?"

"It's everything I could have hoped for."

Said like a true debutante swooning with love, Fanny thought dolefully.

"You've certainly made more than a ripple, my dear. Only in the best possible way," Fanny added quickly in response to the flare of concern in Odette's eye.

"You're certain I shouldn't be aware of...anything that might be of concern?"

"Not at all," Fanny said warmly. "Why, I overheard Lord Derry telling my nephew George he hadn't seen a more charming and delightful young woman as you in all the seasons he's been hunting for a wife."

Odette blushed charmingly, and Fanny could see how she appealed to Jack. Yet Odette had not the depth and spirit her Katherine did. She was sure of it. Nor did she love Jack like Katherine, she thought fiercely.

"Yes, warm praise indeed for such a notoriously difficult to please gentleman which is why, I daresay, he remains unwed. Now, where has Jack got to? Ah, there he is, talking with his father. Or rather, uncle, I should say."

Introducing the element of uncertainty regarding Jack's parentage might be of no account, but it couldn't hurt, Fanny thought. But then, if Odette really loved Jack, that would not signify.

Having just spied Bertram, Fanny was weighing up how safe it was to navigate their way in his direction. Bertram was a wild card, yet he'd been the only one to come up with anything resembling a plan to bring together two unlikely hearts that were elsewhere engaged. If only some great drama could be orchestrated, she thought wistfully. Bertram was the king of drama, but unfortunately they usually didn't go according to plan.

She was about to take Odette's arm and gently steer her in her brother's direction when the girl said, "I do wish Jack wouldn't talk of his parents as if they were a charitable institution." She ventured an uncertain look at Fanny, then, perceiving encouragement, went on, "They've been so good to him, not distinguishing him from their other children, yet he speaks all too often as if he really were some foundling child adopted by Mr and Mrs Patmore."

"But he *is* a foundling child," Fanny said cautiously. "And Mr and Mrs Patmore have been very generous to him in giving him their name." To anyone else she'd have fiercely claimed Jack was just as good if not better than anyone else in the room, and most definitely the equal of the Patmore's natural children. "Is there something about that that troubles you?"

Odette looked ashamed, then fierce, then sorrowful. "Sometimes I have to cover my ears with my hands when he says the reason he's driven to work so hard is that for all he knows, his father might have been a highwayman for whose misdeeds he must atone. Or even a murderer. I hate hearing him talk like that."

Dismayed that Jack should continue to be tormented for such fantasies when Fanny knew the truth of his parentage, she swallowed and asked, "What do you say?"

"I tell him that he *is* a gentleman in my eyes, and that he should just go on about his business to the rest of the world on that basis. I don't think he should tell people he was adopted, and he certainly shouldn't spout all this nonsense about criminals and highwaymen, or else people will question whether he deserves their respect."

"Perhaps you respect him more for having worked so hard to get where he has despite his origins?"

Odette shrugged. "I'd fallen in love with Jack long before I found out he was adopted. Papa never told me. It was quite a shock, but I resolved that I wouldn't let it stand in the way of how I felt about him."

"You just wish he'd never talk about it?"

"That's right." Odette darted a worried look at her. "You don't think that's wrong of me, do you?" she asked.

"I think it's important we're all honest about our feelings, my dear. Otherwise, how can we trust each other if we keep secret what we really feel?"

Sadly, she thought of her Katherine, bottling up the secret of her love for Jack all these years. And, intercepting a fleeting look between Jack and Katherine and realising the depth of her feeling was more than reciprocated, her resolve hardened that the no doubt worthy Odette must be replaced.

"Come, my dear. Have you met Lord Derry? You have? Ah then, as he's talking to my brother who was interested to know how you enjoyed your visit to the tower, there's no need to introduce you if we join them, is there?"

CHAPTER 23

Diana was certain that hiding under the bed would solve all her problems. The moment she'd heard her grandmother's voice in the hallway five minutes ago, she'd taken advantage of the fact that her nurse-maid had just left the nursery to look for a cloth to clean up the paint water she'd spilled.

Now, as she heard Betsy calling her name, her breath came in shaky bursts as she contemplated the consequences of being found.

Her grandmother wanted to take Diana back to her house. "To spend a few nights there so we may become better acquainted," she'd overheard the old woman saying.

Diana couldn't imagine anything worse. She imagined days spent pressed against the stiff purple silk of Lady Hale's clothes, which smelt musty and nasty, while her grandmother read her stories with Diana perched unwillingly on the chair beside her. It was like a nightmare. As was the fear that her grandmother might steal her away.

At the evening party her great-uncle Lord Quamby had held the night before, Diana had overheard such a possibility being suggested by two men, one of them Lord Quamby's son George whom Diana didn't trust at all, and the other, Lord Derry, the gentleman who was always mooning over her mama. Although Diana had known him all her life and, in fact, didn't object to him like she did her mother's cousin, George, she'd been frightened by what she'd heard.

She remembered it with terrible clarity. Cousin George had sauntered over to Lord Derry who was standing by the sofa near where Diana was hiding behind a large pot plant, and said, "Lady Hale thinks Diana should spend a few days with her as per Freddy's dying request that the two become better acquainted after his death."

"Katherine wouldn't let his mother over the threshold after she insulted her that memorable evening, and I don't blame her. Lady Hale is a deplorable woman." Lord Derry had taken a sip of his drink, sighed, then said, "Well, if you think that can help influence Katherine, I'd be enormously grateful. I don't want to force her into anything against her will, you do understand; I just feel that I can help her to be happy."

Diana had thought that those words were very strange: I can help her to be happy.

Diana knew he couldn't. Her mother only ever smiled when she spoke of her happy memories of being a child and when she first came to London, and how everything changed the night the carriage came.

The carriage.

She strained her ears for the sound of Betsy's footsteps then pulled herself out from under the bed and ran to the window. Standing on a chair, she saw Lady Hale's carriage and, in front of it, the carriage belonging to the nice man from across the sea who always made her mother smile, though her mother looked even sadder when she watched him leave. Diana was very attuned to what made her mother smile and what made her sad. Lord Derry made her mother anxious and sad, and Mr Patmore made her mother smile when she was with him and sad when she wasn't.

Jack. He was a nice man. Diana also didn't mind the lady he always brought along. She was pretty and laughed a lot. But Diana would rather that Miss Worthington stay at home instead of going everywhere with Jack.

Still, she might have some of those clotted cream caramels she'd given Diana last time she'd visited, and she certainly wasn't cross like Diana's grandmother.

As she watched Mr Patmore step from his carriage, then help out the pretty lady who looked a bit cross today, followed by another older lady, she thought how nice and cosy the carriage would be to hide in. It both amused her to think of how cross Lady Hale would be as she'd no doubt be when she sent Betsy off in a fluster to look for her. Suddenly, it seemed a very good idea to leave the house and run across the lawn and jump in.

Diana was reasonably confident Mr Patmore wouldn't be cross with her when he discovered her there after he returned to his townhouse only a few blocks away at the end of his visit. He was always nice to everyone.

Especially to her mama and to Diana.

"I'M SURE I LIKE LADIES FENTON AND QUAMBY, BUT THERE are other people to visit," Odette whispered to Jack as they waited upon the doorstep of Quamby House to be admitted. "Please, let us not stay long. Aunt Harriet, you don't want to, do you?"

Jack wondered if Odette's reluctance to be here had anything to do with Katherine. The thought made him uncomfortable. He'd tried so hard to deny his feelings for Katherine and, when that proved impossible, make himself immune to them. He hoped Odette was not aware of the frisson of intense emotion that swamped him each time his old friend was anywhere near.

"We'll stay as long as necessary to be polite, and then you can remind me of your dressmaker's appointment," he told her, trying to summon warmth towards Odette when she smiled her gratitude and squeezed his arm, saying, "You are the most thoughtful man a wife could have, Jack."

Last night, when Lady Fenton had invited a small group to join her and her sister for a morning tea this morning, there'd been no room to refuse. Jack had been both glad and otherwise. It was becoming increasingly harder to deny that his attraction to Katherine was becoming almost unbearable, not to mention difficult to hide.

Odette squeezed his hand as they heard footsteps in the lobby, and he returned the gesture. Odette's father was dying, and she needed to know she could rely upon him.

"Miss Worthington and... Miss Worthington. Jack, welcome!" Lady Quamby greeted Jack, Odette and her chaperone. Jack was surprised to see that Lord Derry and Bertram Brightwell had been included in the morning tea when they were shown into the drawing room. Katherine was not among them.

Disappointment was quickly followed by forced relief, until the sound of Katherine's voice in the passage made his pulse skitter and the blood scald the surface of his skin.

There she was standing in the doorway, no doubt looking as beautiful as he remembered though he forced himself not to jerk his head around at her entrance for fear he'd give himself away. Instead, he allowed Derry to be the first to move forward, the older gentleman taking Katherine by the hand in the most familiar of gestures before leading her to a chair.

"You look flustered, my dear. Is everything all right?" Derry enquired.

Jack would have liked to have asked Katherine the same thing. He didn't think it was Derry's excessive attentiveness that accounted for the flushed look on her face for she'd looked harried the moment she walked into the room.

Katherine glanced at the others and, seeing that only Derry was paying her any attention—Jack was pretending to listen to what Odette had to say—muttered, "Lady Hale has come to visit Diana unexpectedly, and my daughter is not behaving as an exacting grandmother would like."

"Or her mother?" Derry enquired, patting Katherine's hand consolingly.

Jack noticed Katherine pulled it away though not rudely.

Katherine lowered her eyes. "I don't like her grandmother either so I can hardly blame her. I've asked Lady Hale to join us in a few minutes as Diana needs to be punished for yesterday's naughtiness and do an arithmetic lesson instead of have a story. I thought a white lie that involved draconian measures would be more likely to have the desired effect."

Jack was surprised at Lord Derry's warning tone as he addressed Katherine. Several others had begun to talk, but Jack's ears were attuned to the intimate discussion between his friend and her... He wasn't sure what to call Lord Derry, who was saying gravely, "You know Freddy was quite particular in his final wishes that Diana spend more time with her grandmother. You don't want her to decide she'll take Diana on a more permanent basis."

Katherine's hand flew to her mouth. "She couldn't. Diana's my daughter."

"But a father's last wishes count for a great deal more than the desires of a mother in the eyes of the court."

Jack wanted to shake Derry. What was the man playing at? Meanwhile, he was doing his best to attend to two conversations at once, and only realised how poor a job he was doing when Odette patted his knee and asked, patiently, "Jack, dearest, isn't that right? We can't stay very long today as—"

He was relieved when Lady Quamby interjected cheerfully, "I believe, Jack, that you are taking Odette to see your father in the country after this. You'll stay for lunch, naturally. It's three hours to Patmore Farm by carriage. I was expecting you'd stay for proper refreshment. I thought that's what we'd agreed."

He felt Odette stiffen beside him at the same time he caught Katherine's clear-eyed glance across the table. She was still upset, and his heart tumbled to his boots at the knowledge he could do nothing to help her; that he was, in fact, contributing in another way so greatly to her pain.

He forced himself to look away, his only consolation that Katherine's decisions had been made by herself. She'd thrown herself into her marriage with Freddy Marwick incautiously, recklessly, when he'd advised her to show restraint.

But wasn't that one of the things he loved about her? Her exuberance, her impetuosity.

There was little evidence of it now, though. The past seven years seemed to have quashed so much of that spirit, and Jack wondered sadly how much remained. Enough to extricate her from a marriage with Derry that she didn't desire?

For there was Derry, now, murmuring words of comfort in her ear judging by the conciliatory pat upon her sleeve and frown of concern.

As Jack accepted Lady Quamby's invitation, he heard Katherine's steely rejoinder and was pleased at the fact she could still assert herself. "Diana will not be spending any more time with her grandmother than absolutely necessary, Derry. I don't care what Lady Hale has been saying to you.

Nor can I imagine why she would voice such sentiments to you."

FANNY TRIED TO APPEAR BRIGHT OVER LUNCH, BUT THE downcast spirits of her daughter, earlier, and Jack's obvious solicitousness towards Odette depressed even her. Time was ticking towards Jack's nuptials, but Bertram's plan to bring together Derry and Odette seemed increasingly doomed to fail, if not ridiculous. The surreptitious glances Jack and Katherine sent each other endorsed the fact they were secretly in love, but Odette's shining love for Jack and her frail dependence upon him would make it impossible for him to forsake her. Fanny knew him too well.

As for Odette and Derry, it was clear the pair enjoyed one another's company when on the dance floor and during the few minutes she'd ensured they sat alone together at her little gathering. But what possibility was there of them suddenly being overcome with wild romantic love for one another without provocation? And what provocation could possibly be instigated?

When Jack and Odette rose, declaring they must leave, there was nothing to suggest that fate would run its course. Katherine and Jack, she feared, would again be denied.

CHAPTER 24

It was only three hours to Patmore Farm, and travel was to be conducted during the day. So when Odette's aunt declared herself suddenly unwell, it was agreed by all over pudding that it would be acceptable for Odette to travel in the same carriage with Jack, unaccompanied.

"What a treat," she murmured, pressing her cheek against his shoulder when the door was closed upon them and the horses moved forward. "Soon we can be together, forever, always. You're all I have left, Jack. Papa will be gone soon, and I will have no one. No one except you."

Jack squeezed the little gloved hand she placed in his and tried not to think of Katherine. She'd looked so beautiful and so tragic over lunch today. If Jack were free to offer her the world, offer her his heart, he would do so. But with Odette depending on him so heavily, he could not.

"And my adoptive parents," he added. "They've been so good to me when under no obligation. I owe them the world. You will be like a daughter to them, I know it."

She smiled. "I hope so. But Jack, I do wish you'd stop referring to them as your adoptive parents. They gave you their name and their backing. There's no need to tell the whole world you're adopted, and there's certainly no need to tell them you're originally from the foundling home."

"It's the truth, and I'm proud of it," Jack said. "Would you not consider it worse if I were to say nothing and then have people think I was trying to deceive them or present myself in a false light?" He paused. "Would you have felt differently about me if you'd known earlier that I was an orphan who had no idea who his parents were? You say you fell in love with me from afar and long before you met me. And your father never said anything to you about my origins—but if you'd known, would you have felt differently?"

He'd been gazing through the window at the passing countryside now they'd left behind the city and straggling villages clustered on its outskirts. He glanced at Odette. She was toying with the fringe of her flounced skirt, biting her lip, and when she looked up at him, there were tears in her eyes.

"Your unknown origins—as you refer to not knowing about your parentage—means nothing to *me*, Jack," she whispered. "But it would be wrong to pretend other people feel the same unconcern." Her shoulders trembled, and for once Jack felt no desire to hold her to him. Odette's frail need had once appealed to his sense of manliness. He'd wanted to protect and nurture her. In India, she'd seemed like a fragile flower in a hot and hostile environment. Since coming to England, however, she'd shown a steely resilience that had at first impressed him but now had him questioning who she really was, since she alternated so greatly between fire and frailty.

"So, what are you saying, Odette? That I should pretend to the world that the Patmores are my real parents? Why, half of society knows the truth."

"Well, there's no need to tell everyone on your first meeting with them," she muttered.

"Do I?" He squared his shoulders feeling aggrieved, for she made him out to be some angst-ridden get-ahead man who hadn't reconciled the truth of what he was. Dread assailed him. But he had, hadn't he? He'd long ago accepted he was a bastard, just as he'd reconciled himself to not knowing what his parents might have been. A prostitute for a mother, and a murderer for a father? He'd accepted the worst possible pairing he could come up with so that he was prepared, should he ever be served up the truth. Not that that was possible unless someone visited the foundling home twenty-five years later looking for him and revealed the truth, which may or may not ever be delivered to him.

"It's not like you blurt it out in the first conversation, but you have a habit, as you progress your acquaintance, of ensuring that people know the Patmores are your *adoptive* family and that you are an orphan. And then, if they ask, you furnish them with details of coming from a *foundling* home, Jack." She put her hand on his sleeve and obviously tried to look ameliorating. "I don't mind admitting that I cried myself to sleep when I learned the truth months after I'd fallen in love with you—"

"You never said, Odette." His words sounded cold even to his own ears. It was not like him, but a great hardness towards her was welling up inside him. Her words sounded like a terrible betrayal, even though he knew it shouldn't since she'd simply offered him the truth and still professed to love him, as she once again reiterated.

"You know my heart belongs to you, irrespective of all that," she said urgently, gripping his lapel. "Yes, I worry about our children and how society will judge them, and that's a truth I'm both ashamed to admit—for your sake—but which I think is only natural. But wouldn't you rather the truth, Jack?"

He stared at the heartfelt look in her eyes and found no

answering surge of feeling. He'd have expected to feel a great warmth at her honesty for hadn't she been brave in admitting that when she must have known it would have been unpalatable to him?

Swallowing down his disappointment, he lightly squeezed the hand she thrust into his. She was desperate for his acceptance of all she'd said, and if they were to be married—as they inevitably would be—he had to exonerate and forgive her for feelings they both might not like. The most important thing was that she'd admitted the truth and the truth trumped all.

"Thank you for being so honest, Odette," he said, forcing himself to smile. "If I could have given you my name, I would have. I am proud of the name Patmore and the lineage. But it isn't mine." Saying the words aloud was more painful than he could possibly have imagined. He closed his eyes. "I shall, however, endeavour not to embarrass you with my candour when I go out and about in society, but nor shall I dress up the truth with lies."

"Oh, Jack—"

Her words ended in a squeak as the carriage went into a deep rut, sending them swaying perilously to the side before it righted itself and continued. But the pile of rugs on the opposite seat had fallen to the floor, and Jack was about to reach out to pick one up to put over Odette's knees when out of the woollen layers emerged a little head.

"Oh!" said a little girl, staring wide-eyed at them from the floor.

Odette gasped while Jack exclaimed, "Diana, what are you doing here?"

She rubbed her eyes. "I was sleeping."

Odette leaned forward to peer closer. "Diana! You naughty child! You shouldn't be here." She sounded so cross, whereas Jack felt only a great affinity with the child whose chatter he'd found quite endearing on several occasions. She reminded him so much of her mother when Katherine had been a child.

"I am not naughty. I was sleeping," said the little girl, staring at Odette with a rather challenging look.

"But why...in our carriage?" Odette demanded.

Diana stuck out her chin. "Running away from my grandmother. Where is she? I don't want to have to go to her house like she said."

Jack smiled. "I think you're safe enough since Lady Hale is having lunch at Lord Quamby's residence, and we are a good one and a half hours away from London."

"What on earth are we going to do with the child?" Odette threw up her hands before rounding on Diana. "Do you know what an inconvenience you've created? We're exactly halfway between London and where we're going. Now what do we do with you?"

ॐ

KATHERINE HAD JUST PUT HER KNIFE AND FORK TOGETHER and was listening to Derry waxing lyrical on the state of the sharemarket when Lady Hale reentered the room with a look of great consternation. The fact that Besty, Diana's nursemaid, was right behind her looking flustered was what made her own fears rise up in a way that Lady Hale's ill temper alone could not have done.

"My granddaughter has completely disappeared. Are you hiding her from me?" Lady Hale demanded as Betsy corroborated, "We bin lookin' this past 'our, ma'am and I canna find 'er anywhere." She looked on the verge of tears, whereas Lady Hale looked as if she were about to spit out a cobra of the variety Katherine had often wished lately had done its worst with regard to Odette Worthington when she'd been in India.

Uncharitable, and not reflecting well on her, she knew. But true.

Now, every mother's fear rose to the fore as she pushed back her chair and stood, saying with as much control as she could, "Have you looked inside the kist at the end of the bed in the blue room. She usually hides there when she doesn't wish to be found."

"I went into the blue room and called loudly," declared Lady Hale.

Katherine nodded. "That would have had little effect." With a sigh, she dropped her napkin onto her plate and turned. "She can't be far. I'll look for her."

"She'll be punished for her naughtiness!" declared Lady Hale, turning, but her words caused Katherine to swing round and say between gritted teeth, "Diana is a child who, like all of us, responds favourably to those who treat her well. And I decide upon her punishment."

She was aware of her mother watching tensely at what appeared to be a growing public altercation. Derry looked horrified while Aunt Antoinette, Uncle Bertram, and Lord Quamby simply looked enthralled.

"My late son was Diana's father, *if you recall,* and he conveyed to me his express wish that his daughter's propensity to develop the wild, hoydenish ways of her mother be properly reined in." Lady Hale's bosom rose impressively. "You are proving unfit for the role of custodian, Katherine. I'm sorry to say it so publicly, but it's the truth." She sent a venomous look at the assembled company. "Freddy invested in me the power to make decisions that would be in the best interests of his child, and I'm fast coming to the conclusion that you, alone, Katherine, are completely unequal to the task of ensuring Diana grows into the well-behaved young lady of which he'd be proud."

"How dare you!"

Katherine felt a surge of gratitude at her mother for defending her with all the fierceness of a mother wolf defending her cub. She'd always looked to Aunt Antoinette for advice on the personal matters she felt uncomfortable discussing with her mother, but when it came down to it, when she needed her unconditional support, her darling, beloved mother was there to give it.

"Get out of this house, Lady Hale. If you feel you can slander my daughter and her abilities as a mother, you are not welcome here again."

Lady Hale's nostrils flared as she rounded on Lady Fenton. "This is not your house, Lady Fenton, just as I remind you again that I have the authority through my son's wishes from the dead, conveyed to a solicitor, that I have equal say in Diana's welfare." She swung round to Katherine. "You've courted scandal since my dear son died, yet you've done nothing to put an end to the gossip surrounding you and Lord Derry. Of course, there are more than just whispers about your reputation, since Lord Derry has been on the scene since before you married Freddy. Lord knows, but it was a scandal you should entice my son to elope! Now you've whipped up the gossips with all your carryings-on with his lordship." She shot him a fierce look.

Katherine noticed one of the servants bending to whisper in Lord Quamby's ear before her loyal uncle interjected in his usual, affable manner, "I believe your carriage is waiting for you round the front, Lady Hale. We will inform you when Diana has been found, and she and Katherine can pay you a visit in the next couple of days. I'm so sorry for the inconvenience."

Lady Hale's eyes flashed at the subtle dismissal. She gathered her mantle around her and said, dignified, "I trust the child will be punished when she is found. Her lack of deference to her grandmother should not be tolerated."

"Have no qualms, Lady Hale," said Lord Quamby. "I'm sure we all concur that discipline should be meted out appropriate to the crime."

As soon as she'd gone, Katherine sank into her chair and put her hands to her face a moment before looking up at the assembled company. "I don't blame Diana for hiding. The woman is poison," she muttered. Lady Hale's threats were deeply troubling, but her propensity for vitriol had become well known to Katherine after her years of marriage to Freddy. Son and mother had never got along, and Katherine was surprised at the sudden interest Lady Hale was showing in Diana when she'd not been too troubled by whether or not she saw her granddaughter when Freddy had been alive. She did, after all, have three grandsons by her other sons, Freddy's brothers.

"Would you like me to help you look for her?" her mother offered, but Katherine declined. "I know where she is. I'll have a talk to her."

She rose and left to go to the blue room, calling along the way and surprised to find the kist where she'd thought to find her daughter, empty.

"Katherine."

She looked up to find Derry standing in the doorway. He closed the door behind him and took a few strides towards her, something in his expression sending a lurch of foreboding to her stomach.

"Please, Derry, I think you know my feelings—"

He cut her off. "Katherine, I think you have not accorded Lady Hale the power she has over Diana's future."

She shook her head. "No, Derry, it's not true. I am Diana's mother. Lady Hale has no power."

"Indeed she has. She's visited the solicitor and discussed her legal standing."

Katherine stared. "And why would she tell you that?"

He shrugged. "Her sensibilities are offended by what she terms your carrying-on with me, and she's afraid Diana may be tainted if you don't legalise our union."

"That's outrageous!"

He shrugged again. "I'm sorry for it, but it is the truth." He closed the gap between them and took her hands. "Katherine, you know how I feel about you."

"And you know how I feel about you," she whispered, raising her head to see his eyes clouded with unhappiness.

"Yet we could make each other happy," he suggested. "I know you don't love me, but it would be in Diana's best interests if you and I were wed."

"I am not responsible for the scandal attached to our—"

"Friendship," he supplied. "You and I know that's all it is but the rest of society has drawn its own conclusion. I'm sorry, Katherine. I would not have put you in such a position, but think of the future. Many unions grow strong from far shakier foundations. I think you and I could be like that. You're lonely...and it's not as if there is anyone else. Please, think about it."

She closed her eyes and gently pulled her hands away. Derry wasn't an unkind man. After all, she'd been drawn to him before she'd married Freddy. But she was not in love with him. And after seven years of knowing him, she knew she never would be.

"Miss Katherine! Miss Katherine! Katie says she seen Miss Diana." It was Mary, bursting into the room, her eyes red-rimmed.

Katherine stepped away from Derry and hoped the maid-servant wouldn't infer anything inappropriate may have passed between the two of them.

"Then tell me where she is."

"Katie says she were lookin' through the window when

she seen Miss Diana climb inter that other carriage that were 'ere. The one belongin' ter Mr Patmore."

"Lord, why didn't Katie stop her?"

"She says she thought Miss Diana were s'posed to be goin' on a carriage drive, an' wiv the two carriages behind each other—Lady Hale's an' Mr Patmore's—she didn't think 'bout whose was whose."

Derry glanced at his timepiece. "They've been gone some time. I wonder why they didn't just turn back when they discovered the child."

"P'raps Miss Diana fell asleep an' they didn't notice," Mary suggested, twisting her apron around her fingers. "'Tis a large carriage, an' she might 'ave climbed into one of them boxes strapped ter the back." She drew a quavering breath and said with growing alarm, "P'raps they don't know she's trapped an' bouncin' along. Oh, Lordy!"

Katherine bit down on her fingers as Derry said, "I came on horseback, and that's the fastest way to catch up with them." He strode to the door, turning, and clarified, "They were on the northern road heading for Patmore Farm? Right! I'll be off this instant to bring her home."

❧

Jack considered the dilemma. Odette was tired and emotional. She didn't want to return to London with the child, but he saw no alternative.

Sighing, he signalled to the coachman to stop by a road-side tavern.

"Some refreshment will do us all good," he said, persuading Odette to take his hand so he could help her out into the fresh air. Diana looked perfectly content curled up against the opposite door, but she leapt up exclaiming 'My favourite!' when he suggested they ask the tavern keeper if they perchance had apple pie.

She tucked her hand into his while Odette clung mulishly to his other arm, muttering, "It's just the kind of thing a daughter of Lady Marples would do."

"I'm sure I don't know what that's supposed to mean," Jack said mildly, raising his eyebrows at her.

"Just that your friend is impulsive and so is her daughter."

"Impulsive?" Jack took offence on Katherine's behalf though he tried to hide it.

"She eloped, for goodness' sake. Who but the most wild and impulsive young woman elopes! And now her name is linked in another unsuitable liaison, Jack," she said under her breath as they mounted the steps to the front door which was opened by a maidservant in a clean white apron over a print dress.

When Odette saw Jack's knitted brows, she said quickly, "I know you're very defensive of your friend Katherine, and I don't mean to malign her, but it's the truth, and you know very well that society considers her behaviour scandalous. It's not just me saying it. Poor Diana obviously needs someone to keep her in check."

"Oh, there *is* apple pie!" exclaimed Diana excitedly, breaking off a hurried separate conversation with the maidservant who'd been leading them up the corridor. "And they'll bring it to the private parlour." She looked as if she were on a grand adventure as she ran ahead into the room to which the maidservant led them.

The weight on Jack's shoulders intensified as he took a seat opposite Odette and Diana, who couldn't sit still she was so excited at the prospect of apple pie. He smiled when he caught her eye. Diana reminded him so much of Katherine.

Odette leant across the small space and shook her finger at Diana, her voice stern.

"You were very naughty to jump into a carriage when you didn't know who it belonged to or where it was going," she said. "What will your mother say?"

Diana leaned back in her chair. Her feet were dangling well off the ground, and she looked contemplative rather than contrite.

"She'd be cross," Diana agreed. Her lip began to tremble. She seemed suddenly to be reflecting on her actions rather than taking the adventure as it came. When she gazed into Jack's eyes her own looked bright with unshed tears. "I think maybe because I did what *she* did she'll be even crosser. Oh dear!"

"Well, at least your mother knew where her carriage was going," Odette muttered, obviously referring to Katherine's escapade seven years before. "You didn't, Diana. You could have got into awful trouble."

Diana shook her head and sat up straight. "Oh no, Mama *didn't* know where her carriage was taking her. That's why she'll be even crosser with me for doing what she did." As if a realisation had suddenly descended upon her, the little girl gasped, "I'll have a lifetime of sorrow." She suddenly burst into such tears of genuine fear and tragedy both Jack and Odette looked at each other in confusion before Jack reached across to pat the little girl's arm and say, "Of course you won't, Diana. We'll take you back to your Mama straight away."

She rubbed her reddened eyes and looked back at them. "After the apple pie?"

Jack smiled, wondering if he could press her on her enigmatic words, for a rather odd sensation had followed Diana's revelation, and he didn't know if it might also have registered with Odette.

"Naturally. You can have my serving as well, if you like."

It was as if the sun had lit her up from within. Jack swallowed, for Diana's smile was as genuine and without artifice as Katherine's had ever been; it sent him hurtling back in time. He remembered the pure joy he used to feel at the prospect of leaving the foundling home to see his old friend each week. Being welcomed by Katherine, running across the lawn to meet the dogcart in which he would invariably be conveyed had been like stepping into a magical kingdom.

"I'm sure your mother didn't threaten you with a lifetime of sorrow if you hid in someone else's carriage," he prompted mildly. "It's a rather unlikely thing to do."

Diana shrugged. "It's what Mama said she got when she got into the wrong carriage. She was punished with a lifetime of sorrow. Oh, goody! It's the apple pie!"

There was no opportunity now of getting into the specifics. Distracted by the little girl's words, Jack pushed across his plate of apple pie and imagined possible interpretations. Had Katherine inferred to Diana that she wished she'd not been so impulsive in choosing to jump into Diana's father's carriage that fateful night?

Or was there something more to it?

Odette clasped his hand, and he looked into her face, forcing himself to smile. She'd hate to know how often his thoughts dwelled on this little girl's mother, and how suddenly the past seemed to be in doubt.

As did the future.

"Ah, Jack, but you're a good man, sacrificing your apple pie to bring happiness to a perhaps not-so-deserving child, but one who is grateful nonetheless."

His betrothed's eyes sparkled at her attempt at humour, and Jack wondered if a similar analogy with regard to his own situation with Odette were not too dissimilar.

CHAPTER 25

With great irritation, Odette had just agreed that she and Jack had no choice but to return from whence they'd come in order to take Diana home when a short, sharp rap upon the door of the private parlour heralded the tavern keeper. Bringing up the rear was Lord Derry, who, after a quick glance about the room, settled his gaze upon Diana with relief.

"Lord, my girl, but you've set the cat among the pigeons with your carryings-on," he said, not unkindly but not in the ameliorating way that might have won him the child's approbation. "So! I have instructions from your distraught mother that when I find you you're to return immediately with me."

Diana rose to her feet with a vengeance. "With you? I will not!" She put her hands on her hips and stared directly at Jack. "I'm going with Mr Patmore. He already promised." She pointed a little finger accusingly at Jack. "He let me have his apple pie on condition I go home with him, and I gave my solemn pledge."

Odette seized her opportunity as she smoothed her mulberry and grey check skirts and jutted out her chin.

"You've already been so naughty as to run away, Diana. Of course you'll do as you're told and go with Lord Derry."

Jack looked dubiously at Derry's riding clothes. "You don't propose to put her in front of you and gallop all the way home, do you?"

Derry nodded, his look slighting, as if he disliked being called to account by a sapling like Jack. "She's as light as a feather, and it'll not do her any harm."

Jack stared from the indignant and reluctant child to the older man while concern niggled. "Surely Katherine didn't expect Diana would be jolted all the way home with..." He was going to say someone she hardly knows, but supposed this was not true. Perhaps it was why Diana did not wish to go with him.

Lord Derry hovered near the doorway impatiently. "It'll be less than an hour on horseback, and the sooner I can put her mama's mind at rest, the better. They still don't know where she is, of course, and are in quite a panic. Come, Diana. You love an adventure!" He said this with an enthusiasm that had no influence upon Diana.

She looked at Lord Derry disdainfully, and in that moment, Jack realised he must be the one to win Diana over. Not just for her but for her mother's sake.

He crossed the room and knelt down in front of her. "Miss Worthington and I can take you back in our carriage," he said cajolingly. "It'll be much more comfortable. Lord Derry can ride ahead to tell your mama. How does that sound?"

Before Odette could respond, a commotion in the passage was followed by another arrival. Jack glanced up as the tavern keeper's wife swept into the room followed by a large, voluble middle-aged woman loudly declaring her pleasure to discover that Miss Worthington was in residence.

Her bonnet was trimmed with more roses than Jack had

ever seen and her purple gown was expensive and vulgar yet Odette greeted her like an old friend, rising quickly and clapping her hands.

"Mrs Monks. Why, I haven't seen you in more than a year," she exclaimed, smiling warmly and introducing the woman as their former neighbour and dear friend of her late mother's. When she established that Mrs Monks was resting for the day before resuming her journey to London the following morning, Odette was quick to suggest that Jack could take Diana in the carriage while she remain.

"I'm very tired after the long journey, Jack, and if Mrs Monks is here until tomorrow, I shall be perfectly well looked after while you're gone." Odette sank into a seat opposite her new chaperone and smiled up at Jack as if the matter was already settled. "Lord Derry can ride ahead to reassure everyone at Quamby House that Diana is safe, or send a message."

To Jack's surprise, the idea of travelling alone and not having to keep up small talk with Odette was liberating.

He hesitated and Mrs Monks said warmly, "Excellent arrangement, Odette. Now do join us for refreshment, Lord Derry. I knew your dear mama, you know."

Jack rather thought she meant that she knew *of* Derry's mama. He couldn't imagine the two on an equal social footing.

He was glad that Odette seemed comfortable with the new plan and surprised that she didn't think it vulgar when Mrs Monks glanced about the sitting room with approval, saying, "This will do very well for an old woman to rest her weary body, and you shall be just the panacea I need, Odette, after having to listen to my husband who is now snoring upstairs!"

Derry looked less than enamoured of the idea of spending

time in her company, Jack noticed, quickening his pace towards the door in case Odette changed her mind.

"I shall be back within a few hours," he promised, "if you're certain you don't wish to accompany me."

He was relieved when she shook her head while Mrs Monks suggested that she and her husband could take Odette in their carriage and deliver her to Patmore Farm if Jack was delayed. It was an offer Jack wasn't going to refuse though he told himself he wasn't going to linger at Quamby House. Not even to talk to Katherine.

"So, are you ready, Diana?" he asked, surprised at the enthusiasm in his tone.

She nodded, clearly much happier with the arrangement to leave with Jack rather than Derry.

"You make sure you apologise to your mama, young lady," Derry said, finally lowering himself into a chair opposite Odette and Mrs Monks, and clearly relinquishing Diana as his responsibility for he turned eagerly as refreshment was offered.

Jack wondered what Katherine's reaction back at Quamby House would be. He found it odd to think of her as a mother with cares and responsibilities when she still looked so much like the innocent girl he'd fallen in love with.

Fallen in love with. The thought caught him by surprise and he made a mental note to remember how long ago that had been. And that she was a friend. Only.

They were halfway home when the coachman unexpectedly drew to a halt.

When Jack put his head out to ask the reason, he was told that Lord Quamby's carriage was coming towards them. Indeed, as he recognised the handsome equipage that had stopped just in front of them, a well dressed woman stepped out and onto the road.

"Jack! I knew you'd find her!" Lady Quamby called out

gaily, as Jack opened his door and climbed out to greet Katherine's aunt.

He was disappointed, he found, that in all good conscience, he could relinquish Diana to her aunt.

Which would mean he'd not see Katherine.

"Lady Quamby, your hunch was correct." Quickly, he explained the arrangements that had been put in place then turned to call for Diana. However, when he started to tell the child that her aunt and, as it turned out, her Uncle Bertram, too, would take her to Quamby House, Lady Quamby interrupted with a trill of laughter. "I really have no wish to retrace my footsteps, Jack. Would you be so good as to save us the journey and take Diana back to London? Bertram and I are on our way Patmore Farm, in fact. We were confident you'd find Diana and all would be well. We'll see you at your parents' home, then?" She smiled hopefully.

Jack hesitated, desire to comply warring with what he knew to be the safest course. A great deal of potential heartache could be avoided if he simply turned around and went back to Odette. He realised this now as he recognised the disappointment he felt at being denied a chance to see Katherine again.

Jack was a sensible man. And he had made his bed.

Just as Katherine had all those years ago.

"Odette is waiting for me at the Northcote Arms about half an hour from here. No doubt she'll be bored if not anxious."

"I thought you said just now that Lord Derry was keeping her company." Bertram Brightwell had now brought his portly self to bear, smiling benignly at Jack from over his sister's shoulder.

"Lord Derry is with her, that's correct—"

"Then she's being entertained as well as she might be. Chaperoned, of course, by Mrs Monks," he added quickly.

"Well chaperoned, but no doubt anxious to resume her journey."

"And what a happy situation that we are going to the very same destination," declared Lady Quamby. "Such a lovely girl, your Odette is. I feel I don't know her as well as I would like to, and this will prove the perfect opportunity. You were always so dear to us, Jack, and we'd like very much to further our acquaintance with the wife you've chosen." Lady Quamby ruffled Diana's hair, which earned her a scowl and then a smile as Diana's aunt said, "You don't mind continuing to see your mother in the company of Mr Patmore, do you, Diana?"

She shook her head. "Not if he tells me more about the elephants in India which I could ride if I lived there. He's very interesting."

"Just as Lord Derry is!" Bertram said robustly.

"Lord Derry is very boring. He's never ridden an elephant." Diana put her nose in the air. "And he only wants to talk to Mama, besides."

Jack felt a small tug in his chest cavity. Lord Derry would soon marry Katherine. He was besotted, and little wonder.

"But Mama doesn't want to talk to Lord Derry. She says she has to, though."

"Goodness, child. What a thing to say!" said her aunt, and Jack would have expected her to shut down whatever indiscretion might be about to issue from Diana's mouth. Instead, she prompted, "Why does your mama have to talk to Lord Derry if she doesn't want to?"

A furtive look crossed Diana's face as she hesitated. "Mama might be cross if I tell."

"Oh, not if you tell *me*," Lady Quamby assured her, leaning down to her level so that the flowers in her bonnet trembled like a bouquet in the breeze. Jack had to admire the woman for her style. And her subtle insistence on having her way which she achieved through the greatest charm. "Your mama knows how anxious I am to help. Tell me why you think your mama feels she has to talk to Lord Derry if she doesn't want to."

Diana gave a loud sigh and pursed her lips. "Mama always has to be nice to Lord Derry. Papa told her she had to."

"Really?"

Jack's ears felt like they were burning. While he wanted to know more, he understood Katherine would not be happy to learn her daughter was so happy to divulge that which was probably not intended to be public knowledge.

Diana nodded as she clasped her hands demurely in front of her and said, "Lord Derry helped Papa when he had his cribbage crisis so mama had to be nice to him."

"Oh...my goodness, Diana. *Cribbage Crisis?* Are you sure?" There was a definite note of prurient interest in Lady Quamby's question.

"Of course. I heard everything," replied the little girl who looked like she was enjoying the attention. Her tone became more enthusiastic. "I was hiding under the chair by the window. They didn't know I was there, but Mama said she didn't want to do what Papa said because it would put her in a comp... " she struggled with the word, agreeing happily when Lady Quamby suggested, 'compromising', then adding, "but Papa said it was the only way, and she had to. Now now Mama has to always be nice to Lord Derry." She turned to Jack. "Will you tell me more elephant stories, Mr Patmore?"

"Only if you're very sure you want to come along with me," he said cautiously. "I'd hate you to dislike the idea of talking to me—"

"Oh, you're much more interesting than Lord Derry," Diana assured him, turning back towards his carriage and waving to her aunt. "Besides, if I have to go with Aunt Antoinette I know Uncle Bertram will start snoring as soon as the carriage starts moving, and he does make such a terrible noise when he does that. I'm sure it's the main reason he has such trouble with the ladies."

"Snoring? I'm sure I don't!" protested Bertram, but Jack was too caught up with his own musings to take much notice. Since he'd tried everything to get out of delivering Diana, he couldn't possibly be blamed for the time he would be able to spend with her mother. Courtesy would demand that he furnish Katherine with the answers to all her no-doubt anxious questions.

"Please reassure Odette I'll return as quickly as is practicable," he said, helping Diana into the carriage.

"I rather think she'll enjoy a little respite. You and she have been inseparable since you returned, and that's certainly not a healthy way to start married life." Lady Quamby nodded decisively before she turned back to her own carriage.

Jack was just thinking the same as he closed the door behind him, before he was immediately called upon to give a full accounting of all the animals he'd seen, ridden, shot or eaten when in the Far East.

But even while he spoke at great length in the most descriptive terms, his mind was dwelling on his forthcoming encounter with Katherine and how much he was looking forward to witnessing her joy at seeing him emerge from the carriage with her daughter.

He was familiar with all her expressions and his favourite was the look of pleasure that crossed her face when she encountered someone she cared for deeply.

Like when she'd seen Jack again after so many years. There was a magical quality to their encounter in the darkness seven years ago. He thought of that disembodied kiss, often. It had sustained through much loneliness during his time away.

And her pleasure at seeing him after he'd returned with Odette sent tendrils of warmth coursing through his body.

Quickly, he reminded himself how easily firm friendship that lasted forever could be mistaken for the transient affection of the heart.

Yes, he was indeed lucky to be able to claim Katherine as a friend for life. He was sure Odette understood they were almost like kin.

So Jack could see Katherine, innocently and respectably, whenever he wanted and there'd be nothing untoward in their fond reunion when he arrived at Quamby House after his journey.

The thought should have been comforting.

But it wasn't.

***

KATHERINE WHO'D BEEN WAITING FEARFULLY AT QUAMBY House for news of her daughter, saw the carriage turn into the driveway from her position at the window. She flew down the corridor and out of the front door, reaching the bottom of the steps as the carriage drew up.

"Diana!" she cried, whisking her daughter into her arms and raining kisses upon her head before the little girl had stepped onto firm ground. "What were you thinking? You weren't, were you? What could have possessed you to climb into a strange carriage? Do you have any idea where you could have ended up?"

"I wouldn't have minded, as long as it wasn't with grandmother. And Mr Patmore's told me wonderful stories and given me apple pie. He's very nice, Mama." She paused and sent Katherine a searching look. "Don't you think so?"

Katherine felt a very sharp tug at her heartstrings. She ventured a glance at Jack. "He is," she agreed, clearing her throat, then looking at him more directly before she had the courage to put her hand on his arm. "I don't know how to thank you, Jack."

"I put no conditions on helping where I can," he said, sounding surprisingly formal though something in his gaze was at odds with his pronouncement.

Nevertheless, Katherine winced. "I must get Diana up to the nursery. It's been a long day for her but do say you'll stay a while. You can't be thinking to return immediately." To her consternation, Jack had cast several glances at his carriage as if that was exactly what he intended doing.

"Jack! We're serving tea in the conservatory. Do come and join us!"

Katherine was glad her mother had made the offer sound impossible to refuse. She was afraid that her own entreaties would have sounded a note that sat ill with his notion of what duty required of him. Odette was, mercifully, not with him but the pull she exerted was apparent. Duty was like the dead spouse whose memory must be served up at the appropriate times to preserve propriety, she thought suddenly.

"Katherine, go and see to Diana. I'm sure you don't want to say all that needs to be said here for all the world to hear. I'll take Jack to the conservatory." Lady Fenton's hand was firmly about Jack's upper arm as she began to lead him into the house.

There, he couldn't refuse now, could he? Katherine thought with a surge of desperation that he stay.

With as much haste as was seemly, Katherine returned from upstairs where she'd transferred Diana into the capable hands of her nursemaid, who was ecstatic to see her young charge safe and in her usual bright spirits. "I'll be back soon to have a proper talk with you about the decisions you made today, Diana," she said, trying hard to sound stern but desperate to leave in case Jack should be gone before she returned.

To her relief, he was ensconced in the conservatory with her parents, but not long after Katherine arrived her mother said, somewhat abruptly, "Jack, do you remember the old almond tree?"

He looked surprised. "I spent a lot of time eating cake up in its branches."

"With Katherine. Yes, I always knew where to look to find her. Katherine, why don't you take Jack to see the almond tree? I'm sure he'd enjoy such a visit into the past. I thought I might find Diana there. What a naughty child!" But she said it with a twinkle in her eye.

Katherine felt a jolt of excitement at the idea of leading Jack, with her mother's sanction, to the almond tree, though surely her mother realised the mission was hopeless.

She was even more convinced of this when she saw Jack's obvious reluctance. "I think Jack wants to be on the road before too long," she said, eyeing him. "He's worried about Odette."

"Fiddlesticks! Odette now has three chaperones: Mrs Monks, Antoinette, and Bertram and it's highly likely they're already with Eliza who's now happily ensconced at Patmore Farm and waiting to welcome Jack to his old home. Jack's been on the road all day. He must be exhausted. Of course he can't turn right around and begin another tedious stretch of travel straight away. Now, you two go to the almond tree and tell me if you don't suddenly feel like children again."

Katherine sent Jack a stricken look as she raised her eyes. Her mother was *treating* them like children. Furthermore, she was adopting that tone that suggested she not only had a plan but matters well in hand and was confident of a happy outcome.

The only positive aspect of all this was that it was clear

Lady Fenton sanctioned Jack over Lord Derry, but she'd clearly not factored in the strength of Jack's attachment to Odette.

Still, a little kernel of hope lodged in Katherine's heart as she saw the betraying flicker of longing in Jack's eye. He did want to go to the almond tree with her. He did want to be alone with her. Had his time in the carriage with Diana given him a different perspective on how their futures might be?

A twist of pain, longing and fear burrowed into her and nervously she smoothed her hands over her skirts. Had he realised whose child Diana really was? Would it be enough to make him relinquish his ties to Odette? Katherine couldn't tell him. It would be coercion, but if he deduced it himself...

By the time Katherine had risen and was at the door beside Jack, a myriad of possibilities had flowered in her breast. Maybe her mother was right in not simply accepting as Katherine had done—that Jack was irrevocably pledged to Odette.

She barely knew what to say as they walked silently, side by side, towards the almond tree by the lake.

It was only natural they stop and turn to face one another when they were beneath its laden branches.

Without hesitating, Jack put his hands on Katherine's forearms and looked her in the eye. In the distance, the clouds had amassed, grey and darkening, while a gentle breeze stirred her hair and brushed her cheek; just as she wished Jack would do in that wonderful, familiar way of his when he was talking to her.

In the moment before he opened his mouth to speak, she tried to read what was in his heart. It was a better gauge than what he might say to her, she feared, and yet she could still hope. It was all she had left.

"Katherine." Her name hung in the air. He cleared his

throat as if what he had to say were momentous but he had no idea how to go on.

She stared at him. Waiting. *Say it, Jack. Tell me you love me for that's the truth. Tell me whatever else you have to say for Odette's sake, but at least say what's in your heart,* she silently willed him.

At last he spoke. "A year ago, I acknowledged to my employer at the time, Charles Worthington, that I owed him a great debt. My success, my reputation as a man of business, was all due to him."

So this was how it would be. There would be no words of affection to soften the blow. No words of affection that might blossom into a mutual recognition of what they might share together. The hope that had bloomed so suddenly just minutes earlier was just as quickly cut off at the root. Katherine dropped her eyes. What was the point in hearing him out? He was letting her down, as gently as he could.

"And that is when you pledged your loyalties: to him *and* to Odette?" she interrupted, softly. "There is no need to go on, Jack. Please don't try to save my feelings or my dignity."

She was more wounded than she'd have allowed.

He looked into her eyes and she saw pain and conflict in their depths. "Katherine, if circumstances had allowed it—if Odette's father weren't dying and I hadn't made a promise—I would sacrifice my life to be with you." His words hitched. "But if I ignore those realities, I'd be sacrificing much more: my honour, my pride, my dignity. And without those, I am nothing. Whatever was left would be worthless to you. Please understand."

"Am I so transparent, Jack?"

"That your heart belongs to me?" He gripped her arms tighter. His voice rose and for the first time she saw cracks in his self control as he struggled to push out the words. A whisper of wind stirred the branches dislodging a flurry of droplets. "At first I could hardly hope to believe it might be true. When I kissed you last, Katherine, it was an accident...a fatal accident. I tried to remind myself of my duty to Odette, but I could think only of you."

"I felt the same, Jack. I..." She wanted to tell him so much more of what she felt. To unburden her heart would have been cathartic, but he seemed reluctant to hear it for he put his finger to her lips as he pressed his own together.

"Katherine. Sweetheart, it's impossible. You know that."

She stared. She knew it. She should have known it, but it was a torment to hear him put into words.

"I shan't marry Derry," she whispered.

A spasm of pain crossed his face. He shook his head. "You owe Derry an obligation that he's calling upon you to fulfil. I suspected as much from what Diana said."

Katherine nodded. "But I shan't marry him, Jack. I don't care about my reputation."

There, maybe if she told him how much she was prepared to sacrifice he'd be prepared to do the same.

"Katherine! Don't do this to me, I beg of you," he muttered, a shuttered look coming into his eyes as he stared over her shoulder before returning his gaze to her face. "Your reputation will suffer, and you will be ostracised, but it will be bearable if the alternative is to wed a man you do not love. My punishment will be at the cost of my soul. Do you not see?" He shook her gently even as he pulled her slightly closer. "I cannot abandon Odette. I simply cannot and still call myself a gentleman. A man of honour. Even though you are as dear to me as anyone I have ever known, even though I need you like the air I need to breathe, I cannot wed you at the cost of Odette's happiness."

"What about my happiness?" she whispered through tears. She'd thought she'd be stronger than this when the moment came but the devastation of learning how baseless was the hope that had sustained her was almost more than she could bear.

"I'd bring you no happiness, Katherine. Not if I despised myself. And I would. You know I would."

She did. It's which stopped her from revealing everything. What use would it be to heap further torment upon him when he was tormented enough already? She knew he loved her. She could feel it through the pressure of his hands; through the intensity of his look.

It began to rain. The gentle shower caused a steady drip through the branches, but they could not break away.

"I will release you, Jack," she whispered brokenly. "I'll do it quietly, and I'll accept it." She drew in a painful breath. "On one condition."

He tilted his head. Afraid? Hopeful?

"That you kiss me."

❧

HE'D SACRIFICED SO MUCH, BUT HE COULD NOT SACRIFICE this—not his last opportunity to hold the girl he loved in his arms and expedite her last request; the only demand she'd ever placed on him. Katherine was pure and good and did not deserve the pain he promised her if he came to her as half the man he could have been. Should have been.

For Odette, he could be enough. He could live with that in order to draw the delicate balance between living with his desires and succumbing to his demons.

It was to be a gentle kiss upon the lips, immediately withdrawn before he'd make his excuses and leave. Honour could be served if he managed that and only that.

But the sweet, gentle pressure communicated too great a memory. The touch of Katherine's lips sent fingers of need and memory silently, invisibly, searching deep within the hidden depths he'd revealed to no one but her. Grasping, searching, drawing out of his very soul all that he'd locked away for so long: his need for connection; a connection only Katherine had ever satisfied.

His arms tightened about her shoulders as he drew her well-remembered curves against his chest. Her lips parted beneath his, soft and yielding while her hands strayed to his face, touching his cheeks in a tender display of affection that brought the memories of their stolen moments all those years ago crashing over him. He'd been embarking on adventures bigger than their love. So he'd thought. He'd needed to prove himself, both to himself and to the world—and he'd done that.

But at what cost?

Losing Katherine?

With a groan, he dragged his mouth from hers and stared into her luminous face.

"I've always loved you, Jack."

She hadn't said it to make him stay. Or to make his decision harder, he knew that.

Katherine spoke the simple truth.

"And I love you, Katherine." He dragged in a breath. "But I can never have you."

The rain had increased in intensity, and a soft rumble of thunder made them raise their heads and stare at the hills over which grey storm clouds were rolling.

"It reminds me of the West Indies," he said , taking her hand and squeezing it gently before he released it. "I thought of you whenever a storm rolled in. You'd have loved it."

"I'd have gone with you if you'd asked me."

He smiled and brushed back a strand of wet hair from her cheek. Though light, the rain was dense. "It was not a life for a young girl. I told myself that often enough when I wished I *had* asked you. Come." He started to walk, turning and holding out his hand to her, but not to make contact. He couldn't afford to do that.

It was safer if they talked as they made their return to the house. With no physical contact. He'd need to be on the road shortly if he were to make it to Patmore Farm before nightfall. "Besides, you were testing the competition with some enthusiasm, if I recall." Levity might make their conversation more bearable.

"Freddy?"

He slid a glance across towards her darkened expression. "I'm sorry, Katherine. Sorry it was not the marriage for which you'd hoped."

"It was a marriage I'd never intended," she muttered. "But there it is, Jack. We cannot change the past, can we?"

"I would to God we could." Jack stopped in the middle of the lawn, suddenly overcome with the need to communicate his longing when before he'd been intent more on communicating the reasons why their love could never be. "Or the timing, Katherine. I said if you ever needed me, you had only to call on me, and now that you do need me, I cannot give you what you want."

"I only want it if you want it too, Jack. If you want it enough, that is." She turned her head away and continued walking b his side, saying just so he could hear, "But...pay me no heed. I've become churlish when your parting kiss should have been everything I needed to sustain me." She stopped as they reached the gravel drive that skirted the house and turned abruptly, her tears mingling with the raindrops. "I'm sorry, Jack. I didn't mean to make this harder than it is already. You are a good man. An honourable man. That's why I love you, I suppose. But I understand what you've told me. And I understand that now it's time to say goodbye."

CHAPTER 26

Back at the Northcote Arms, Antoinette and Bertram were becoming increasingly frustrated by the lack of progress in expediting their plan. They'd not told Jack they planned to detour via the Northcome Arms en route to Patmore Farm. That would have smacked of collusion though surely the young man understood the lengths to which they'd go in order to reunite the childhood sweethearts.

"They've barely spoken a word to one another, Bertram," Antoinette hissed as she went to the window in order to examine the approaching bad weather, calling her brother to her side, supposedly to get his opinion.

The siblings glanced over their shoulder at Miss Worthington and Lord Derry, who both appeared to be gazing into space, while they sipped tea. Mrs Monks had returned to her bedchamber.

Bertram scrunched up his face as he contemplated the matter. "Leave it to me," he said after a pause.

"Oh dear, that's what you said last time." Antoinette bit her lip. "And poor Aunt Brightwell ended up in a hot-air

236

balloon with dreadful George Bramley trying to make love to her thinking it was Thea."

"Ah, but you missed the point, Antoinette." Bertram scratched his nose and darted another glance at the unresponsive Miss Worthington and Lord Derry. "That was a necessary if unfortunate precursor to Thea and Grayling pledging their troth. It was all part of the grand scheme of things, for you know as well as I that matters must become very dire before all is happily resolved."

"Well, since the weather is hardly conducive to sending anyone up in a hot-air balloon, what do you suggest?" Antoinette felt increasingly dejected as time ticked by. At this rate, Jack would be back to fetch his intended, and Katherine would forever be denied the love she deserved. If she had to admit what was truly in her heart, Antoinette did feel somewhat culpable for what had happened all those years before. But how could she have known Katherine and Jack were so utterly in love when Katherine had kept it such a secret?

She put her hand to her head, toying with the floral trimming as she sought for inspiration. And, suddenly, it came to her. "We'll push her down the stairs!"

"Miss Worthington? Good God, Antoinette, even I would not countenance something so extreme!"

"I don't mean murder her, for God's sake, Bertram. What do you take me for?" Antoinette shook her head. "I mean so she sustains a little injury and Lord Derry has to look after her, after which he'll become inevitably attached. It happened very successfully in a book I've been reading. In *Pride and Prejudice,* the dreadful matchmaking mama sends her daughter Jane off on horseback when she *knew* it was going to rain, and sure enough, the girl got soaked and caught a chill so spent a week as a guest of her hero during which time he fell in love with her. Just as her mama had hoped would happen."

An approving look crept into Bertram's eye and he nodded. "So, who shall do it? You or I?"

A bit of throat clearing from the other side of the room was followed by: "Weather's not looking so good. I'd best be on my way now that my horse has been fed and rested."

Antoinette swung round to face Derry who was rising from a bow in Odette's direction.

Bertram made a strange noise before he hurried forwards, running his fingers around the inside of his collar. "Did you not hear, old chap? The message wasn't passed on?"

"What's this?" Derry frowned as he straightened.

"Your horse. Poor creature's lame. I was sure the message had come straight to you that the ostler was trying to rustle up a replacement."

"Odin's lame?" Derry repeated, a touch of urgency straining his voice as he strode towards the door.

Bertram waylaid him, almost barrelling into him as he rushed to put his hand on the door knob first. "Very minor, but he can't turn about in this weather and churned-up mud, can he, now?" He sent Derry a meaningful look. "You just see to Miss Worthington and I'll bring back a report. I was off to the stables myself, in fact, as we need to ensure we're set to continue our journey with no delays. Antoinette!"

She sprang to attention, relieved that Bertram had come up with this interim plan. It was obviously up to her now to smooth the way. "Odette, I see you've finished your tea. Perhaps we should continue onwards to Patmore Farm." A sudden thought assailed her. "Lord Derry, your estate is very close, is it not? And the rain is not *so* very bad. I'm sure Miss Worthington would love nothing more than to view Derry House. After all, her in-laws will be your neighbours within an hour's carriage ride."

Lord Derry hesitated and scratched his head, thinking. There was a slightly harried look about him, as if the condition of his horse had blinded him to the immediate social niceties required. Still, he managed to turn to Miss Worthington and say with commendable charm, "Would you indeed like to pay a call to Derry House along the way, Miss Worthington? It would be but a ten-minute detour."

"What a splendid idea!" Antoinette clapped her hands together. "Odin may well only need just a *little* more rest, but of course you can procure a mount from your own stables and then choose to return to London in the morning. Lord Derry, you will, of course, come with us in our carriage. I'll see that Mrs Monks is informed."

The plan was considered an excellent one to suit the circumstances, and within the hour, the party was drawing up in front of the portico of Derry House.

As the double doors were thrown open by the stately butler, Antoinette slid Odette a surreptitious look and was rewarded by the awe on her face. Derry House was indeed colossal, and although the girl was to inherit a fortune when her papa died, the family's money came from trade. A landed estate would be her dream, Antoinette imagined. And her father's dream, too.

"Such a sweet place you have, Derry," Antoinette said as her host helped her out of the carriage, then reached in an arm to draw Odette out into the increasingly heavy rain, holding up an umbrella to shield her from the weather.

They hurried up the stairs and into the lofty hallway where the ladies were relieved of their mantles and the men of their coats and hats.

"Do tell Odette the history of your home, Derry," Antoinette pressed him as they were shown into the drawing room where a crackling fire was a welcome contrast to the deteriorating weather. "The original part is more than three hundred years old, is that not so?"

With obvious pride, Lord Derry expanded on the role his

family had played during the Civil War, losing their home in the middle of the seventeenth century when the Roundheads were victorious, but having it returned and being awarded additional lands when a new king was returned to the throne some ten years later.

"But of course, Odette, you also will be mistress of a fine home which Jack has purchased with the fortune he has made," said Antoinette as they were served Madeira once they'd settled themselves. "He has made his money just like your father, and although there are those who spurn trade, you have a great deal to thank him for, namely his business acumen." She took a sip and smiled at Derry, adding, "Everything simply landed in your lap, eh, Derry? And now you're looking for a wife, and if my hunch is correct, my niece will become mistress of all this." She waved an expansive arm about her, conscious of the scandalised look Odette sent her, and the rather startled expression on Lord Derry's face. Still, he didn't seem to take offence, and in fact appeared relieved when Antoinette suggested he take Odette on a tour of the lofty building.

"Lordy, I don't know how that went," muttered Bertram when they'd gone. "But at least they're alone."

"And at least I've sown the seed." Antoinette, who was more than ready for an aperitif, searched for the bell pull. "This is just the kind of estate Odette would aspire to. And don't you think Odette is just the kind of wife Derry needs? One with a great fortune—regardless of where it comes from. Katherine, by contrast, brings nothing."

Betram nodded gloomily and Antoinette exhaled gustily before adding, "*We* know Jack and Katherine are perfect for one another, but will *they* discover it in time?"

WHILE ANTOINETTE WAS DETERMINED NOT TO LOSE HOPE in her plan to achieve her niece's happiness through throwing Derry and Odette together, her sister was fast losing hope as she stared through the Quamby House's rain-flecked drawing room window and took in the expressions of her daughter and the handsome young gentleman she'd hoped would be her husband.

With a sigh she turned to her husband who was reading the newspaper in his favourite wing back armchair before the fire. "I'd so hoped sending them to the apple tree would rekindle memories that couldn't be denied. But Katherine and Jack look as if they're carrying the woes of the entire world upon their shoulders. Oh Fenton, darling, I can't bear it!"

At the first hint of genuine distress, Fenton was always Fanny's greatest stalwart. Now he was at her side in an instant, his arm about her shoulders as he followed her gaze. He sighed and when he spoke his tone as bleak as Fanny's. "Honourable fellow's just ended anything there might have been between them," he muttered. "I can see it on his face."

Fanny turned into her husband's embrace. Fenton was her rock. He teased her when she took things too seriously but he was always the first to understand the gravity of something like this. "Oh Fenton, darling! Katherine has been miserable for seven years! She deserves to be loved as *she* loves. To see her last opportunity snatched away is just too terrible. Oh, George!" She stopped abruptly, uncomfortable to discover her sister's son hovering in the doorway. It wasn't often George looked ill at ease. He had the kind of bravado that meant he brazened anything out, and walking in to see his aunt looking distressed was likely to do the opposite of tugging at his heartstrings, she thought.

He took a few steps forward as he followed the trajectory

of their vision through the window. "Jack didn't tell me he was coming back," he said.

"I'm sure Jack doesn't have to inform you of his movements," Fanny said tartly. She disliked George intensely and was sure he would revel in Katherine's unhappiness if he knew.

"No, of course not." George frowned as he took up position at the next window and Fanny wondered what he thought of the scene. It seemed suddenly prurient to be observing Katherine and Jack when they had no idea they were being watched. They were walking side by side, heads lowered, expressions glum. There was none of the joyful luminosity Fanny had hoped to see wash over her daughter's face.

George cleared his throat. "I thought I should mention that Lady Hale is back again. She's in the hall asking after Diana."

Fanny shot George a sharp look. "We could well do without that meddlesome creature at such a time, couldn't we?"

Fenton was more ameliorating. "Come now, Fanny, she's the girl's grandmother. Of course Lady Hale would want to learn news of Diana. And here she is," he added in a lowered tone before saying expansively, "Good afternoon, Lady Hale. Yes, what good news Diana has been found, isn't it? And you look as up to the mark as ever."

❧

KATHERINE DIDN'T THINK SHE COULD BEAR IT. NO SOONER had she and Jack parted, Jack to go to the stables in preparation for leaving, and she to return to the house, than she was hailed by the unwelcome tones of her mother-in-law.

The black bombazine-clad figure with her black spotted net veil was like a harbinger of doom

"You'll be pleased to know, Lady Hale, that Diana has been found, safe and sound," Katherine pre-empted the old lady who was advancing towards her on the gravel path. She forced a smile even though her heart was breaking. Jack was about to leave and he was never coming back.

"I heard the naughty child climbed into a stranger's carriage and was whisked miles away!" Lady Hale cried, her voice shrill. She looked like a formidable galleon in swathes of grey and black silk bearing down on her. "What is she being taught of common sense and how to make wise decisions, I ask? That girl needs a firmer hand." Lady Hale drew level as she continued to berate Katherine.

"Diana is only six, and she knew the carriage belonged to someone visiting." Katherine tried to keep her tone mild. "It was unfortunate that we had the worry of it, but she was never in any danger."

"Ah, but she might have been, Katherine. She might have been in very grave danger. A husband is what you want, Katherine. A husband with a firm hand is what you and the child both *need*."

It was hard to pay attention, for Katherine could hear the shouts of the stablehands and clink of harness from the stables behind as they prepared the conveyance Jack was taking back to Patmore Farm. She knew he'd have preferred to have ridden. He'd have covered the distance in a very short time, and his riding would be confined to his own pleasure. Odette was not a horsewoman. She disliked horses, and a carriage that shielded her as much as possible from the creatures would have to be the consideration from here on. Jack would expend a lot of effort to ensure his bride enjoyed the creature comforts with which her indulgent papa had showered her, but Katherine doubted he'd even look out of the window to wave in parting to the woman he loved. For she knew that he loved her.

"Yes, but I'm not looking for a husband," Katherine said, tightly. "I'm still in mourning for your son."

Lady Hale made some noise that denoted disapproval. "Not that anyone would know it," she said, looking pointedly at Katherine's gown that, while black, was brightened by the colourful Indian shawl Jack had sent her during his travels.

"Well, I don't know how you can suggest I marry again at this juncture of my life when Freddy is barely cold in the ground." The words sounded cruel and harsh as they fell upon the air, frosting in front of Katherine's face like a reproach in the gathering cold. She raised her face quickly to Lady Hale to apologise but met a beetling look and the surprising response, "Freddy was a good-for-nothing. We both know that. It's why you need to find a replacement who'll treat you with the respect you deserve."

Katherine gasped out loud as Lady Hale went on, "Freddy was an inveterate gambler and had no compunction in taking his pleasure without conscience. The night I heard he'd eloped, I felt both pain and pleasure, Katherine, I'll be honest."

Katherine's heart beat quickly. She could hear the sound of carriage wheels on gravel behind her and knew it must be Jack, but Lady Hale was facing her down with words that were so painful and loaded with prophecy and portent she couldn't turn around. She might crumple into a heap of despair if she did.

She bunched her hands into fists to give her strength, and closed her eyes as the irony of the situation engulfed her. Jack —the future she'd wanted the whole of her adult life—was passing behind her at this very moment, and she couldn't feast her eyes upon him one last time because the mother of the wastrel she'd married pinioned her like a butterfly with the words that revealed her estimation of her own son was as bad as Katherine's.

"Pain...because I wondered how long it would take before the young woman he'd tricked into marriage realised the deadly error of her impulsiveness, and pleasure...because at last I could share the worry over Freddy's antics with someone else."

"I was married to Freddy for seven years..." Katherine took a deep breath and sent Lady Hale a combative look. "And I do not think I'll marry again."

"You have a child to consider, Katherine. Freddy's daughter and Freddy, as a husband, is as strong beyond the grave as he ever was in life. His dictates will be taken very seriously in a court of law, and you know what his wishes were as regards Diana."

For a few moments, Katherine had believed her mother-in-law stood in solidarity with her. Some of her dislike had melted away, but now it hardened, encasing her heart as she muttered, "Freddy ceded decisions surrounding Diana to you, it is true, but you've never shown any great interest in her. Why would you take her away from me?"

Lady Hale drew back her shoulders. "I don't want the care of the child, it's true. But I want to see her future is guided well, Katherine. I want a responsible man at the helm. Not a string of fly-by-admirers who'll mire both you and Diana increasingly in scandal and erode my granddaughter's chances of making a good marriage."

"You have so little regard for my morals?" Katherine asked, outraged.

"Your family has not been renowned for lofty morals, Katherine."

Katherine turned on her heel and began to walk away. There was no answer to this. Her mother-in-law had gone too far by tainting the entire Brightwell clan with her outrageous claim. As she raised her head, she saw Jack's carriage turning out onto the main road that led north towards Patmore Farm. She stopped to stare.

What was left for her now? If she couldn't have the man she loved, she had only her daughter to brighten her dull days.

"Marry Lord Derry and I'll not instigate a claim for Diana!"

Lady Hale's harsh words carried from the path where she still stood. Katherine halted, but she didn't turn. A fury greater than she knew she could control was threatening to overcome her. She had to breathe very carefully and steadily before she could turn to look the old woman in the eye. Otherwise, she'd run, screaming, across the short distance that separated them and put her hands around Lady Hale's neck.

"Marry Lord Derry? You want me to marry Lord Derry *so much*?" Katherine shook her head. She squeezed shut her eyes and clenched her fists. Then she picked up her skirts and walked steadily along the path and disappeared around the corner of the house, leaving Lady Hale standing where she'd left her.

"Oh my, Katherine! I'm sorry!"

Katherine stepped backwards after bumping hard into her cousin George's chest. She was going to continue onwards with no word, but he put his hand out and gripped her wrist, drawing her round to face him.

She didn't need this right now and struggled to release her arm.

"You're forgiven, George," she muttered, about to move on, but he angled himself in front of her.

"You look upset, Katherine. Can I help?"

Katherine raised her face to see his eyes, small and calculating, boring into hers and a great revulsion made her tremble.

With an effort, she tried to normalise the encounter. It wasn't appropriate to slap his face when that would simply be an outlet that would give her great satisfaction and provoke him—with good reason. "Jack's gone to Patmore Farm where Miss Worthington has no doubt made her way with Aunt Antoinette and Uncle Bramwell. Did he say goodbye to you?" She phrased it like that to give him greater pain—like the pain she was feeling.

George shook his head. "I came out to wish him Godspeed, but he was talking to you so...I didn't want to interrupt. And then he was gone."

"That was surprisingly thoughtful of you, George." Katherine picked up her skirts and moved past him. "And now I should check that Diana hasn't run away again. Lady Hale has a dim view of my mothering abilities."

He put out his arm to stay her, and as Katherine swung around, she was glad to note that Lady Hale was no longer where she'd left her, so that was one objectionable person out of the way. Now she just needed to get rid of George.

"She's just worried about Diana, I'm sure." His voice carried in the cold air behind her. How she wished he would just go.

"And what would you know about such concerns, George?" Katherine snapped. She could feel the tears starting behind her eyes and hated that George should witness her weakness.

"I feel concern, Katherine. I feel concern for you, though you might not think it."

Katherine breathed in through her nose. "Really, George. Do you? Then find a way to get Lady Hale out of my life so I can keep Diana in it!"

Suddenly he sounded urgent. "You could marry me, Katherine. That would solve that problem. Lady Hale wants you to have a husband who can steer both of you in the right direction. She's concerned by your propensity to court scandal, that's all and—"

"Oh, shut up, George! I did not court scandal. It was thrown at me like a....mud pie."

He put his hands on her shoulders. "I just asked you to marry me, Katherine." His voice was softer, and his eyes held something she'd not seen before and which she couldn't identify, until he put a hand to his heart. "I've loved you all my life, Katherine." His voice was soft; his words surprisingly heartfelt.

"A strange way you had of showing it," Katherine responded warily. She really didn't know what to say.

"You know I wanted you. You did, Katherine. Do you remember when you were preparing for your come-out and we'd practise dancing? You knew how much it meant to me that I could hold you on the dance floor. How I hoped we could be more than just cousins."

"But..." Katherine shook her head. "How could I take you seriously, George? You were so young and...always trying to cause trouble for me."

"I wanted to cause trouble for anyone who might have a superior claim to your heart."

"Like Jack?"

"You still love him?"

The words hung between them; their answer like a portent of doom. Katherine had only to admit it, and he'd wring every last drop from her. He'd make her suffer.

But how could she suffer more than she suffered now?

She felt her shoulders slump. "Jack is to marry Odette. He told me just now. Nothing will change his mind."

"You could marry me."

She shook her head.

"I know you don't love me, Katherine, when that is all I ever wanted, but if you can't marry Jack, what will you do?

You need to marry to keep Diana. I heard Lady Hale. Yes, she thinks you're loose and dangerous without a strong man to guide you, and that you'll be swept up into worse scandal than the scandal that ensued when you recklessly eloped with Freddy—"

Angrily Katherine shook her head. "I did not recklessly run off with Freddy. I didn't know it was Freddy. I thought it was Jack who sent that carriage. I thought he'd changed his mind, and that with the delay caused by the storm, he was offering me one final chance to brave everything to be with him. And I was willing to do that. I didn't need the glitter and comfort of all this!" She was crying as she encompassed Quamby House and its manicured grounds with a sweep of her arm. "I only wanted Jack. And I still only want Jack!" She began to walk. The rain was heavier now, and the wind had gathered momentum. She raised her skirts to step over the puddles that had formed in the path but George moved quickly to waylay her, gripping her upper arms and pushing his face into hers.

"Marry me, Katherine!" he cried. "Marry me, and all this will one day be yours. You'll be Lady Quamby, not some ordinary domestic housewife with an estate that has been bought through trade. That's all Jack could have offered you!"

"Good God, I'd rather marry Derry if that was all the choice I had, for I would *never*... no, not in a thousand years, marry you, George!" She slapped away his hands and began with greater purpose than ever to walk towards the house, turning to cry out as he tried one final gambit, "Get out of my sight. I can't bear to look at you, George. You always were so filled with malice that this must be meat and drink to you. To see me brought so low. To see me so reduced that if the world ended right now, I'd be happy not to suffer a moment's torment more of what I'm suffering. Now get out of my sight!"

❦

She'd hoped to make it silently to her bedchamber where she could cry her eyes out in private, but her mother waylaid her in the passage and brought her into the drawing room where her father was solicitous, and her mother tried to say soothing words.

Some while later they heard loud stamping in the hallway and the sound of slamming doors, and when Lady Fenton asked what the commotion was about, she was told that Master George was in a fury and had gone out riding.

"In this weather?" Lady Fenton queried for the rain was teeming down from an almost black sky. "George isn't one for exercise even in the most clement of conditions."

"I hope he breaks his neck," Katherine muttered, unable to bear a moment more of anyone's pleasant or unpleasant temper as she stepped out of her mother's orbit and headed towards the door. "Goodnight, Mama. I think I'll have an early night. Please offer my excuses at dinner."

CHAPTER 27

George hated the rain. He hated riding in the rain, and right now he hated everything in this world except Katherine.

Even though she hated him. Oh, she'd made that clear enough. She'd hated him her whole life, it seemed, and no doubt she'd be happy to hear the news that he'd broken his neck.

Still, he urged his mount on, over roads that were turning into rivulets, across streams that existed when none had but an hour before. Rage and hurt drove him on until exhaustion and self-pity had him slumping in his saddle as he neared the Northcote Arms where he knew Jack and Odette had stopped along the way. Presumably, Lord Derry was with them as he hadn't passed him on the return journey.

When he learned they'd in fact headed towards Derry House, George turned his mount in that direction and was announced just as dinner was being served.

Apparently, the rain had made travelling the final distance to Patmore Farm too much of an undertaking that evening, he was told as he stood, dripping on the flagstones. However, instead of inviting George in to join the others, Lord Derry's butler seemed to infer that while the inclement weather had been reason enough to offer Odette and George's mother and uncle accommodation, George might consider taking himself off to the Northcote Arms.

He was not about to do that.

"George, you look like something the cat dragged in," his mother told him, not looking at all pleased to see him when the clearly reluctant butler showed him into the dining room. "And you're making great puddles where you stand. You're as bad as a ten-year-old. Really, you must change your clothes but did you think to bring something with you? I cannot believe you did not."

Derry, realising something of import must have occurred to have his friend riding hell for leather, apparently did not want to bring attention to their collusion, for he merely directed his valet to take George away and provide him with something appropriate.

But first, the others wanted to know if he'd passed Jack along the way. Jack. That's all they were concerned with. They were cross when he told them he'd passed Jack's equipage but had not stopped.

The others seemed to see this as a deficiency in George, and he'd been only too pleased to leave before he'd answered all their other questions.

When he presented himself, dry and respectable, in the drawing room after dinner, some of the urgency had dissipated, and he was starting to feel foolish. Not only that, he felt as if his presence were being regarded more like an intrusion. Not even his mother was pleased to see him.

Why Katherine's cutting words had spurred him on so, he had no idea. What had he been thinking, racing off like that when Katherine had made it clear she'd be happy if she never saw him again—or whether he lived or died? It was cruel and painful. Then he saw Derry lounging against the mantelpiece, looking tall and debonair in his ancestral home; the home that was not quite as grand as Quamby House, yet he looked like the lord of his domain in a way George had never felt. Truth be told, George had spent his whole life feeling like an interloper. The odd boy out. The boy nobody wanted to talk to but was obliged to.

Jack had been good to him. But Lord, it was only because of George that Jack had ever been invited to Quamby House. Jack was supposed to have been George's playmate. Instead, he and Katherine had become as thick as thieves leaving George on the outer.

George approached Derry, who looked up and ran a hand through his hair, saying, "Miss Worthington and I have been discussing the weather." His nostrils flared and he looked quite unwelcoming.

"The weather?" George repeated stupidly. He'd come here on a life-altering mission, and yet all these people could talk about was the weather.

"Yes, the weather," Miss Worthington said. She was seated demurely by the fire nearby.

He eyed her suspiciously. Was she mocking him?

Her clear-eyed gaze seemed to neither approve nor deride. Good God! Couldn't she decide whether to accept or reject him? Was he so unworthy of notice? Of any kind of feeling either way? A powerful compulsion to stamp his foot and smash every ornament off the mantelpiece before delivering a great punch in his lordship's self-satisfied face, was replaced by a mild enquiry as to whether they supposed the weather would be fine enough to continue the ride in the morning.

"I'm sorry you didn't stop to learn from Jack his plans," remarked Miss Worthington.

George clenched his fists as he tried to rein in his temper. Why, even Miss Worthington thought he wasn't up to the mark. She was criticising him like all the others as to the decisions he'd made in coming here. They didn't want him. None of them did. They made him feel as if he were as welcome as the dirt he'd brought in on his boots.

For a long moment, he stared at her. Then he said, "If he's headed for the Northcote Arms, it's only half an hour's ride by carriage from here. He'll arrive soon enough." He couldn't hint at the truth, which was that he'd gone through hell to get here himself—falling from his horse twice, which had only hardened his anger towards Jack so that he didn't trust himself to face his old friend knowing what only he and Katherine did. Well, maybe Jack did know that Katherine loved him. But not that she'd loved him for seven years and had intended to run away with *him*. That she would have if Freddy hadn't intervened. And by God, George had had his hand in that one. Yes, when Katherine had turned him down all those years ago he'd felt *glad* that he was hurting Katherine in denying her Jack.

Well, Jack would never know any of this from his lips. Not that it would have made a jot of difference. George knew Jack's reasons for marrying Odette had nothing to do with love and everything to do with honour. That was another reason George hated him so much right now. Jack, who'd had nothing, had proved himself the bigger man. Everyone loved Jack even though he was an orphan.

No one loved George.

Everyone thought Jack a great hero filled with virtue and honour.

No one attributed a jot of the honourable to George.

Miss Worthington sighed. It was a peevish sound that set up George's bristles. Lord, he didn't think he could survive a lifetime married to such a creature. Jack deserved her.

"Jack should be here any moment now. He must have

reached the Northcote Arms and been directed here quite some time ago. Don't you think, Lord Derry?"

Not George. Oh no, she didn't address George. He was beneath her notice.

Derry smiled at Miss Worthington. He actually looked at her with indulgence as if what she'd said weren't the most clinging and pathetic of utterances. "I'm sure we'll hear him pounding on the door before we've finished our Madeira. Another glass, Miss Worthington?"

"I might just have one myself, Derry," said George, looking down at the borrowed trousers that were straining across his thighs and too long at the ankles. He felt as ridiculous as he surely looked. He drew himself up. When he was the Earl of Quamby, everyone would want to be his friend. He'd have money and influence. Lord, he had all the money he knew what to do with now, for his father didn't keep him on short strings like some. True, from time to time Quamby drew in the reins, usually at his mama's instigation if he'd been on a losing streak for too long. But George didn't need money. Not generally, although it had been useful to contemplate the funds that would be his price for bringing Derry and Katherine together.

A spasm of pain caused by his disordered thoughts ripped through him, and for the first time, someone showed him concern.

"Are you quite all right, George?"

He smiled gratefully at Miss Worthington. She had a heart, after all. He forgave her.

She frowned at him. "For a moment, I thought you were about to cast up your accounts all over my shoes, as my father is wont to say, though I daresay it's very vulgar. Still, it's what came to mind."

She tittered, and Derry tittered too, and George decided he'd had enough.

With a fulminating look at them from over his shoulder, he marched to the door. Let them all have joy of one another or rather being endlessly unhappy as George had been his entire life, he thought piteously.

His mother sent him a concerned look as he strode past her but she made no attempt to stop him. He traversed the entire length of the drawing room past Uncle Bertram, and nearly tripped over the trailing hems of his trousers before he reached the door, and still no one stopped him.

It had been a wasted effort. He'd come here to make a difference. He wasn't sure exactly how, but he knew Katherine and Jack loved each other, and he'd hoped to facilitate something good for them. For the first time that he could remember, his motivations were entirely selfless, but no one appreciated his nobility, and he was damned if he was going to exert himself if this was all the appreciation he was going to get.

His bedchamber had been assigned to him—the red room on the second floor. He'd changed there and now he was returning, but Derry detained him at the bottom of the stairs.

"I say, old chap, you're in rather a flame of indignation, eh? What's got you so hot under the collar?" he asked. "Why are you here, really?"

George felt some of the advantage had returned to him by being able to turn on the third step enabling him to look down at Derry, who was lounging against the newel post.

"Why am I here?" He repeated it in clipped tones, trying to inject the words with sarcasm. "Why am I *here*, Derry? Because a little matter on home territory has changed matters somewhat, and I wish to have no part in any wager that feeds you to Katherine through blackmail, coercion, or underhand lies."

Derry blinked. "My, my, George, but that's rich coming from you."

George bunched up his fists.

Derry smiled. "If I recall, it was you who proposed the wager."

"A foolish lad's throwaway line seven years ago. I never imagined it would come to anything. But tell me, does Katherine wish to marry you?"

A shadow crossed Derry's face. Evading the question, he said, "I spoke to Lady Hale earlier today, and she assured me she had no intention of allowing Katherine to keep Diana unless Katherine married me."

"I believe the stipulation was that Katherine was simply to marry a man who'd keep her wanton impulses in check. Which means that husband could be either you, or it could be me."

"You!" The derisive way Lord Derry laughed at that was enough to make George lunge at him and wipe that smirk off his face, but George was stronger than that. Or rather, he had ammunition stronger than fists.

"Katherine has no desire to marry you. I think you know that, Derry."

Derry raised his chin. "You have no idea what you're talking about, George."

"Katherine has no wish to marry you or to marry me. She has no wish to marry anyone except..." Would he say it? Was more harm to be caused by revealing the truth or not? George held back.

"Except who?" Derry's eyes narrowed. "You're not going to tell me the stupid girl is still in love with Jack."

"Is it not as plain as the nose on your face that Katherine is in love with Jack, and Jack is in love with Katherine, only Jack is pledged to Miss Worthington, and his honour is stronger than the inconvenient beating of his heart whenever his childhood sweetheart is near." George blinked at his unusual expressiveness, just as Derry did.

When Derry seemed unable to respond, George went on, "Do you have so little pride that you'd coerce Katherine into marrying you using Diana as your weapon? Would you?" he prompted. "Would you really want to marry Katherine when you know her heart belongs to Jack, and it always will? She's loved him since she was seven years old, and he her. Nothing will ever change that. I thought I could. But even I can't." His words felt lame, but there had been power in speaking the truth. Little matter that George was relinquishing all hope of Katherine or the thousand pounds he would make through seeing a wedding occur between Katherine and Derry.

It was satisfying to see the bleak look on Derry's face.

And finally he felt like the bigger man when he turned and, leaving Derry with no words, continued up the stairs towards his bedchamber.

JACK WAS EXHAUSTED BY THE TIME HE REACHED DERRY House. It was late, and the travelling had been tedious. Three times they'd been stuck in mud past the axle.

He supposed he'd be welcomed. Odette was there, as were Lady Quamby and her brother, he'd learned.

During the entire journey, he'd replayed in his mind his last encounter with Katherine. Had he phrased what he'd needed to in a manner to inflict the minimum pain? Regardless, she'd let him off easily.

Then he wondered whether it was cowardice. Was he too afraid to break it off with Odette knowing she'd scream and wail and accuse him of deceiving her?

He was very certain by the time he arrived that he'd acted in the only way possible. He'd ascertained that Odette's father was in tolerable health before he'd left. There'd been no cause to bring her home, nor did his relief stem from the fact that there was consequently no reason to bring forward the wedding?

He realised he'd have been happy to postpone it for as long as possible, yet every moment was one closer to that when he'd walk down the aisle with his joyful bride. And that was what he'd pledged—to make Odette happy when her world was falling apart around her. She'd lost her mother when she'd been a child. Her brother had died of fever the previous year. All that was left to her was her father and when he died, whom did she have to rely upon? A disinterested cousin and elderly aunt who played chaperone from time to time?

The mood seemed strangely jovial when he was ushered into the drawing room with its lofty, gilded ceilings and expansive pale green Aubusson carpet. Lady Quamby appeared to have consumed a great deal of champagne; her brother was even more intoxicated. Even Odette seemed oddly affected as she stood up and wended her way a little shakily towards him, although he'd obviously bade her remain seated as he went to her.

"You took your time, Jack." George was pressing a glass of brandy into his hands. He was very oddly dressed, Jack thought, before he dismissed any thoughts regarding George apart from wondering what he was doing here.

"Jack! Are you pleased to see me?"

It was a very odd question from Odette, Jack thought, narrowing his eyes at her. Her cheeks were flushed, and her hair looked a trifle disordered. But then, it had been a long day's travelling.

"Did you think you had to ask such a question, my dear?" He knew his words sounded stilted, but perhaps that was because he was the only sober member of the party. Yes, he was sure of it.

Odette hooked her arm through his and walked with him to a cluster of chairs a little apart. "Tell me what you thought about during your long, dull journey?" she asked, putting her head close to his, leaning across the small space between their two wing-back armchairs. "Did you think of me, and me alone? Did you wish it wasn't so long before our wedding? Did you regret having to go back to Quamby House with that child? Oh, do let's get out of here, Jack. Let's go for a stroll along the Gallery."

Jack didn't know how to answer as she led him up a rear staircase to the old part of the house where they wandered past a collection of old suits of armour and pikes. Odette, however, seemed content enough to do all the talking. She stopped to gaze through the window. "You came into my life just when I needed you, Jack. *You* were my knight in shining armour. Indeed, you were. And Papa loves you. He loves you like the son he'd lost; I think you know. He was very good to you when you worked for him, wasn't he?"

"He taught me so much. I credit him with my success; you know that. I owe him everything."

"And me, Jack. You owe him the care of me."

Her words sounded slurred. Jack looked at her with concern. He turned her to him, holding her shoulders so he could look into her eyes.

"Kiss me, Jack." She closed her eyes and offered him her lips, and there was nothing Jack could do but as she asked. But every fibre of his body rebelled against the touch, even as she twined her hands behind his neck to deepen the kiss.

With the greatest effort, he purged his mind of thoughts of Katherine. It was so wrong to compare the intoxication he'd felt only hours before in that forbidden, dreadfully sinful encounter with the lack of enjoyment he was feeling now.

She stepped back, and he forced himself to smile while he berated himself internally for his disloyalty and wicked, unforgivable behaviour.

But he'd atone. He'd spend the rest of his life atoning.

For a long moment, she stared at him, as if reading in his face all the hopes and dreams she harboured for their long union together.

Then she reached up her hand and touched his cheek, her smile one of the sweetest he'd seen. Yes, she was perfect for him. She was.

"Let's go back now, Jack. After all, we're not married yet, are we?"

۞

ANTOINETTE REACHED OUT HER ARM TO ARREST BERTRAM'S progress and waggled her fingers. "What a thoughtless brother you are. Can't you see my glass is empty?"

"I think you've had more than enough, Antoinette."

Since Bertram gave an inelegant hiccup at this juncture, Antoinette considered she was within her rights to up her demands, until Bertram wove his way over to the sideboard where Jack was sipping a glass of claret a little distance from George, though neither appeared to have anything to say to the other.

After downing her drink quite quickly, Antoinette felt the need to succumb to the call of nature. There was no one to whom to offer her excuses, so she left the room with no fanfare, sailed up the passage, and then happened to glance left where a small flight of stairs descended to a dim passage that snaked through the darkness to the bowels of the house. The sight that greeted her made her first wonder if her eyes were playing tricks on her, then whether someone had put something in her drink, and finally to wonder if she truly was a sorceress before she realised the need to make as silent a passage past as possible.

"Mother, are you all right?" George asked her as she returned to the drawing room. Jack was now talking to Bertram, and George appeared to have been eyeing the doorway with unusual keenness.

"Of course, darling." She brushed him off, hardly able to wait until she could tell Bertram the wonderful news.

However, Bertram's conversation with the other gentlemen appeared to have gained intensity so, unable to stop herself fidgeting, she went to the window and looked out into the darkness.

"It was awfully good of Jack to deliver Diana all the way home. It's been a long day's travelling for him."

Antoinette glanced up to see George at her side, as if he'd come to see what it was she was staring at. Irritated, she waved a hand in the air. "Oh, it's just the sort of thing Jack would do. He wants to be everybody's hero."

"Mother!"

She put her hand to her mouth, realising the cruelty of her words, when in truth, she'd been thinking of Jack's need to be Odette's hero in particular, at the expense of Katherine. Indeed, she'd been unable to think of anything else.

"Darling, don't imagine I intended to be the slightest bit cutting. It's just that Jack *is* everybody's hero. He's always there to do the right thing." She blinked hazily at her large, oafish son. "I mean, unlike you, he'll put himself out for a good cause. Oh, that wasn't at all meant to be cruel, either, George darling, but you were never hero material, were you? Which isn't to say I don't love you. You're my son, after all."

She patted him on the arm for he did seem to have taken her words in quite the wrong way. She tried to explain herself without wounding him further. "I mean, George darling, you were such a very needy little boy, and that's why we thought

Jack would be good for you. Jack had had no advantages, unlike you. We thought he'd build you up. And yes, he benefitted, but we did it all for you. You mustn't look down on him—"

"I don't." His words were clipped. "And do you think I profited having Jack as my moral guide, Mama?"

"Darling, no need to sound aggressive. You have always liked Jack, haven't you?"

"Like a brother, Mama, though, like you, I'm sure he thought me oafish and…lacking."

"I never expected anything more given your father—" Antoinette stopped abruptly, putting her hand to her lips, for the words seemed to have flown out without a care when Antoinette had spent her life being so very careful. At least where George's parentage was concerned.

"What do you mean by that, Mama?"

He looked puzzled, though surely he could not have interpreted anything from what she'd said?

"Oh, pay me no mind, George. Though I will tell you I was extremely disappointed to hear that you were the instigator of that terrible wager that encouraged Freddy to run off with Katherine all those years ago."

"You were entirely complicit in ensuring Katherine married Freddy, Mama, so please don't put all the blame at my door."

Antoinette dropped her gaze to her feet. "Well, it hardly makes it any better, George, does it? I love Katherine like my own daughter. I would never have caused her unhappiness if she hadn't led me to believe she was madly in love with Freddy Marwick." On a wave of spite, she added, "You, on the other hand, have always been so jealous of your cousin, haven't you? You couldn't bear it that anyone other than you should get a jot of affection and interest because that meant there was less for you. As if love were a finite thing."

"Oh, you never led me to believe that, Mama. You had all the love in the world to spread around. I've seen it my whole life; that bountiful, endless flow of love you've bestowed upon my tutor, the actor who was giving Papa lessons. So much love, but not a kiss or caress that was heartfelt have you shown my father—"

"Oh, for God's sake, he's not your father!"

The words seemed to snap his head back. George stared, and Antoinette was left feeling like a tiny little star swirling in a morass of confusion. What had she said?

She closed her eyes as she tried to decide what to do now. Surely she hadn't blurted out the one secret it was imperative she keep?

Vaguely, she waved a hand in his direction as she sought for something with which to change the subject. "Ah, here comes Odette and I'm sure Lord Derry won't be long. I can't imagine what they were doing at the bottom of the stairs in the dark. Bertram, I thought you'd completely forgotten you even had a sister. No, don't offer George any. He's had far too much. He can't seem to remember anything properly, and I've asked him three times already to fetch me another glass of champagne."

CHAPTER 28

Katherine didn't usually rise late, but this morning she was in no mood to get up at the insistent knocking on her bedchamber door, before her maid entered in some excitement waving a letter which she informed her mistress must be responded to immediately.

It took only a moment for the fuzziness to clear from Katherine's brain. Truly, she'd existed in a cloud of grief, barely able to sleep until the early hours of the morning, and the urgency in Mary's voice brought with it her greatest hope.

"Jack?" she cried before she could censor herself, though fortunately Mary hadn't seemed to notice, thrusting what turned out to be a hastily scrawled letter into her hands.

Eagerly, Katherine scanned the salutation and immediately her hopes plummeted.

George! It was from George!

She reread the note while fury roiled inside.

"Please, miss, the rider wot brought it is waitin' fer an answer."

Katherine focused a gimlet eye on Mary. "Tell the rider," she said, crisply, "that he can gallop right back where he came from with the message that I will *not* be jumping in any carriage—Papa's or Lord Quamby's—if it's to find myself anywhere in the vicinity of where George is. And certainly not after what he's just revealed."

Mary's eyebrows shot upwards, and she opened her mouth to speak before closing it firmly with a nod. "Very good, ma'am. Though p'haps ye'd better put that in writin'. I ain't convinced the young boy wot brought the message is goin' ter remember all that."

Once Mary had left to deliver her mistress's letter, Katherine plumped up her pillows and unfolded the crumpled paper to reread it.

She fisted her hand and put it in her mouth while she tried to regulate her heartbeat. Of all the audacity, this was the most brazenly outrageous George had ever been. Well, he'd confessed to part of his crime, she supposed, though it hadn't been difficult all those years ago to guess he'd had a role in the bad business that had forged her to Freddy with no way out.

And he'd apologised. Apologised for setting up the wager that had given Freddy the enthusiasm and financial incentive for marrying Katherine, in particular, when his devastating losses at the gaming table had fuelled his urgency in allying himself with a monied bride before his losses became public.

"I know the moment you read this message, knowing that it is from me, you'll doubt my motives, but this time I want to atone, Katherine," he'd written.

"Please come to Derry House at the earliest. I know we parted badly when my jealousy reared its ugly head and you saw in me the spoiled boy you've always scorned.

"It's true that my greatest happiness would be to learn you'd reconsidered; that you'd marry me even if you didn't love me. But believe me when I tell you that in writing this message, I'm

motivated by your greatest happiness. And your greatest happiness would be served by you being here, Katherine.

"I can make things right again for you. I promise I can. Just come!"

This time Katherine didn't just crumple the message, she ripped it into tiny shreds and tossed each one in the grate. Of all the people in the world who wanted to see Katherine undone, George was at the front of the line-up.

⁂

GEORGE STARED AT THE FEW WORDS KATHERINE HAD written in such precise letters on the now soiled piece of parchment. The lad to whom he'd entrusted this mission held out his hand for payment. George stared at the grime on his fingers that had transferred to the paper and felt a surge of revulsion and anger. He'd sullied what was to have been the perfect overture to Katherine. He'd made grubby the pure and pristine nobility of George's mission, which had been to secure Katherine's happiness.

After rummaging for a coin to secure the lad's departure, he rested the back of his head against the window and stared into the empty drawing room as a great pressure pulsed behind his eyes. Why couldn't he even play the hero without having mud slung at him? Nobody wanted him about. Nobody believed him when he spoke the truth. Nobody thought...well, much of him at all.

Derry's drawing room, when not hosting a crowd of people, appeared heavy and dismal; the mahogany sideboard and overstuffed sofas flanked by dead animals in glass domes more like a mausoleum than a place to gather for entertainment. And this was destined to be Katherine's palace. She would replace the tawdry trappings Freddy had considered up to the mark when he'd fallen in the world, with the heavy, stately, suffocating majesty Derry had inherited from his own parents. There'd be no room to accommodate her brightness, her liveliness.

And did Derry even love her like he certainly once had? Was his desire merely based on the competitive need to acquire what he'd failed to acquire seven years before when he and Freddy had been such great rivals?

But George loved Katherine.

And Jack loved Katherine.

And Katherine deserved to be with someone who would appreciate her for her spirit, her personal qualities. Not as the prize she'd always represented to Derry.

"George, darling, you don't seem to be feeling quite the thing. Are you all right?"

"I'm quite all right, Mama." He kept his eyes closed, though he felt a tear breach its barrier and then roll down his cheek.

"My dear boy, you're not thinking about what I said last night, are you?" She gripped his arm and gave it a little shake. "Look at me." She seemed anxious this morning, which was out of character. For the first time he noticed the tiny crow's feet beneath her eyes. "Last night, everyone drank far too much, and I'm sure we all said things we didn't mean or that weren't true."

"Not all of us, Mama," George said coldly, contemplating her with dispassion. Despite the slight puffiness beneath her eyes, the harsh sunlight did nothing to mute her beauty. No grey peppered her hair, and her skin was still like alabaster.

George, on the other hand, must have inherited his father's looks. Whomever his father really was, that is. Not Lord Quamby—and yet he'd accepted George as his heir. George had been groomed for the role with no sign of ill will from the man who...*wasn't* his father.

He felt lost.

It was midday, and the party was preparing to continue on to Patmore Farm. George hadn't been invited, even though his mama and uncle had just now been happily speculating on the fine table Eliza Patmore promised. She was known for the expertise of her catering, and many times his mother had remarked on the superiority of the tasty fare from a humble farmhouse which arrived hot to the dining room, compared with the cold offerings that were so often served up at Quamby House.

"I meant everything *I* said, Mama. As I recall," he added stiffly.

"Really, George. I'm sure you can't remember half of what you said."

"I remember telling Jack he was wrong to think he'd be making anyone happy if he married Miss Worthington—including Miss Worthington herself—if he was really in love with Katherine."

His mother blinked, and the bland façade she so often adopted when she spoke to him fell away. "Why did you say that, George? Since you're in love with Katherine..." Her voice faltered.

"She's not in love with me. Oh, she made that very clear when I last spoke to her." He raised his chin, wounded pride coursing through him once more. "Nor is she in love with Derry."

"Why, George. That was a noble thing to do. To tell Jack the truth, I mean." His mother squeezed his arm, and her face lit up as if she were about to impart some marvellous news. And perhaps it was. "I saw Lord Derry alone with Miss Worthington last night in a dark corridor." She lowered her voice. "I passed by just when I think he was about to kiss her. I don't know if she expected it or not, and I know that both of them had had too much to drink, but she didn't claw his eyes out. It's a beginning, don't you think? If we're to get Jack and Katherine together, I mean."

Murmured voices in the hallway became louder before the door was opened and Jack and Odette entered, deep in conversation, unaware the room was occupied as they wandered to the other end towards the French doors.

Words indicating wedding preparations punctuated the stillness as if to debunk any of the hopeful possibilities George and his mama had just been discussing.

"It won't work, Mama," George said softly. The room was so large the others couldn't hear. "I sent a message to Katherine asking her to come, but she refused. She hates me, you know."

"I'm sure she doesn't hate you, George. She probably just didn't believe you'd be requesting her presence for any noble reason."

"Nobody ever believes me when I try to do good." He sniffed. "I was so sure if I could get Katherine here so soon after I'd told Jack that she loved him, then her presence would change everything."

"But George, Jack knows Katherine loves him. That's not the problem." Lady Quamby spoke to him as if he were a child. "And Jack loves Katherine. But Jack is too much a man of honour to renege on the promise he's made Odette. And I'm sure I don't know how to overcome that obstacle. Not with Derry and Odette refusing to cooperate and properly fall in love with one another."

George closed his eyes, thinking, then opened them to see Jack put his arm about Odette's shoulders as if he were comforting her. A hero could be the most insufferable of all human beings, yet hadn't George always wanted to be like Jack? Not *just* because he wanted to be the recipient of Katherine's love.

"Katherine would come if she thought Jack was in danger," he said.

"Really, George. That's too dramatic. In danger...at Patmore Farm? With his own parents?"

"Or if she were told Jack had had an accident."

"So, now you're proposing to set upon Jack so Katherine can be told he was wounded in a brazen attack by footpads?"

George frowned at his mother. "You're so ready to dismiss my every idea, aren't you, Mama?"

"Really, that's not fair, George." Lady Quamby bridled. "But you do tend to run on without thinking matters out to their final consequences."

"I'd suggest that's just what you did when you clearly *had* to marry Quamby. But that's hardly done you any harm."

Ignoring his mother's gasp of outrage, George went on, returning to the subject at hand, as he outlined the plan he'd recently devised in a hurried whisper. "Nothing will progress if Katherine isn't here, Mama. We both know that, I'm sure. And Katherine won't listen to me. But what if *you* wrote to Katherine and told her Jack had suffered a severe fall from his horse and was asking for her. Of course, it would be a lie, but it would bring her here if she recognised *your* handwriting. She'd come then, wouldn't she? I mean, nothing would keep her away if she heard that from *you*."

Lady Quamby regarded her only son with approval. "Why, George dearest, I think that's the cleverest plan you've ever come up with. Bertram and I have already paved the way. As have you. I feel sure it will only take the vision of Katherine bursting through the doors of Patmore Farm and crying out her deepest distress to learn that Jack lies in mortal danger of succumbing to his injuries, for everyone to understand there really is no other reasonable outcome than for Jack and Katherine to be together."

CHAPTER 29

What a dreary day, thought Katherine as she strolled through the gardens of Quamby House the following morning.

The drizzling rain would soon have her drenched to the skin. Perhaps she'd catch a chill, but what did it matter? It would make her mother be even more displeased with her, of course. Or was her mother displeased at something else? Did Katherine really care?

Did Katherine really care about anything other than the fact that Jack had made it clear he returned her feelings, except his loyalties towards Odette were greater than they were to Katherine? She tried to hate him for ruining her life but couldn't.

At the bottom of the hill, she stopped to look up at the fine old Queen Anne building. It looked sad and lonely beneath the grey sky. A gravel path wound its way from a side door, cutting through the grass towards the small lake around which Katherine was now meandering slowly, her heart a sad, empty vessel.

But now a figure had emerged from the side door and was

poised upon the threshold, scanning the surroundings before locating Katherine and hurrying with more than usual haste towards her.

"Katherine! You told no one you were going out! I've not known where to find you these last ten minutes!" Her mother sounded panicked, which was unlike her.

Katherine's heart began to pound, and she picked up her skirts and ran towards Lady Fenton who was waving a letter in the air.

"Your aunt has just written to say that Jack had a bad accident this morning. He's asking for you!"

"Jack's hurt?" The back of Katherine's legs felt cold. A terrible malaise seemed to grip her from the inside before she was able to throw off her panic. "Is he going to be all right?" She put her hand to her mouth as her breath came in short, staccato breaths. She closed her eyes. Jack was hurt? Jack was asking for her?

"I don't know!" Her mother sounded as afraid as Katherine felt. "Antoinette doesn't say."

"I have to go to him!" Katherine scanned the lawn and the house as if she might gain inspiration for what she needed to do.

"The carriage is here," her mother said. "I'll have it brought round."

"The carriage will take three hours, Mama!" Katherine cried. "Three hours when I have no idea how bad Jack's injuries are. I can ride the distance in an hour."

"On horseback? Heavens, you can't possibly do that, darling," her mother responded with firm conviction. "No, must arrive by carriage looking a vision of loveliness and Jack—"

"Oh, stop saying such things! What do I care what I look like when Jack's life is hanging in the balance?" Katherine cried, her voice breaking as her fear increased. "I'm taking

Stargazer." Already she was striding towards the house, saying over her shoulder, "Ask Tom to saddle him up for me while I change into my habit. And please tell Betsy I'm leaving immediately. You'll see to Diana, won't you?"

"I won't let you go alone, Katherine! You can't possibly! Even if Jack's life is in danger, you can't thumb your nose at convention and set tongues wagging at your latest antics, for that's what they'll do."

"Then tell Tom he has to come with me, if it'll make you happy, though I'm sure it hardly matters what society has to say about me, don't you think, as long as Derry's prepared to marry me and prove that his devotion is stronger than the credence he gives to society's opinion of me."

"You're being too dramatic, Katherine—"

But Katherine was out of earshot to hear the rest. Within twenty minutes, she was dressed in a stylish dove-grey riding habit and smart, high-crowned hat, the energetic Stargazer restless beneath her. Urgency, excitement, and terror mingled in her veins, but at least her mission—terrible though it was —promised her some release. No more languishing in the drawing room dwelling on her disappointed hopes. No more passive acceptance of Jack's choice to prioritize Odette's happiness over Katherine's own, simply because to do anything else rendered Jack less than the man he wanted to be to the woman he chose as his wife.

She waited for Tom to leap into the saddle of his own mount, and then they were off, galloping up the northern road in the direction of Patmore Farm a little over an hour's journey away when the weather was fine, but probably closer to two, today, due to the fact the rain had not eased and parts of the road would be churned to mud or washed away by river or stream.

Katherine didn't care about the discomfort posed by the weather. The wind that lashed the heavy hanks of wet hair that had escaped from her bun across her face was welcome for making her *feel*. She cared nothing for the pain that spasmed across her lower back due to the hectic jolting she'd become unused to. Freddy had forbidden her from riding in public after she'd been admired for her 'dash and spirit' and speculation as to whether she'd been sewn into her habit in one of London's scandal sheets.

After he'd sold her horse, Katherine had done only a little riding, though Lord Quamby had given her the use of Stargazer whenever she wished. The risk hadn't seemed worth it since she knew Freddy would question the servants about whether she'd kept her promise to stay out of the saddle.

Now she felt freer than she could remember. Freer than she had during her seemingly endless marriage. Freer than she had since Freddy had died, for by then Derry had made it clear he was there to fill the breach.

And she had owed him a very large debt.

Thanks to Freddy.

Before they were even halfway, the road had become a quagmire, and the horses were tiring. Tom slowed, and Katherine drew to a halt beside him in the shelter of a small beech forest.

"Do not suggest we turn back because we're closer to Quamby House than Patmore Farm," she warned him, channelling her pain into anger. She was still panting from the exertion of negotiating terrain far more difficult than she ever had before. Although she'd always been considered a good horsewoman, she had little experience of riding in such adverse conditions.

"I'm yer servant, ma'am. I wouldn't dream of it."

Tom had been Lord Quamby's retainer for as long as Katherine could remember. She'd always liked the way his eyes twinkled in his ruddy face as he pulled at his whiskers when he addressed her. He'd been doing so since Katherine was a child. Now the whiskers he pulled were greyer and bushier and his cheeks weather-beaten to brown as he went on, "But I am thinkin', ma'am, that it's reckless ter fight the elements like this when yer could secure a post-chaise in the village over yonder." He pointed to a small hamlet nestled in the lee of a hill.

Katherine shook her head. "I know we've been journeying an hour, and we still have some distance to go, but a carriage is far more likely to become bogged or held up by rising waters than we are on horseback." She emphasised this with a scornful look, just as she had done when she was a child and teasing him. "Are you getting too old for such discomfort, Tom? Shall I find another groom in the village who can keep up with me?"

He didn't respond in the bantering tone of the old days. Instead, his brows knitted and he sucked his gums before saying, "With the greatest respect, it is ye who are tirin', ma'am, an' that ain't b'cause yer not a mighty fine horse-woman. This kind of ridin' needs practise, however, else yer likely ter come a cropper."

Katherine bit her lip. She knew she was out of practice, but she was not giving up. "We're going on, Tom. Just another hour and we'll be at Patmore Farm. Jack is injured, and I won't rest until I know how badly."

"Ah, but it ain't no surprise, all this madcap ride." He made a sweeping gesture with one arm. "Ye and Jack were always thick as thieves. 'E'll be mighty glad ter see yer at 'is bedside, I don't doubt. Well, we'd best get on wiv it, eh?"

The rest had been much needed, even if they hadn't dismounted. Katherine was relieved Tom hadn't exercised his stubborn streak, though she knew he disapproved. Strangely, not as much as she'd expected for he seemed to fully endorse Katherine's mission, even if he was less enthusiastic regarding her means of expediting it as quickly as possible.

With relief, they crested the last hill before reaching Patmore Farm and stared down at the familiar house nestled in the valley. Now her breath came in even sharper bursts, hurting her side. She closed her eyes as she dug her hand into the pain as if to slice it in half.

"We're nearly there, Tom," she said, watching a gaggle of geese waddle across the lawn of the pretty farmhouse in the distance. "Fifteen minutes down the hill and across the river."

He shook his head. "We can't cross there, miss. Water's too 'igh. We'll need ter go upstream ter find someplace safer 'an narrow—if it can be done at all in this weather."

Katherine squinted as she bit her lip. They were too close to allow a diversion.

"We can find us a boat, miss. Leave the horses 'ere. Aye, mayhap that's safest."

But the idea of searching for a cottager who might have a boat he was prepared to lend them was too much in the way of delay for Katherine.

"We're too far away from the water to tell for certain," she said, urging Stargazer forward. The current was flowing strongly, and it was much higher than it usually was.

"With enough speed, I think Stargazer can jump it." She had to talk herself into it as much as Tom, and her mouth felt numb.

"No, miss." He shook his head. "Stargazer may jest as easily not make the distance 'an then where would yer both be? I'll not be responsible fer draggin' yer corpse from the river when the current finally abates."

"What a morbid turn of phrase you have, Tom," Katherine managed to quip. It was easier to revert to banter than to acknowledge the very real danger that concerned Tom.

"Come, miss; let's go back up an' follow the road. See if it takes us ter a more fav'rable crossing."

Katherine brought Stargazer's head round, and followed Tom back up to higher ground. His horse was tiring and obviously found the going harder than Stargazer. But then Stargazer was younger; a nimble, flighty mount who'd been known to take a fancy to surprising his rider and making a dash in the direction opposite the one he was intended to go.

So why shouldn't Katherine adopt the element of surprise and turn the tables on the little horse who'd done just the same so many times when Katherine had been a young and inexperienced rider?

With a bolstering shout, she wheeled about, her heels digging into Stargazer's flanks as she gave the little horse his head and urged him down the hill.

Faster and faster he went, gathering speed like a steam engine on a downward incline only more agile and with the ability to tuck his legs beneath him when Katherine launched him into a graceful arc across the muddy, choppy waters that he needed to negotiate in order to prevent a landing of the most disastrous proportions.

CHAPTER 30

Jack was hardly in the mood for charades, but it had been Odette's idea and he was prepared to humour her, especially in view of his disloyal heart *that must be conquered.*

Besides, when she had her way she was very sweet and loving, and what new husband didn't enjoy having his brow stroked and told how clever and handsome he was? Odette had never stinted on her affections, and now he must make a particular effort to ensure that he was as fondly attentive *as he needed to be.*

Sitting on a red-velvet sofa that had been dragged into the drawing room to supplement the clusters of seating, he was the loudest to applaud when Lady Fenton guessed Odette's rendition of *The Wild Swans*, Hans Christian Anderson's recent children's book.

"What a fine and majestic creature you did look, Miss Worthington, with your swanlike neck and bold eye," remarked Derry.

"Though I should beware, if I were Jack, of inadvertently doing something to stoke that wild inner spirit no one would expect you were harbouring," said George, standing up to act out his turn.

"Ah, hidden depths are much to be admired," responded Derry, his own glance admiring as Odette blushed and dropped her gaze as she returned to Jack's side and took his hand, whispering, "Did you like it?"

"Naturally," he responded. And then, because this sounded lacklustre in contrast with her other admirers, "You were marvellous, as always."

He hoped this pleased her, and was glad when a hush fell upon the room as George clutched his heart and stared like a moonstruck calf at the ceiling, prompting his aunt to say excitedly, "George is in love! Who can it be, George? Oh, that's not the point. But the first word is love, isn't it?"

With this agreed, George then adopted a look of great ferocity and brandished what was clearly an imaginary sword. It took a few false suggestions before Jack came up with 'conquers', his offering immediately drowned out by Lady Quamby who leapt up crying, "Love conquers all! That's it, isn't, George? *Love conquers all*! Oh, but no truer words were ever spoken. What a tragedy for those who enter the state of matrimony without fiercely beating hearts and the desire to conquer the world for their one true love."

She put her hand on Lord Quamby's pudgy knee at this declaration and pressed her cheek against his, so that the veracity of her statement would have been clear to all those in the room who knew them, Jack thought. Yet there was a real fondness in the look the mismatched couple shared, and Jack's immediate wish was that he, too, could manufacture the desire to conquer the world on Odette's behalf, but then it was replaced by the sop that perhaps, in time, they would forge a comfortable happiness during what promised to be a long and blessed union together.

"And now it's your turn, Jack," George urged. However,

just as Jack rose to make his reluctant way towards the front of the room, a great commotion sounded in the passage. Pounding footsteps stopped abruptly at the door, which was thrown open and Eliza Patmore's parlourmaid entered, bobbing a quick curtsey as she cried, "Miss Katherine's broke 'er neck! Oh Lordy, it were 'er groom wot said it!"

She'd barely finished before the butler, a far more dignified personage who was clearly not as swift as his loose-tongued inferior, emerged looking no less appalled. "Get back into the kitchen, Mabel," he hissed to the weeping maid who defended her tears with, "But 'tis terrible! Miss Katherine's—"

"Get into the kitchen!" he repeated more loudly and sharply, pushing the girl out of the room before facing the horrified contingent.

"What's this, Dunbridge?" Jack was the first to surge forward. The pounding of fear in his ears was so intense amidst the loud and excited babbling of everyone else, he could barely make out what the butler was saying. "Quiet!" At his commanding shout, the room instantly went silent. "Where is she? Who sent this news?" He raked one hand through his hair as he faced the butler.

"Her groom has come this moment to apprise us of the situation, sir. She's down by the river."

"Good God! Down by the river?" cried Lord Quamby in querulous tones, while Lady Quamby gasped and Jack responded with disbelief, "In this weather? What on earth is she doing even on the ride? Here? Riding?"

It made no sense. There must be some mistake. He shook his head. "Broken her neck? No, it can't be." As the words sank in his horror grew. Katherine...dead? A world without her was no world in which to exist. He squeezed his knuckles into his eye sockets then whipped around. "I must go to her! Mother, prepare a bedchamber for her!" He glanced at the white faces about him, adding, "And a brandy for Lady Quamby. Stay with her until we get back." He stopped as he passed the aunt of the girl he loved, who was weeping piteously, and put his hand on her shoulder. "The maid spoke out of panic. I'm sure it's not as dire as we all fear."

"I should never have sent that letter!" wailed Lady Quamby, recumbent on the banquette Jack had recently vacated while her son and husband tried to soothe her.

"What letter?" Jack's mother asked.

"Yes, what letter did you send, my dear?" This was from Lord Quamby.

"I sent a message to Katherine telling her that Jack had suffered a terrible accident and that she must come quickly. I never thought she'd take me so literally and *ride* here in this weather."

"Why did you tell such a lie?" Eliza asked, but Jack had already left the room, and the reply couldn't be heard as he ran towards the front door which was now being opened again by the butler. Katherine's mud-spattered groom was shouting across the courtyard to one of the stable lads who was bringing round a horse which, by God, Jack had no intention of letting anyone else ride, even though he wasn't dressed for it.

"I'll take it!" he cried, about to dash down the steps when a soft hand touched his. He swung round.

"I hope she'll be all right, Jack," said Odette, her eyes luminous, as if she were blinking back tears. She surely couldn't be so concerned about Katherine, he thought, nodding at her distractedly as he cast off his morning coat, far too constricting for riding and handed it to her.

"See that Lady Quamby is all right, Odette," he called. "Make sure there's hot water and liniment and anything else you can think of!"

By now, he was already astride, wheeling round the frisky mare and galloping away hard on Tom's heels.

The rain had not eased, and the ground was slippery as the horses half slid down the steep hill that led to the river. What was Katherine doing on horseback here in weather like this? It made no sense unless...

Fragments of the conversation he'd overheard at Patmore Farm whispered in his mind. No, he'd not countenance that such a trail of deceit should lead to this. Had Katherine's aunt really summoned her here on the pretext that Jack was in danger? The fact Katherine had come so peremptorily, and thereby risked her own life riding in these conditions, was no balm to his ego when set against what he feared he would find.

A small group had gathered by the edge of the river which, dear Lord, he realised she'd tried to cross in one bound. He couldn't countenance it—it was madness! Utter recklessness!

But at their feet lay Katherine, so small and vulnerable and unmoving.

He could barely swallow, and prickles of fear chilled him to the bone. He'd never felt such fear at the unknown. When he'd left all he held dear seven years ago—namely Katherine —to make his way in the world, the unknown had been a big adventure. He had youth, energy, fearlessness, and he'd thought, more to gain than he had to lose.

Now, with success achieved in that he'd secured a future for himself and the deserving woman who would be his wife, he realised he had everything to lose.

Love. The only true love he would ever have.

As the villagers shifted, turning as he hailed them in his progress down the hill, he caught a glimpse of her prone form, the dove-grey of her sodden riding habit half-covered in the mud through which she'd been dragged as her first rescuers had moved her to higher ground.

Yes, the chance to ever love properly was what he risked losing.

He dismounted and crouched by her side. "Katherine." He spoke her name softly as he put his hand to her neck. A weak pulse beat there, and a surge of hope made him snap his head up and shout, "She lives. We need a door or a wide plank of wood on which to carry her. Katherine!"

She stirred, and he lowered his head to hers in the hope he'd hear something distinguishable from her lips. But she remained unintelligible, though, thank God, she was struggling to sit up.

A makeshift stretcher would take too long to get here. Jack contemplated the distance to the cluster of cottages that might yield something suitable, then bent down and put his hands beneath her knees and about her shoulders.

He'd carry her, even if he collapsed from the effort, for the weight of sodden skirts and petticoats was considerable. He couldn't put her on his horse and jolt her all the way back, though hopefully a carriage or cart could be found. In the meantime, he'd relish the chance to have her pressed close to his chest even if it was the last time...

No, he'd not think about anything that might truncate the future for either of them. The only moment was now, and by God, he'd make the most of it.

The feel of her curves pressed against him was achingly familiar as he carried her through the mud that sucked at his boots, back towards Patmore Farm. Suddenly, nothing seemed more right than that Katherine should accompany him home to where his parents would be waiting anxiously for their return.

And anxious they should be for Katherine had fallen back into unconsciousness and the extent of her injuries remained unknown. Jack hoped he wasn't exacerbating them with each footstep but what else could he do? He wasn't going to let anyone else have the care of her.

In the meantime, he hoped that someone had thought to fetch the doctor.

THEY HAD.

Dr Lovegrove was pacing by the window, turning as Jack staggered into the bedchamber to which he'd been led and gently laid Katherine upon the blue-and-gold counterpane. Dr Lovegrove had attended to Katherine when she was a child during the summers she'd visited Patmore Farm. Like Jack, he'd have fond memories of the little hoyden who climbed trees and took foolish risks on horseback. Katherine ought to have grown out of such daredevilry, and indeed, the generally sober demeanour she'd presented since Jack's return suggested she had.

But something dramatic had happened to make her cast caution to the wind and embark upon what anyone would consider the most foolish of risks—trying to cross a river in flood. He couldn't reconcile the talk he'd overheard as he left Derry's drawing room. Would Katherine really have been spurred to such action through concern for Jack's welfare?

He stepped back to allow the doctor access to Katherine's side, gazing at the perfection of her features so pale and still against the pillow. She was beautiful. Beautiful from the inside out, and his heart hitched as he closed his eyes and the constriction in his throat made it hard to breathe.

Lady Quamby was weeping as she hurried into the room, her tears not feigned, for Jack had seen often how judiciously she manufactured emotion to achieve her own ends. Now she appeared panicked and remorseful as she knelt at the bedside and snatched Katherine's hand, George looking downcast, shuffling into the room in her wake.

"Katherine, dearest girl, forgive me." Lady Quamby held her niece's hand against her cheek and closed her eyes. "Forgive me for not helping you all those years ago when I truly believed you loved Freddy."

Jack blinked. And his eyes widened when George leaned over his mother's shoulder and said softly but urgently, "*I* was to blame, Mother. *I* proposed the wager. I encouraged Freddy when he thought he had no chance of winning Katherine." He took a handkerchief from his pocket and mopped his brow, adding, "Though I swear I did not know he'd lost everything at the gaming tables the night before the blackguard tricked her into getting into his carriage. Do not blame yourself, alone, Mother. You always wanted only what was best for Katherine. Unlike me. Until now." His voice broke. "Only to see our plan go so horribly wrong."

Plan? Jack was about to interject and quiz them with urgent ferocity, but the doctor was now rising after he'd gently wiped the mud from Katherine's brow, and everyone moved aside so he could reach his bag of instruments.

"How bad are her injuries?" Jack managed to ask, clenching his fists to stop them trembling.

The doctor stared at Jack a moment, his eyes flickering in the effort, it seemed, to place the situation in its rightful context.

"I'm afraid I can't tell you just yet. I fear, however, that'll she'll not manage to walk up the aisle in—when did your mother say the wedding was?"

Jack blinked rapidly. The doctor had confused Katherine with his intended bride. He shook his head and said, wishing the words to hell though he had no choice but to utter the truth, "Katherine is my...friend. I'm to marry Miss Worthington."

"I...I'm not sure that would be wise."

He swung round at the sound of the soft, regretful words and found himself staring into the tearful gaze of his real bride.

Struck dumb, he saw the effort it took Odette to draw in a shaking breath. "I have my dignity too, Jack," she whispered. She looked stricken, and Jack felt the most dishonourable cad that ever lived as she went on, "How can I marry you, Jack, knowing every time you look at me you wish you were looking at Katherine?" She turned her head and gazed at the young woman on the bed. "*She* obviously feels the same... otherwise, she wouldn't have taken such risks to be here thinking..." She looked at Lady Quamby and George before adding, "That you were injured."

"Odette." Jack took her hand as remorse and dismay and confusion warred within him.

"You can't help the way you feel, Jack," she said sadly, gently extricating her hand. "And I admire your loyalty and honour, but I won't hold you to what you are *only* doing out of loyalty and honour. It's not fair to either of us." She stepped backwards, towards the door. The room was silent; everyone's attention riveted on Odette while Jack remained rooted to the spot, knowing he should argue with her, take her hands in his and refute everything she'd said.

But he couldn't.

She offered him a small, sad smile. "I shall, with dignity, withdraw from our intended contract. My father is ill. He needs me more than you do, let us say. Neither of us shall be deemed to have acted dishonourably." Her lip trembled. "And don't we all deserve to be happy?" She cast a final glance at Katherine before putting her hand on the doorknob. "I hope Katherine recovers fully but...even if she doesn't, Jack, I won't be your substitute love."

CHAPTER 31

It was just as she'd dreamed. Katherine was lying in a cloud of comfort, the curtains billowing into the room, a blue sky beyond, the air fragrant with the scent of roses.

And there was Jack, sitting at her bedside, holding her hand and smiling down at her.

She smiled back and squeezed his hand, surprised at the lack of strength in her grip.

"Jack dearest," she murmured. "I knew one day we'd be together. I didn't mean for it to be like this, though." Her thoughts seemed jumbled and hazy, but she was surprisingly undisturbed. Simply being with Jack infused her with happiness, for Jack would only be holding her hand and looking at her with such intense adoration if they'd both died and gone to the hereafter.

"Did you have a happy marriage with Odette? I hope you did. I only ever wanted you to be happy."

Jack pulled out a handkerchief and dabbed at his eyes, glancing up at the sound of someone entering the room. Katherine caught a whiff of the peony scent her mother favoured these days and felt another surge of joy. But, of course it couldn't be her mother. In Heaven with them, too? That was just too much of a coincidence.

She heard the words: "She's rambling, Jack, but she's awake. Thank God she's awake." And then the muffled sound of weeping.

"Rambling? I'm not rambling. I'm talking to Jack. I want to learn everything he's been doing since we parted. Do you have children? Oh, Jack, I wanted to tell you so much about Diana, but I couldn't." Now she was the one who started to feel like weeping. A tear breached the corner of her eyelid before Jack tenderly wiped it away with his forefinger. He kissed it, then, which made Katherine very happy.

"What did you want to tell me about Diana, dearest?" he whispered, putting his head close to Katherine's cheek, before kissing her lips ever so softly.

"Why, that she's yours, of course. You surely must have guessed that, though. And even if you didn't, it was not something to talk about, was it? Not with you marrying Odette, when you had no choice. You made it very clear, and I understood. You know, about how you couldn't have lived with yourself if you'd not done what honour demanded of you."

"Katherine." He tightened his grip on her hand. She thought he had something in his throat. "Katherine." He said it again, and she thought he sounded strangled by some strange sentiment like remorse, which was strange, for being in a place like this, none of that mattered anymore. Not now that they could be together.

"I didn't know. I...never guessed."

She opened her eyes, and there he was, staring at her, tears welling behind his eyes. He shook his head, real shock in his expression. "I must have been the blindest fool. I *was* the blindest fool. Diana is...*mine?*"

Katherine smiled happily. "She's lovely, isn't she? I hope

she's happy. As happy as I am right now. I want her to know love as I've known love with you, Jack."

Jack made an odd noise. "I didn't see so much of what was staring me in the face," he muttered. "And then George told me what he had done."

"George?" She heard the derision in her voice as she widened her eyes. "He did badly by me. Very badly." She ought not to feel such anger when she and Jack were together now, and the past was barely remembered. Then she shivered, remembering the seven years of unhappiness she'd spent with Freddy.

"But he did his best to atone, Katherine. Yes, it's true he set up the wager, and he encouraged Freddy's plan to send a carriage after he'd sent the note to you. He never thought you'd actually get into it!"

"I thought it was you sending the carriage for me, Jack!" Katherine jerked forward, and Jack took her in his arms. How warm and comforting the feeling was. She knew the carriage didn't matter. George, Freddy, the accidental elopement. None of that mattered because she was now where she wanted to be. But she was afraid Jack mightn't know everything, and it was important that he did.

She put her face close to Jack's and lovingly traced the contours of his face. "I got into the carriage because I thought that when bad weather prevented you from sailing that day, you'd reconsidered and were asking me to throw my lot in with yours. I thought *you* had sent the carriage!"

࿐

JACK CUPPED HER FACE AND RESTED HIS FOREHEAD AGAINST Katherine's. "So it's true, my darling Katherine." He felt weak with emotion. "I couldn't believe it. Not even when Diana made so many references to it: the wrong carriage...staring out over the sea. I berated myself each time for having the ego to think that I was the source. Lord, I *would* have taken you with me across the seas if it could have been managed. If there'd been time. After I realised how much our last two nights together changed everything and I could never love another like I loved you." He drew back so she could see the sincerity in his eyes. "Yes, I made a success of it all, and I'm a rich man, but I could have done it faster with you by my side." He swallowed. "And been a great deal happier for many years more."

Her eyes shone with unshed tears. "I can't blame anyone other than myself...*darling* Jack," she whispered. "I hadn't read the letter properly when Mama stepped into the room, and I threw it into the fire, my heart threatening to explode with excitement at the thought that this carriage that was in the street just outside my bedroom window would take me in just a few hours to where you were!"

He held her tighter, and she shuddered within his embrace, sagging as she put her head on his shoulder. "But instead I found Freddy waiting for me," she wept. "It was not too late to extricate myself, I thought. But then there were people at the tavern who recognised both Freddy and me. I knew I'd be ruined if I didn't marry him after that."

Jack shook his head as he gathered the rest of the story from the snippets that had been told to him. "And your aunt thought you were truly in love with Freddy. She could have helped you, otherwise. Pretended she was staying at the inn, she says. If she'd only known." He breathed deeply, managed to smile, then raised one eyebrow as Katherine raised her head to look at him. "Your Aunt Antoinette claims she's rather good at smoothing over potentially scandalous situations. Claims to have been doing it her whole lifetime. But..." Here was the question he could barely wait to return to. "Diana. You *know* she's mine?"

"Oh Jack, you only have to look at her. She has the same coloured hair, the same dimple in her chin that you have—"

"The same hands, and the same cast to her nose that the three of us have, in fact."

Jack swung round as his mother quietly entered the room, smiling as she took a seat in a rusle of checked skirts. He would have preferred to have continued this precious moment with Katherine but there was a strange urgency behind his mother's smile as she asked, "I hope you don't mind if I join you, Katherine."

A look like fear flashed across Katherine's face. Concerned, Jack squeezed her shoulders, even while his mind dwelled on the oddness of his mother's last words.

"Where are we?" Katherine asked. "What are you doing here, Mrs Patmore? I thought I'd died and gone to Heaven when Jack...kissed me." She blushed hotly. "For he's—"

"No!" Jack said quickly. "Odette's gone back to London with Lady Quamby and Lord Derry after she understood how matters were between us. There was really no hiding the truth after you were brought in from the river."

"The river?"

"Why, after your fall, Katherine. Don't you remember?"

She put her hand to her mouth. "Yes, of course! I was riding here to see you, Jack." She struggled to sit up unaided, and Jack rearranged the pillows to help her. "Aunt Antoinette sent me a note to say you'd been injured most horribly," she went on urgently. "Of course, I had to come as fast as I could."

Emotion welled up in Jack's gullet, stronger than ever. Strange how all his manly attributes seemed to have deserted him. All he wanted to do was crush Katherine against his chest and murmur to her how much he adored her. But his mother was here, with her cryptic words, and there was so much else to explain to Katherine.

"But I wasn't injured, Katherine. It was a plan hatched by Lady Quamby and George. You see, George was doing his best to get you here, certain that we could mend matters between us—"

"George!"

"Darling, you really should modify your tone every time you utter his name. You'll hurt his feelings most terribly, and he's probably listening in the passage."

Katherine tossed her head. "George is always eavesdropping, and what you've said can't be true. George would never—"

"He would, and he did. And when you wouldn't come, he suggested that his mother write a note to tell you I was injured, never imagining you would take such risks to be here. My precious girl, *I* can't believe you'd take such risks to be with me."

"I would cross raging seas to be with you, Jack."

"But you wouldn't tell me Diana was my daughter to bind me to you if you felt I was honour-bound to marry Odette?" The truth that had seemed so unreal before was now washing over him, filling him with a plethora of emotions—not all of them tender and loving. "How could you keep such a thing from me? My own child? Do you know what that means to me? To know I have a child? My own flesh and blood? When I've never known my own flesh and blood. Only the charity of good people."

"Please don't be angry, Jack." Katherine reached out her arms, but this time he just took her hands. He would come to terms with this, of course, but he felt keenly the hurt of having been denied the knowledge.

"I did what I thought was right at the time," whispered Katherine. "I couldn't use Diana for my own ends—even though I longed to be with you. I had no choice but to marry Freddy when you were across the seas. I didn't know what else to do. Besides, I married Freddy before I even knew I was with child. A letter would have taken months to reach you and what was the good of telling you something that would just torment you when there was nothing to be done about it?"

"And she was so young, Jack."

He'd forgotten his mother was there, sitting silently to his right. He turned, surprised to see the tears coursing down her cheeks. Suddenly, he wanted her gone. This moment should be between Katherine and himself.

Until his mother said in a voice so soft and laden with shame, he had to put his head closer to hear her. "You think you were brought up not knowing your own flesh and blood, Jack. That Rufus and I took you in out of the goodness of our hearts. Did you not *know* how much we loved you?"

"Of course, I knew. And I made my own love and appreciation for you both very clear." Yet all he could think about was Diana. He understood Katherine had no choice; that he'd put her in an impossible situation. It made him feel even more wretched.

"You did. And that's why I thought it didn't matter if I withheld from you the fact..."

She couldn't go on. Jack had never seen his normally self-contained mother so overcome as she put her head in her arms and leaned forward.

"What fact, Mother? What fact did you withhold?"

She put her hands in her lap and looked at him. "That you were the son I was forced to give up when I was even younger than Katherine was when she had Diana."

"What?" His brain felt suddenly filled with fog, and he felt Katherine reach for him as she too gasped. With difficulty, he tried to breathe evenly again. "I don't understand you, Mother. Why would you keep such a thing from me?" Anger like he'd never known surged through him. He felt a whole lifetime of angst at not knowing his true parentage was mocking him. A thousand voices were laughing in his ears.

"Don't be angry, I beg of you! Please Jack!" his mother begged. "I couldn't tell anyone you were mine after I found you again, having lost you for seven years and believing I'd never see you again. Seven years...almost the same length of time you've lost Diana," she added in a tone of wonder before Jack snapped, "Did you not think it was important for me to know the truth? When I've wondered my entire life if my father was a thief, a murderer? I was so grateful to Odette for accepting me as I was and taking the chance that the blood of villains might taint the blood of the children we would have..." He stopped himself. He was with Katherine now. This was not the moment.

But...

"Katherine, did you know this?"

She shook her head. She was even paler than she had been. "I, too, loved you for who you were, Jack. I didn't care who your parents were. But...Aunt Eliza? You are Jack's *real* mother? I...I don't understand?"

It was almost too much to comprehend. Diana was his daughter, and Eliza Patmore was his mother. He'd learned both these facts in the space of five minutes. He had kin. A real mother, and a real daughter. And both had been kept from him for seven years. He stood up. He didn't know if he could remain.

"Please, Jack! Understand here what's important, I beg of you!" His mother tugged at his coat. "I did what I did to protect you and keep you safe. Katherine did what she did at great self-sacrifice. It's not like you to think only of yourself."

His mother's anger snapped him back to reality. He sat down with a thud. It was not often he was berated by anyone, but wasn't it so true that he'd been treated with loving kindness and respect his entire life? Despite the fact his origins were mired in obscurity.

"Forgive me," he muttered. "We all do what we think is right at the time."

"Of course we do, Jack. And I was prepared to marry George's uncle—commonly referred to as 'odious George' so his cousins, Ladies Quamby and Fenton tell me." Her mouth quirked, but she went on quickly to answer his look of enquiry, "You were Young George's playmate, and George Bramley was in residence with his uncle, Lord Quamby. I recognised you when I dragged you from the lake after all you children nearly drowned. I recognised the tiny sixth finger on your right hand. And I knew the only way I could be reunited with the child I'd had out of wedlock and that had been taken from me was to marry George Bramley. Odious George." She paused. "So I thought at the time."

"But you married Uncle Rufus instead...and he accepted me as his own." Jack was struck by wonder at such generosity. "Why did you never tell me, Mama?"

She shook her head. "You grew up such a lively, happy child. And suddenly you were eighteen and about to cross the seas to make your own way in the world." She looked down at her fingers intertwined in her lap, the knuckles white. "I never found the right opportunity," she said, looking up. "You knew you were loved. And that seemed all that mattered."

"It *is* all that matters."

Katherine's lashes were wet as she echoed his mother's words.

And as Jack looked from Katherine, the girl he'd adored since she'd pledged her friendship to the foundling home lad, and his mother whom he'd loved as deeply as any son could, biological or adoptive, he knew there were no truer words.

Jack leaned down to pat Diana lightly on the back as the eight-year-old was about to run to the tea table that had been set up beneath the apple tree in honour of her birthday.

"Be nice to Uncle George, now, won't you?" he cautioned. "He's very proud of his new lavender coat that I heard you making fun of earlier, and I can't tell you strongly enough how unkind it is to taunt people—for any reason."

He smiled as Katherine glided up to his side, slipping her hand into his and resting her head on his shoulder to look down the grassy slope to where Aunt Antoinette had organised the family gathering.

Diana, who had paused at this instruction, put her hands on her hips. Her dark hair was brushed back and tied with a pink bow and two lace-edged pantalettes peeked beneath her new flounced pink and blue checked dress. The fashions were different but to Jack, his daughter was the image of her mother when she'd been a child.

"Can I tell him what I think about his new side curls, then?" Diana asked.

"Not if that means speaking the truth, darling," said Katherine causing Jack to raise an eyebrow as he waited for her to go on. Throughout the eight wonderful months of their marriage—which had taken place the day after Katherine's twelve months of mourning had come to an end—she'd never ceased delighting him with her acute observations and candour.

And the depth of her love.

Diana looked puzzled.

"It's called tact, darling," her mother explained, glancing from Diana to Jack then back to Diana again. "Your father has always had so much more of it than I have. Tact is a skill and I suspect, if you're like me, you'll need to work on that skill for it might save you a lot of heartache throughout your life."

Jack understood Katherine's veiled meaning. If she'd not wounded George, how different things might have been.

"What is tact, Mama? Is it lying?"

"Only if it's to be kind. Yes, tact means being kind to people, even if you think they're..."

"Silly? I think Uncle George's side curls look very silly but Miss Burnside thinks he cuts quite a dash." Diana's eyes sparkled with mischief.

"Yes, I overheard that remark, too," said Jack. "But did you notice how happy it made George when Miss Burnside said that?"

Diana nodded thoughtfully, prompting Katherine to go on, "And didn't it give you a nice feeling to see Uncle George happy? A much nicer feeling than if he'd looked all sad if you'd told him his side curls looked silly?"

Diana contemplated this with a frown. "It would have been funny to make George cross but..." She looked from her parents down the hill to where George was sitting next to Miss Burnside, the daughter of one of Aunt Antoinette's gentleman friends, a widower who'd started calling on the pretext of writing a history of several notable houses in the area. He and his daughter had become regular visitors. "Uncle George is much nicer when he's not cross."

"Exactly, darling," Katherine said approvingly. "Uncle George is very nice when people are nice to him. And that's the way it is with most people. So try not to tease and make fun of Uncle George."

Diana nodded gravely. "I'll try not to, Mama. Papa." The promise seemed to have unleashed the gaiety within her for now she was running down the hill while Jack and Katherine followed at a more sedate pace.

"She reminds me so much of you, when you were her age." Jack slipped an arm about his lovely wife's waist and stopped so that he could enjoy the smile she sent him. For Katherine always smiled when she looked at him. The great joy at rediscovering all that had been lost for those long years apart was as strongly felt by her as it was by him, he knew.

"She was my treasure when I didn't have you." Her look was so loving it caused him something akin to pain.

"But now you have me for always. *And* we have Diana."

"And as many others as we choose, thanks to a little knowledge that most married couples are denied."

Raising his eyebrows and smiling, Jack looked from Katherine to her aunt a few yards away. Lady Quamby was waving the cake knife in the air, waiting for Katherine and Jack to fill the two remaining seats for they were all there with the notable exception of Lady Hale who'd declared she'd never again set foot over the threshold of Quamby House where she'd been so insulted. She'd been true to her word, showing as little interest in her supposed granddaughter after Katherine had married Jack, as she ever had done before her surprise meddling when she'd desired a match between Katherine and Lord Derry.

The biggest surprise was that her thwarted desires in the matchmaking department appeared to have found a new outlet: Odette Worthington. Jack supposed there were mutual benefits. Odette was an heiress in need of a husband and Lady Hale had contacts. Jack didn't miss Odette and was surprised, and impressed, by the dignified manner in which she'd dealt with their separation. Perhaps she'd not loved him as much as he'd supposed. Or perhaps her aspirations had changed. A husband with a title was well within her reach and Jack had discovered Odette was more ambitious than he'd at first thought.

Derry had shown a surprisingly sporting attitude, too. His concern for Katherine after her accident had been sincere but he'd housed Jack and allowed him complete licence to be at the bedside of the convalescing Katherine.

Jack supposed it must have been as clear to him as to everyone else how deeply Jack and Katherine felt for one another. Not a single person had stepped in to voice any objection or to denounce them when their love was so apparent after Odette had broken off their engagement.

For a week Jack had remained at Derry House. While he read to Katherine, and talked with her, Derry had organised the practicalities. He'd seen to the medical care of Katherine's mount, Stargazer, who had fortunately not had to be put down and had now made a full recovery. In fact, Katherine rode him regularly, during the early morning canters she and Jack enjoyed so much. Derry had also offered Odette hospitality and sympathy following the dissolution of the young woman's engagement. A year later, the pair was occasionally to be seen on the dance floor. They seemed to have become good friends.

Jack scanned the table of guests. Surprisingly, Lord Quamby was stroking his wife's hand as he discussed some matter with her, his curls as vermilion as ever. Instead of Lady

Hale, Diana's real, though unacknowledged grandmother was there to enjoy the celebration. Jack was conscious of a great warmth and sense of gratitude as he caught his mother's quick smile when she transferred her look from Rufus Patmore beside her, the man who had been so much more to Jack than most fathers. Meanwhile, Katherine's own parents Lord and Lady Fenton, had their heads together in private conversation while George and Miss Burnside looked hopeful and happy in the midst of their own discussion.

"Knowledge is golden if one knows what to do with it," Jack remarked, thinking of all the knowledge he—and Katherine—has misused before they'd found their wonderful happiness together.

They reached the table as Diana unfolded her napkin and said in clear earnest tones to George, "I know Mama says it's impolite to bring up your side curls, Uncle George, but I've been considering the matter all afternoon and I think I agree with Miss Burnside. You do cut quite a dash with your new hair cut."

Jack had felt Katherine tense when their daughter had begun her little speech but she relaxed as Diana offered her verdict. He and Katherine exchanged a smile, their amusement increasing when they were rewarded by the play of interesting emotions cross Diana's face as she took in her Uncle George's fiery blush, his stammered thanks, and then the great pleasure in his expression as he self consciously touched his hair before resuming his conversation with Miss Burnside with even greater enthusiasm.

Diana ignored the glass of lemonade that had just been put in front of her and sent her parents a sign of acknowledgement in the form of a clumsily executed wink that she'd heeded Katherine's earlier advice. Then, with a quick, satisfied glance at Uncle George and Miss Burnside, she announced loudly and imperiously to the gathering at large,

"I think we're all very happy now, Aunt Antoinette. Would you please cut the cake?"

"*I'm* certainly very happy, my darling." Jack put his lips to Katherine's ear as he pulled out her chair and helped her into it. "Isn't our daughter a treasure? She's just like her mother."

For a moment, Katherine retained his hand as she tilted her head to look at him. So much was communicated by the intensity of the gesture and in her look and for a moment Jack was almost glad that their separation had given him an excuse for throwing his all into this journey of rediscovering everything he thought he'd lost forever.

"I think Diana has inherited the best of *both* of us," his beautiful, much-loved wife whispered.

A whispered affirmation of the most wonderful secret that had ever been revealed to him.

THE END

NOTE FROM THE AUTHOR

The Accidental Elopement is Book 4 in my *Scandalous Miss Brightwells* series and takes up the story of Katherine and Jack who play together as children in **The Wedding Wager.**

In **The Wedding Wager**, we meet Eliza who agrees to marriage with a selfish man as the only means of getting closer to her long-lost love-child, Jack.

Here's what the readers say:

"A lovely and heartwarming story." ~ Kindle Reader

"Oh my gosh, what a tremendous love story with so many twists and turns."

The Scandalous Miss Brightwells

Wicked and lively Fanny and Antoinette Brightwell have made spectacular marriages—despite scandals and the treachery of a disappointed suitor determined to besmirch their reputations.

So, who better to play matchmaker when a deserving candidate waltzes into their orbit?

Here are the first four stories in the series, each following on from each other, although each can be read as a stand-alone.

1. Rake's Redemption

The beautiful Brightwells—clever Fanny and her easily-led sister, Antoinette—battle scandal and spurned suitors to achieve gilded marriages against the odds. A love match in Fanny's case and a very satisfactory compromise in Antoinette's.

"Fanny and Fenton's story is full of drama, humor and sizzle." ~ Amazon reader.

Read for FREE in KU or buy here.

2. Rogue's Kiss

How bold would a potential suitor be if he were told the lie that the young lady he desires has only six months to live?

"A great read - one which will leave you sighing for more." ~ 4 Out Of 5 Hearts From Cariad Books

Buy here.

3. The Wedding Wager

A rigged horse race - with a marriage and a lost child riding on the outcome.

Can the matchmaking Brightwell sisters avoid scandal and disaster as they try to rescue two tortured souls and unite their passionate hearts?

"Very intriguing Austen-esque novel with well developed characters and story line. The best historical romance novel I've read in a while." ~ Amazon reader.

Buy here.

4. The Accidental Elopement

Thank you for reading! I hope you enjoyed the series as much as I enjoyed writing about these two scandalous sisters and their matchmaking conquests!

Read for free in KU or buy here.

OTHER SERIES BY BEVERLEY OAKLEY

Enjoy - sizzling romance with passion and intrigue!

The Daughters of Sin series follows the intertwining lives and sibling rivalry of Lord Partington's two nobly born - and two illegitimate - daughters as they compete for love during several London Seasons.

With Hetty and Araminta both falling for men on opposing sides of a dastardly plot that is being investigated by Stephen Cranbourne, now a secret agent in the Foreign Office, there's lashings of skullduggery and intrigue bound up in the central romance.

What Readers are Saying About the Series which is now available as a complete Box Set.

"...lies, misdeeds, treachery, and romance. What an impressive story! Ms. Oakley has a unique way of telling her stories, bringing unknown heroes/ heroines into the spotlight, as they navigate a world of espionage, and intrigue, all while trying to survive and find their HEA. Magnificent and mesmerizing!" ~ **Amazon reader**

"Full of secrets, murders, intrigues and you feel you know the characters and want to strangle some of them, especially Araminta!!! I have since read all in the series and can't wait for Book 5... This is a series I will read again and again." ~ **Amazon reader**

Below is the order of the books:

Book 1: Her Gilded Prison

Book 2: Dangerous Gentlemen

Book 3: The Mysterious Governess

Book 4: Beyond Rubies

Book 5: Lady Unveiled: The Cuckold's Conspiracy

Read the Complete Box Set and Save here!

Or, for something in Kindle Unlimited, you might like my Hearts in Hiding Series

THE DUCHESS AND THE HIGHWAYMAN

A duchess disguised as a lady's maid; a gentleman parading as a highwayman.

She's on the run from a murderer, he's in pursuit of one.

Married off at a young age to a brutal nobleman, Phoebe, Lady Cavanaugh, longs for love—and enters into a risky affair. Framed for her husband's murder, she flees wearing only a blood-stained chemise and is rescued by a handsome 'highwayman' who believes she's Lady Cavanaugh's maidservant.

Hugh Redding has his own reasons for hunting the man whose mission is to see the infamous and elusive Murdering Duchess hanged for murder. And Phoebe, the 'maidservant with aspirations above her station' might prove the very weapon he needs—once he teaches her how to behave like a lady.

Only when Phoebe mysteriously disappears does Hugh realise the real identity of the spirited wench he'd set out to tame—and the danger she's in.

Burdened by the knowledge of his unwitting role in placing Phoebe in mortal peril, Hugh must now polish his skills as a gentleman, not only to save Phoebe from the gallows, but to win back her heart.

What the readers say:

"This love story has so much going for it - strong characters, friendship, "building of trust, a common enemy and of course, a beautiful second chances romance." ~ **Amazon reader.**

"A heart pounding read!" ~ **Amazon reader.**

"I loved how the author gave us an exciting opening scenario and then smoothly and effortlessly built the story up to an exciting and riveting climax. Wow!" ~ **Amazon reader.**

Read for Free in KU here.

HEARTS IN HIDING Series
The Duchess and the Highwayman
The Bluestocking and the Rake
Duchess of Seduction

SCANDALOUS MISS BRIGHTWELLS Series
Rake's Honour
Rake's Redemption
Rogue's Kiss
The Wedding Wager
The Accidental Elopement

DAUGHTERS OF SIN Series
Her Gilded Prison
Dangerous Gentlemen
The Mysterious Governess
Beyond Rubies
Lady Unveiled: The Cuckold's Conspiracy

GEORGIAN MYSTERY ROMANCE Series

Wicked Wager
Her Valentine's Secret

FAIR CYPRIANS OF LONDON Series
Saving Grace
Forsaking Hope
Keeping Faith
Wedding Violet
Christmas Charity

ABOUT THE AUTHOR

Beverley was seventeen when she bundled up her first 500+ page romance and sent it to a publisher. Rejection followed swiftly. Drowning one's heroine on the last page, she was informed, was not in line with the expectations of romance readers.

So Beverley became a journalist.

After a whirlwind romance with a handsome Norwegian bush pilot she met in Botswana's beautiful Okavango Delta, Beverley discovered what real romance was all about, saved her heroine from a watery grave in her next manuscript and published her first romance in 2009.

Since then, she's written more than twenty-five sizzling historical romances laced with mystery and intrigue under the name Beverley Oakley.

She also writes psychological historical mysteries, and Colonial-Africa-set romantic suspense, as Beverley Eikli.

With an inspiring view of a Gothic nineteenth-century insane asylum across the road, Beverley lives north of Melbourne with her gorgeous husband, two lovely daughters and a rambunctious Rhodesian Ridgeback called Mombo, named after the safari lodge where she and her husband met.

You can read more at www.beverleyoakley.com

Please get in touch here:
www.beverleyoakley.com
beverley.oakley@gmail.com